Read...
b...

Catch a Tiger by the Tail

"I love the THIRDS series. It's fun, action-packed, and hella sexy."

—Just Love: Romance Novel Reviews

Smoke & Mirrors

"If you aren't reading this series, well, you absolutely should be. And I, for one, have no qualms about recommending it to you."

—Joyfully Jay

Thick & Thin

"This series has always amazed me and the amazement continued when reading this one…"

—Three Books Over the Rainbow

Darkest Hour Before Dawn

"The briskly paced novel is packed with exciting action, steamy sex scenes, melodramatic passion, and tender moments of romance."

—Foreword Reviews

Gummy Bears & Grenades

"*Gummy Bears & Grenades* was pure fun."

—Birdie Bookworm

By CHARLIE COCHET

LOCKE AND KEYES AGENCY
Kept in the Dark

THIRDS
Hell & High Water
Blood & Thunder
Rack & Ruin
Rise & Fall
Against the Grain
Catch a Tiger by the Tail
Manga: Hell & High Water

Published by DREAMSPINNER PRESS
www.dreamspinnerpress.com

CATCH A
TIGER
BY THE TAIL

CHARLIE COCHET

Published by
DREAMSPINNER PRESS

5032 Capital Circle SW, Suite 2, PMB# 279,
Tallahassee, FL 32305-7886 USA
www.dreamspinnerpress.com

This is a work of fiction. Names, characters, places, and incidents either are the product of author imagination or are used fictitiously, and any resemblance to actual persons, living or dead, business establishments, events, or locales is entirely coincidental.

Catch a Tiger by the Tail
© 2016, 2020 Charlie Cochet

Cover Art
© 2016, 2020 L.C. Chase
http://www.lcchase.com
Cover content is for illustrative purposes only and any person depicted on the cover is a model.

Mass Market Paperback ISBN: 978-1-64108-200-6
Mass Market Paperback published January 2020
v. 1.0

Printed in the United States of America
∞
This paper meets the requirements of
ANSI/NISO Z39.48-1992 (Permanence of Paper).

A big thank-you to Dreamspinner Press for helping me make my dream a reality. To my family and friends for their amazing support. Thank you to all the THIRDS Nerds who've made this an amazing adventure, and to all the readers who pick my stories and ask for more. Thank you.

Cast of Characters

(YOU'LL FIND these cast members throughout the whole of the THIRDS series, some being introduced in different books. This list will continue to grow.)

DESTRUCTIVE DELTA

Sloane Brodie—Defense agent. Team leader. Jaguar Therian.

Dexter J. Daley "Dex"—Defense agent. Former homicide detective for the Human Police Force. Older brother to Cael Maddock. Adopted by Anthony "Tony" Maddock. Human.

Ash Keeler—Defense agent. Entry tactics and Close Quarter Combat expert. Lion Therian.

Julietta Guerrera "Letty"—Defense agent. Weapons expert. Human.

Calvin Summers—Defense agent. Sniper. Human.

Ethan Hobbs "Hobbs"—Defense agent. Demolitions expert and Public Safety Bomb Technician. Has two older brothers: Rafe and Sebastian Hobbs. Tabby Tiger Therian.

Cael Maddock—Recon agent. Tech expert. Dex's younger brother. Adopted by Anthony Maddock. Cheetah Therian.

Rosa Santiago—Recon agent. Crisis negotiator and medic. Human.

COMMANDING OFFICERS

Lieutenant Sonya Sparks—Lieutenant for Unit Alpha. Cougar Therian. Undercover operative for TIN (Therian Intelligence Network)

Sergeant Anthony Maddock "Tony"—Sergeant for Destructive Delta. Dex and Cael's adoptive father. Human.

MEDICAL EXAMINERS

Dr. Hudson Colbourn—Chief medical examiner for Destructive Delta. Wolf Therian.

Dr. Nina Bishop—Medical examiner for Destructive Delta. Human.

AGENTS FROM OTHER SQUADS

Ellis Taylor—Team leader for Beta Ambush. Leopard Therian.

Rafe Hobbs—Team leader for Alpha Ambush. The oldest Hobbs brother. Tiger Therian.

Sebastian Hobbs—Team leader for Theta Destructive. Was once on Destructive Delta but was transferred after his relationship to Hudson ended in a breach of protocol and civilian loss. Middle Hobbs brother. Tiger Therian.

Osmond Zachary "Zach"—Agent for Alpha Sleuth in Unit Beta. Has six brothers working for the THIRDS. Brown bear Therian.

OTHER IMPORTANT CAST MEMBERS

Gabe Pearce—Sloane's ex-partner and ex-lover on Destructive Delta. Killed on duty by his brother Isaac. Human.

Isaac Pearce—Gabe's older brother. Was a detective for the Human Police Force who became leader of the Order of Adrasteia. Killed by Destructive Delta during a hostage situation. Human.

Louis Huerta "Lou"—Dex's ex-boyfriend. Human.

Bradley Darcy—Bartender and owner of Bar Dekatria. Jaguar Therian.

Austen Payne—Squadron Specialist Agent (SSA) for Destructive Delta. Cheetah Therian. Undercover freelance operative for TIN (Therian Intelligence Network).

Dr. Abraham Shultzon—Head doctor during the First Gen Recruitment Program who was personally responsible for the wellbeing of the THIRDS' First Gen Recruits. He was also responsible for the tests that were run on the Therian children. Recently apprehended by TIN for creating an unsanctioned Therian mind control drug, and for kidnapping THIRDS Therian agents for unsanctioned project.

Arlo Keeler—Ash's twin brother killed during the riots in the 1980s.

Beck Hogan—Leader of the Ikelos Coalition. Killed during confrontation with THIRDS agents. Tiger Therian.

Drew Collins—Beck Hogan's second in command. Cougar Therian.

Felipe Bautista—Drew Collins's boyfriend. Wolf Therian.

John Daley—Dexter J. Daley's biological father. Anthony Maddock's best friend, and partner at the HPF. Killed during a shootout in a movie theater during the riots. Human.

Gina Daley—Dexter J. Daley's biological mother. Worked for the CDC in NYC. First to volunteer to work with Therians. Killed along with her husband during a shootout in a movie theater during the riots. Human.

Darla Summers—Calvin Summer's mother. Human.

Thomas Hobbs—Ethan, Sebastian, and Rafe Hobbs's father. Suffers from Therian Acheron Syndrome. Tiger Therian.

Julia Hobbs—Thomas Hobbs's wife, and mother to Ethan, Sebastian, and Rafe Hobbs. Human.

Benedict Winters—THIRDS appointed psychologist.

GLOSSARY

Melanoe Virus—A virus released during the Vietnam War through the use of chemical warfare infecting millions worldwide and killing hundreds of thousands.

Eppione.8—A vaccine created using strains from animals immune to the virus. It awakened a dormant mutation within the virus, resulting in the altering of Human DNA, and giving birth to Therians.

Therians—Shifters brought about through the mutation of Human DNA as a result of the Eppione.8 vaccine.

Post Shift Trauma Care (PSTC)—The effects of Therian Post Shift Trauma are similar to the aftereffects of an epileptic seizure, only on a smaller scale, including muscle soreness, bruising, brief disorientation, and hunger. Eating after a shift is extremely important as not eating could lead to the Therian collapsing and a host of other health issues. PSTC is the care given to Therians after they shift back to Human form.

THIRDS (Therian-Human Intelligence Recon Defense Squadron)—An elite, military funded agency comprised of an equal number of Human and Therian agents and intended to uphold the law for all its citizens without prejudice.

Themis—A powerful, multimillion dollar government interface used by the THIRDS. It's linked to numerous intelligence agencies across the globe and runs a series of highly advanced algorithms to scan surveillance submitted by agents.

First Gen—First Generation of purebred Therians born with a perfected version of the mutation.

Pre-First Gens—Any Therian born before First Gen Therians. Known to have unstable versions of the mutation resulting in any number of health issues.

BearCat—THIRDS tactical vehicle.

Human Police Force (HPF)—A branch of law enforcement consisting of Humans officials dealing only with crimes committed by Humans.

Sparta—Nickname for THIRDS agent training facility at the Manhattan THIRDS headquarters.

TIN—Therian Intelligence Network. Therian equivalent to the Human CIA.

TINMAN—TIN operative. Nicknamed after the Tin Man in the Wizard of Oz as TIN operatives are rumored to have no heart.

Anti-Therianism—Prejudice, discrimination, or antagonism directed against Therians.

Therian Classification—Tattoo marking on a Therian's neck displaying the Therian classification, including Family, Genus, and Species.

Chapter One

HE WAS being hunted.

The shadows around him swirled and drifted as if he were underwater. If he wasn't careful he'd drown all right, in his own blood.

Calvin kept a steady grip on his rifle. He breathed in slow through his nose and released it through his mouth, his breath coming up warm against his skin thanks to the face mask shielding him from the bitter cold. Thank God for his THIRDS thermal uniform. He would have frozen his ass off by now without it. Three degrees. *What the ever-loving fuck?* This was New York City, not Canada. Any day now it would drop below zero; he just knew it. These guys picked the wrong day to fuck up. Felid agents enjoyed a frolic in the snow as much as the next Therian, but not in the middle of the night, and sure as shit not when it was cold enough to freeze their whiskers off. Pissed-off Felids equaled epic hissy fits.

There was a faint cackle in the distance, and he turned with exceptional care, his boots sinking into the blankets of freshly fallen snow. His earpiece came to life, Dex's quiet voice hushed on the other end.

"Calvin, visuals?"

"Negative," Calvin replied, continuing onward. It was eerily quiet. As if the city itself was slumbering and hiding from the unrelenting cold. The only sounds around him were the howling wind and the snow compressing underneath his boots. The wind picked up, and the snow fell in earnest. It made finding the gang of hyena Therians in Central Park's North Woods even harder, especially with their own agents in their Therian forms out there hunting. Maybe his Human teammates were having better luck. He doubted it, considering how quiet his com was. Ethan had caught the scent of one of their suspects several minutes ago and disappeared into the woods. Calvin hadn't heard from or seen his partner since, meaning Ethan was still stalking. Somewhere in the pitch-black night, Sloane and Ash were doing the same. Cael, the lucky bastard, got to sit in the warmth of their BearCat working surveillance.

A perimeter had been set up down E. 79th Street, cutting through Central Park, up Central Park West, across 110th Street, and down Fifth Avenue. If any of these assholes tried to make a break for the city, they'd be met with a shower of tranqs and Theta Destructive's Therian agents in their Therian form. It was up to Destructive Delta to make sure they didn't get that far.

There was another distinct cackle, closer this time. Calvin picked up his pace and spoke into his com. "I heard something. I'm gonna check it out."

"What's your position?" Dex asked, his tone void of its usual humor. Sparks had been kicking their asses in training for weeks since the whole mess with Shultzon and the facility went down, but no one was getting it as bad as Dex and Sloane. The two were being groomed. They all knew it. Hell, even Dex and Sloane knew it. They just didn't know what for. In the meantime, his teammates went along with it. None of them were against strengthening or widening their skill set, especially Dex, who was still trying to figure out what his skill set was. In Calvin's opinion, Dex was secretly enjoying the grueling regime. Eventually he'd get to the bottom of whatever Sparks was keeping from them. Dex always did.

"I'm coming up behind the Blockhouse." Calvin slowed as he approached the old military fortification. It had been built in the 1800s to defend against the British. Now it was a deathtrap. Any number of Therians could be hiding in or around its stone walls.

"Watch your back," Dex said.

"Affirmative." Calvin crouched down by some dense shrubbery draped in layers of fluffy white and scanned the area. Half a dozen or so feral hyena Therians were hiding somewhere in there, all high as kites. THIRDS agents had been issued a warrant and sent to arrest the gang after receiving a tip-off to their location. Before the team could make the arrest, the gang managed to escape by blowing their meth lab into the next town. Luckily there were no casualties, but the group caused havoc through the city before teams from Unit Alpha cornered them in Central Park. That was over an hour ago.

Spotted hyena Therians were anything but the cowards many Humans pegged them to be. In their feral form they were lethal, skilled at hunting at night, had powerful jaws, moved in packs, and defended themselves fiercely. A low giggle met Calvin's ear, and a shadow moved behind the Blockhouse. He readied his tranq rifle before moving in.

"THIRDS! Come out slowly!" Calvin held his rifle firm and took aim at the hyena growling at him from the shadows, its glowing eyes following his every move. Slowly it crept forward, the darkness following it as if it were some otherworldly spirit. It laughed, calling to its friends. The hairs on the back of Calvin's neck stood on end, and he spun just as a hyena Therian lunged at him, knocking him off his feet. His body hit the snow, the Therian's jaws clamping down on his rifle. *Shit!* Movement from his left caught his attention, and he swiped his backup tranq gun from his vest to fire at the approaching Therian. The tranq got it in the neck, and it yelped before scurrying off.

Calvin wrestled with the hyena Therian attempting to crunch his rifle like a tasty bone. Saliva dripped onto Calvin's uniform, and he caught sight of a third hyena Therian circling him, looking for the right angle to pounce. All right, he'd had just about enough of this bullshit. Calvin fired his tranq gun at the Therian chewing on his rifle, and the asshat stumbled off him, the dart sticking out of its neck. It shook its head and laughed that creepy sound of theirs. Multiple sets of glowing eyes and dark shapes popped up in the woods around him. *What the hell?*

Calvin scrambled to his feet and tapped his com. "Dex, there's more than six!"

"What?"

"I don't know where the hell they came from, but I'm looking at seven or eight. Maybe more."

"Shit. Hang tight. We're heading your way."

Calvin fired at the glowing eyes as he backed up slowly. He heard a yelp followed by several cackles, whoops, and laughs. They moved fast as hell. Calvin wasn't in the habit of missing, but his accuracy depended highly on him being able to actually see his target. Every time he aimed at a set of eyes he assumed was attached to the dark blob surrounding it, it shifted or disappeared. He had to draw them out. Fuck. He hated this part.

Slinging his rifle strap back into place, he broke off into a run in the opposite direction, which was a pain in the ass in the heavy snow thanks to the weight of his equipment. He moved as fast as he could, the cackles and laughs getting closer as the Therians emerged from the darkness to give chase. There was a small bridge ahead that crossed over the frozen creek. Hauling ass, he headed for the bridge, chancing a swift glance over his shoulder. Please let this work.

A pack of growling hyena Therians were right on his tail, almost close enough to nip at his heels. He pushed himself harder, his brow beaded with sweat and his lungs burning from the frosty air he was gulping down as he raced through the woods. If he stopped, they'd all descend on him like feral beasts, tearing at him until there was nothing left of him but his equipment. They wouldn't even leave his bones. *Fuck that. He wasn't about to become a meal for these assholes.*

"Ethan!" Calvin cried out, knowing his partner would hear him wherever he was. His best friend would never let anything happen to him if he could help it. Ethan would be there to fight for him, to look out for him, and keep him safe. They had each other's backs, on and off the field. It's how it had always been. The two of them against the world.

From the corner of his right eye, he caught sight of one of the hyena Therians fast approaching. It launched itself at him, and Calvin fired his rifle, but it didn't stop the bastard from barreling into him and knocking him over. It clamped its jaws down on Calvin's shoulder, its teeth sinking through the fabric and hitting his ballistic vest's integrated shoulder plate, giving Calvin enough time to throw a right hook, catching the bastard on the side of the head. With a yelp it rolled off, only to quickly recover, fangs bared as it snarled at him.

The fierce roar that erupted from somewhere in the woods had a paralyzing effect. Tree branches shook, the snow plopping to the ground. Soon enough the hyena Therians snapped out of it and charged Calvin. He readied himself, grabbing his rifle and taking aim, when Ethan leaped out from the darkness and skidded to a stop in front of Calvin. He roared again, huge sharp fangs bare. The sound was terrifying, bringing everything and everyone to a halt for a slip of a moment. Two of the hyena Therians darted off with yips and whines. Half a dozen or so remained.

"Okay, buddy. Let's do this." Calvin got to his feet and cocked his rifle. The Therians scattered and he took off after them, Ethan at his side. Ethan kept the hyena Therians from disappearing into the woods, roaring and leaping out, driving them out into the open areas of the park. It was exactly what Calvin needed. A nice clear shot.

Calvin anticipated their movements, shooting where he thought they'd be instead of reacting. He plugged one in two places. It dropped into the snow. The remaining gang members did everything they could to stay out of Ethan's way while still attempting to get close to Calvin. His claws would take them out in one swipe. Snow flew like waves crashing against a shore as Ethan ran, leaped, and swatted his paws. Realizing they didn't stand a chance against a tiger Therian, they all scattered and took off toward Calvin.

"Where the hell are you guys?" Calvin yelled into his com. Just as he said the words, Ash roared. He emerged from the shrubs, launching himself at two of the hyena Therians. They attacked him, biting at his massive mane and getting nothing but a mouthful of fur. Letty tore through the trees, tranq guns blazing. Sloane was seconds behind with Dex on his tail. Dex aimed his rifle and fired. Another one down. Their Felid teammates corralled the remaining hyena Therians while Dex, Calvin, and Letty approached with rifles at the ready.

"On the ground!" Dex ordered. "Get on the ground now!"

The hyena Therians did as asked, dropping down to their bellies, their ears flattened. Sloane, Ash, and Ethan circled the perps, hissing and growling, their sharp fangs on display as a warning to anyone thinking of doing something stupid. One wrong move and they'd be kitty chow.

Dex tapped his com. "Sarge, area's secure. We have the remaining Therians."

"Copy that," Maddock replied. "Theta Destructive is backing up their truck."

"Copy that." Dex kept his rifle aimed at the perps as he addressed them. "You can either get in the truck on your own or be carried after we tranq you. It's your choice. Try anything funny and our Felid agents will be happy to remind you why cooperating is in your best interest."

The truck arrived, and Theta Destructive's agents hurried out. They rounded up the unconscious hyena Therians and laid them in the cage. The ones not tranqed begrudgingly trotted up the ramp and into the back of the truck. A couple hesitated in front of the cage, but Ethan's roar got them moving quick after that. With the remaining perps locked up and secure, the doors closed, and the truck was off.

"Thank God that's over," Letty grumbled, giving Ash a scratch behind his ear. He scrunched his nose and shook his head, causing snow to fall from his mane.

Ethan sat beside Calvin and pushed his nose against his leg. With a chuckle, Calvin gave Ethan a nice scratch behind his ear and over his head. Not content with a mere ear scratch, Ethan mewed and bumped his head against Calvin's leg. "Yeah, all right," Calvin said with a laugh. He crouched down and scratched Ethan under his chin and the sides of his face, ruffling his thick fur. Ethan shut his eyes in contentment before bumping his head playfully against Calvin's. He chuffed, then let out a low moan, one Calvin was familiar with. Ethan had been worried. It was evident in the noises he made and his rubbing his head against Calvin, as if touching him was the only way to reassure himself Calvin was okay. "I'm good, Ethan. Promise."

"Let's get the hell out of here," Letty said, heading in the direction of their BearCat. "I'm fucking starving." Ash hopped and pounced after her. Clearly he was hungry as well. Sloane bounded after Ash, smacking him on the rump with his paw. Ash growled and chased him, the two frolicking in the snow and pouncing, sending each other tumbling.

"You'd think they'd be tired of the snow by now," Dex said, shaking his head in amusement.

Calvin motioned toward Dex's arm, the one with Sloane's mark. "How did it go? Does it work?" Despite being on callouts for a month now, this had been the first really dangerous call. They'd all been worried about Dex being out among a bunch of feral Therians with his lover's Therian mark on his arm. Before they left, Sparks had called Dex into her office and given him some kind of scent masking sleeve to wear under his uniform. She'd warned him it only lasted a few hours, so he better get whatever he needed done before it wore off. It was clearly TIN issued, because there was nothing out there in the market that could mask a Therian scent like that.

"So far it's working great. If they smelled anything on me, it was Sloane's usual scent. Shame it doesn't have a longer shelf life. Still, I don't know why there's nothing out there like this."

"I'm not surprised, to be honest," Calvin admitted. "Marking is serious. I mean, not even marriage is permanent. That"—Calvin pointed to Dex's arm—"is."

Dex went pensive, and Calvin wondered if Dex and Sloane were aware of the kind of commitment they'd made to each other. The majority of Therians had no idea how deep those scars ran. Humans knew even less.

For the most part, no one at work had challenged Sloane, but then everyone respected him at the THIRDS, whether they personally liked him or not, and none were stupid enough to challenge him. Jaguar Therians weren't to be messed with. A good number of them were grumpy at the best of times, without being challenged over their lover. Taylor was a little funny around Dex and appeared to be doing his best to avoid him, but that was seen as more of a blessing in disguise than a great concern. With this new contraption on Dex's arm, things should go back to normal. Well, as normal as was possible for Dex.

Dex turned to Calvin with a wicked smile. Uh-oh. *He should have known Dex wouldn't remain quiet for long.*

"Are you thinking what I'm thinking?"

"Probably not," Calvin replied with a laugh. He *doubted anyone thought what Dex did.*

Dex held his arms out at his sides and fell onto his back, his body compressing the snow under the weight of his equipment. Calvin laughed as Dex moved his arms up and down and his legs open and closed, declaring cheerfully, "Snow angels!"

It was official. His friend was a nutcase. "How old *are you again?"*

"Old enough to make some awesome snow angels. Come on."

Calvin arched an eyebrow at him. "You want me to roll around in the snow wearing eighty pounds of tactical gear?"

"Yes! No one's watching. We have a few minutes before someone comes looking for us."

Calvin couldn't believe he was even considering it. What the hell. Why not? He walked close to Dex, turned, and spread his arms before dropping back into the thick layers of snow. The two of them laughed like a couple of schoolboys as they wiped the snow with their limbs. He couldn't remember the last time he'd done this. Actually, he could. It was with Ethan, back when they were a couple of lanky, awkward teens. They'd make snow angels in the empty parking lot near their old apartment building and lie there together laughing, watching the clouds go by. Speaking of his best friend,

Catch a Tiger by the Tail

Ethan pounced into the snow next to Calvin, his tail twitching before he started rolling around in the snow.

"What in the hell are you three doing?"

Shit. Calvin sat up, feeling his cheeks burning. Ethan leaped behind him to hide. Like Maddock wouldn't be able to spot his huge tiger Therian butt sticking out from behind Calvin. Dex, on the other hand, was unfazed by their sergeant's scowl. He smiled widely up at Maddock. "Snow angels."

"Let me rephrase that. Why in the hell are you two making snow angels?"

"Because it's fun. Remember when you used to do them with me and Cael?" Dex turned his head to Calvin. "We lost my brother in the snow once. I shit you not. Dad had to excavate him."

Calvin burst out laughing. "What?"

"It's true," Maddock grumbled. "The boys jumped into this huge mound of snow in the backyard despite my telling them not to a hundred times. Dex dug his way out the side of it, but Cael got lost. He was so small, wearing this puffy coat onesie."

"Didn't help that his onesie was white." Dex sat up with a chuckle. He shook his head at his dad. "Not the brightest idea."

Maddock shrugged. "Hey, I told him that, but it's the one he wanted."

Dex grinned. "He looked like a marshmallow."

With a laugh, Calvin got to his feet. He helped Dex up, smiling as Dex and Maddock walked off, reminiscing about the brothers' childhood shenanigans. Calvin followed, holding on to Ethan's tail as his partner walked ahead of him. Felids hated having their tails grabbed, but Calvin had been holding on to Ethan's since childhood. It had been their security blanket back when it was just the two of them.

Inside the BearCat, their team was secured in their seats, with Sloane lying serenely at Dex's feet. Ash sat beside Cael at the surveillance console, his eyes closed and his head on Cael's lap as Cael went on about some new gadget he'd put together. Letty and Rosa chatted, while Maddock took the wheel. It was far too cold for their Therian teammates to want to shift back to Human form in the truck. Most Felids had little tolerance for the cold. Calvin was strapped in his seat at the end of the bench, and Ethan lay beside him on the floor, his large furry head resting on Calvin's lap.

Man, he was beat. Another twelve-hour, ten-day rotation coming to an end. He couldn't wait to get in, have a hot shower, and totally crash. As if sensing his thoughts, Ethan huffed. He rubbed his head against Calvin's leg, seeking affection. Calvin obliged, absently stroking his head or scratching behind his ears as he listened to his team chatting. At one point Calvin dozed off, woken up only when Ethan nuzzled Calvin's face. He couldn't have drifted off long since the truck was still moving.

The near silence around him spoke volumes of how tired everyone was. Even Dex was mostly quiet, murmuring softly at Sloane while nuzzling him. Their team leader's deep chainsaw-like purrs reverberated through the truck. His eyes were closed in contentment, and he didn't care who heard him purr. The change in Sloane amazed Calvin. A year and a half ago Sloane had been ready and eager to kick Dex's ass at the drop of a hat. The mere mention of the guy had been enough to draw a feral growl from Sloane.

It had been rough for all of them. Sloane had been miserable and, quite frankly, an asshole. Not that Calvin blamed him. He knew how much Sloane had been hurting. Now Sloane was so at peace, his tail didn't even twitch. Calvin couldn't help his smile. His friend was happy again. The team had mourned Gabe's loss, and like Calvin, they'd begun to mourn the loss of their team leader and friend.

Dex lifted his head, and their gazes met. A warm smile came onto his friend's face, as if he knew what Calvin had been thinking. With a wink, Dex turned his attention back to Sloane, who nudged at his hand until his muzzle was underneath it. Dex chuckled, leaving his hand on Sloane's muzzle and scratching the top of his head with his free hand.

It had taken Calvin some time to figure Dex out, to see the man behind the big-kid persona. Calvin understood why Ethan was able to talk to Dex. The guy was nothing but genuine in everything he did, loyal to a fault, and would go through the very gates of hell itself to protect those he cared about. Yeah, sometimes Dex did stupid things, but he wasn't stupid. He had his reasons. Like his decision to go after Hogan on his own and keep it from Sloane. Dex's habit of not following the rules got him into trouble, but everything he did came from a deep-rooted sense of justice, a need to do what was right. He simply needed to learn to have a little more faith in those around him.

Inside HQ, Ethan waited patiently in his Therian form outside the en suite shower of the Therian PSTC room they decided on instead of one of the curtained changing areas. This way Calvin could shower and get rid of his cold, wet clothes. Cael and Rosa brought Calvin, Dex, and Letty their toiletry bags from their lockers along with clean, dry uniforms. Once Calvin had showered and dressed, he administered Post Shift Trauma Care.

Like so many other things between them, administering PSTC had changed. Every touch, every look, every breath held a different meaning. It turned into a battle of self-control for Calvin. He made sure Ethan drank a couple of bottles of Gatorade before handing over the power bars. When the dizziness stopped and Ethan was feeling strong enough, he grabbed a towel to slip around his waist, something he'd never done before. Calvin pretended he didn't notice, and he continued gathering supplies as Ethan stepped into the shower. Afterward, Calvin helped him get dressed.

When he fastened the buttons on Ethan's uniform shirt for him, he could feel Ethan's heated gaze on him, his intense green eyes studying Calvin's every move. Ethan could dress himself by this point, but instead he let Calvin do it. He stood silently before Calvin, his thick biceps, broad shoulders, expansive chest, and tapered waist driving Calvin to distraction. Ethan stood with his legs slightly apart and his hands on his muscular thighs.

Ethan had always been big and strong, but Calvin remembered their teenage years. Even tiger Therians were awkward during that time. Ethan's limbs had been too long for him to maneuver efficiently. His clothes and his shoes never fit right. It seemed like he grew a couple of inches by the day. Meanwhile Calvin stopped growing when he reached five foot seven. As they got older, Calvin envied the easy way Ethan's body had filled out, how he built muscle while Calvin had to work out every damn day. Muscle-building came naturally to tiger Therians. They were the biggest of the Felids, the heaviest. When Ethan turned sixteen, he had the body of a guy in his twenties. Eventually Calvin caught up, but he still maintained his boyish looks, making him look younger than Ethan despite being older. Occasionally Calvin would get carded at a bar or club, and Ethan laughed his ass off every time.

Calvin cursed under his breath as he struggled to get a button through one of the wonky holes. Ethan's larger hand came to rest on Calvin's, and he brushed his lips over Calvin's temple to leave a feathery kiss. He took over the task of buttoning up his shirt the rest of the way. Calvin didn't know what to do with himself when Ethan did things like that, randomly doing something to assure Calvin they were more than friends. Ethan was trying. It showed in his intimate gestures when no one was looking. It wasn't that Calvin expected Ethan to be all over him, but his best friend was so reserved with his emotions, Calvin often wondered if Ethan wanted him as badly as he wanted Ethan.

Whenever they were alone, all Calvin could think about was kissing Ethan, touching him, feeling him. The need was overwhelming, and he hated how it put him in a pissy mood. He was trying his best to be patient. They'd fooled around since the incident in the surveillance van where they'd gotten each other off after a heated argument, but those moments had been few and far between, and it was always Calvin who initiated it. Why was he doing this to himself? He was too tired for this right now.

"Let's get some food in you," Calvin muttered. Ethan nodded, his big dopey grin making Calvin smile. Ethan always found a way to pull Calvin out of his funk.

They headed upstairs to the canteen. While Ethan ate his Therian-sized triple quarter pounder with fries and milkshake, Calvin struggled to stay awake. The end of a ten-day shift was tough enough without Sparks and her damn TIN Associate Training Program. For weeks now Destructive Delta had been pushed to its limits with cardiovascular conditioning, speed drills, strength training, flexibility, and Sparks's mixed martial arts specialist, who was kicking their asses three times a week at a secure location. The location was so secret it wasn't even disclosed to their team. Austen drove them there and back in the BearCat, and it was somewhere different each and every time.

Were their regular training schedule and callouts not enough? Between Sparks's guy and Ash training them in Muay Thai and Close Quarter Combat, they were lucky they got a day off to themselves, and usually those days were spent recovering.

Calvin almost passed out on the table but caught himself. "Man, I think I'm gonna crash in one of the bays. I'm too tired to go home."

Ethan nodded and finished his milkshake. He made a brushing movement in front of his teeth.

"Yeah, could you grab my stuff from my locker?" Calvin stood with a yawn. Ethan put his thumb up, and Calvin told him he'd leave the door open so Ethan could find him.

Calvin wasn't the only one too tired to head home. There were a lot more sleeper bay doors closed than usual. From the speed at which Dex and Sloane disappeared, he'd wager a guess they were presently occupying one of those bays, though he doubted there was much sleeping going on. Those two were like a couple of horny teenagers. Calvin found an empty bay toward the end of the hall and walked in, leaving the door slightly ajar. He unfastened his thigh rig and placed it on the desk, followed by his phone and everything else in his pockets. Soon his boots, socks, and shirt were off. He draped his pants over the back of the chair, staying in his black undershirt and blue boxer briefs.

His toiletry bag had a toothbrush and toothpaste, but he just wanted to get that done and over with, so he used one of the newly packaged brushes on offer in one of the bay's many service cubbyholes on the side wall. He brushed his teeth and rinsed at the small aluminum sink before wiping his mouth on the towel provided. The heating kept the room warm enough to sleep with a blanket and not be uncomfortable. Thank God for the sleeper bays. Home away from home.

Calvin sat on the edge of the bed, wondering what was taking Ethan so long. With a groan, he flopped onto his side and drew his legs up. *Screw it. Pajamas were overrated anyway. His head hit the pillow, and next thing he knew he was being pulled back against a hard body. The room was shrouded in darkness, with only the soft glow from the hall coming in through the tiny slit under the closed door. With a soft sigh, Calvin turned in Ethan's arms and snuggled up close. It wasn't the first time Ethan had slept in one of the bays with him, or even in the same bed. Hell, they'd been doing it since they were kids. It was the first time Ethan had held him this close, their bare legs intertwined and Ethan's warm breath against Calvin's skin before he planted a kiss on Calvin's brow. Ethan was in his boxers and T-shirt, his warm skin smelling of soap.*

"Good night, Cal."

It is now that you're here. "Good night." Calvin shimmied lower so he could rest his head against

Ethan's chest, the soft beating of his best friend's heart lulling him. Ethan gave him a squeeze, and Calvin put his hand to Ethan's chest before he drifted off into a peaceful sleep. Unfortunately, it didn't last long.

Sometime in the middle of the night, Calvin was startled awake by Ethan's screams. Calvin bolted upright, ready for a fight. Remembering where he was, he swiftly switched on the desk lamp and turned to find Ethan in the midst of a terrible fit. Whatever he was dreaming, it was bad, and Calvin quickly got out of bed. He knew from experience not to touch Ethan when he was having a nightmare like this. The first time Ethan slept at his house and went into a fit, Calvin had tried to wake him, and Ethan almost broke Calvin's arm. That had been *before* Ethan had grown into his strength. Trying to subdue him now could prove lethal.

"Ethan, wake up," Calvin called out gently but loud enough to try to rouse him. Sweat dripped down the side of Ethan's face, his expression one of terror and pain. It broke Calvin's heart. "Please wake up, Ethan."

Ethan arched his back, a horrific cry tearing from his lips, followed by an anguished, "Sloane!"

As if hearing Ethan's cry for him, Sloane threw the sleeper bay door open and rushed in. As team leader, his handprint would override the security locks on any of the sleeper bay doors, and Calvin couldn't have been more relieved to see him. Dex flipped on the lights, his gaze moving to the bed.

"What's going on?"

"He's having a nightmare. A bad one." Calvin hated feeling helpless, especially where his best friend was concerned, but he was fully aware of his limitations as a Human. In all the years he'd known Ethan, he'd helped his friend through some tough nightmares, but none had ever come close to this.

"Wake him up." Dex moved to the bed, and Sloane threw his arms around him, hauling him back just as Ethan screamed. His fangs started to elongate, and Calvin backed up near Sloane.

"He's going to shift!"

Ash thundered into the room with Cael on his heels. "What the fuck is going on?"

Dex put a hand out in front of Cael, stopping him from getting closer. "It's Hobbs. He's having some kind of fit, and it looks like he might shift."

"Shit. We have to do something." Ash rushed over to the cubbyholes and started rifling through the Therian medical kit. "We need to sedate him. Where's the fucking injector?"

"What happened?" Cael asked worriedly.

Ethan's screams filled the room as his nails grew in and his mass began to shift, his muscles pulling and his body changing. They didn't have much time. If Ethan shifted while he was asleep, who the hell knew what he'd do?

Calvin couldn't understand. "He's had plenty of nightmares before, but he's never shifted through any of them. Whatever he's dreaming about, it's scaring the shit out of him. All I know is that he screamed Sloane's name before he started shifting."

Ash spun on his heels. "He what?"

"He was having a fit. Then he screamed Sloane's name."

"The facility. He's dreaming about the goddamn facility."

Sloane ignored the warnings and climbed onto the bed with Ethan. He wrestled him down, pinning him to the bed. Ethan hissed and tried to claw at him, but Sloane kept his arms down, though with Ethan being stronger Sloane wouldn't be able to hold him down for long. At least it seemed to have stopped Ethan from shifting into his Therian form.

"Ash, help me out here."

Ash ran over and helped Sloane keep Ethan pinned, the two struggling against Ethan's determination to free himself at any cost.

"Hobbs, listen to me. It's Sloane. I'm fine. I'm okay. Wake up, buddy. You're dreaming. We're not there anymore. Open your eyes. Listen to my voice. It's okay."

"Sloane!" Ethan cried, his eyes flying open. He gasped for air, his body trembling beneath Sloane's and Ash's hold. Slowly, Ash backed off.

"Hey, it's okay," Sloane assured him gently. He ran a hand over Ethan's head and smiled. "It's okay. Just a bad dream. You're okay."

Ethan's eyes watered, and he threw his arms around Sloane, hugging him tight. Calvin's pulse steadied, and he gingerly sat at the edge of the bed. At the feel of him, Ethan released Sloane and turned onto his side. He curled up around Calvin, his arm going around Calvin's stomach and pulling him in close against him with a shuddered sigh.

"It's okay. No one's upset with you," Calvin promised.

Ethan squeezed his arms around Calvin's middle, and Calvin ran his fingers through Ethan's hair, comforting him. He knew what his friend was thinking. It always followed a nightmare, or any of the countless things that would make Ethan feel self-conscious. Except, with Ethan's anxiety, his embarrassment was always triple what anyone else's would be. Sloane climbed off the bed, his hand going to Calvin's shoulder and his expression sympathetic.

"Don't sweat it, big guy," Dex said, his tone gentle. "That's what we're here for. If you need anything else, just let us know."

"Thanks, guys. I appreciate it."

Calvin was lucky to have a family like Destructive Delta. It was difficult for people to understand Ethan's anxieties, much less have the patience it required on a daily basis. For Ethan it was a way of life, a constant struggle not to get overwhelmed by his fears. No one on his team ever hesitated when it came to Ethan. Sloane gave Calvin's shoulder a pat and leaned in, his voice quiet in Calvin's ear.

"He needs to talk about what happened."

Calvin nodded. He thanked everyone again and waited for them to leave, grateful when Dex turned off the lights, leaving only the soft glow of the desk lamp. When the door closed and the room was silent, Calvin lay down facing Ethan. It had been a month since Shultzon's goons had taken Ethan, Ash, and Sloane. Ethan refused to talk about what had happened. It was starting to take its toll.

"Ethan, please talk to me. Tell me about the facility."

Ethan was quiet. His eyes were closed, his chest rising and falling steadily. He could have been asleep, but he wasn't. Over the years Calvin had gotten to know every little hitch in his partner's breath and what it meant. He could read Ethan Hobbs like an open book. From Ethan's breathing alone, Calvin could tell if Ethan was asleep, upset, pissed off, or even having a wet dream. Right now Ethan was thinking. Like most of Ethan's fears, his hesitation to tell Calvin meant this was about Ethan judging himself. That's how Ethan's anxieties ate away at him. His perception of how others saw him was skewed, and as much as Ethan was aware of it, he couldn't stop it.

Calvin waited, giving Ethan time to put his thoughts into words, and then he waited for Ethan to take those words and find the voice to speak them. The latter was always the most difficult for his friend.

"When we were taken by Shultzon's men...," Ethan began softly, his voice barely above a whisper. "I woke up in a cage."

Calvin gritted his teeth. He remained quiet, not wanting to interrupt Ethan. What he wanted to do was punch something. That son of a bitch, Shultzon. Wherever TIN had him, Calvin hoped the asshole was rotting away inside his own cage.

"They were supposed to have taken Seb, but Fuller made a mistake. He didn't know there was more than one Hobbs. Shultzon was angry. He said I was... useless, because my disabilities were psychological and not physical like Seb's. He called me...." Ethan's eyes grew glassy, his pupils dilated. "He said I was broken. And then Ash was in a cage next to me trying to get out, and Sloane was strapped down to this horrible chair. They were going to inject the drug into him. I couldn't help him."

Ethan shut his eyes tight, and Calvin pulled him close. With a sniff, Ethan wrapped his arms around Calvin and buried his face against Calvin's T-shirt.

"I dreamed I was back there, and they killed Sloane because I couldn't help him. Because I was too scared. Broken."

"Fuck Shultzon. That asshole was out of his fucking mind, Ethan. He wanted to turn Therians into mindless super soldiers. He messed with your head, and he did the same to Sloane and Ash."

"And yet Ash got out."

Ethan pulled back enough to look into Calvin's eyes, the anguish gripping at Calvin's heart and squeezing.

"Ash got himself out of his cage, and Sloane got out of the chair. I couldn't get out. Could barely move. I'm stronger, and I couldn't do anything." Ethan shook his head, his lips pressed together as he tried to keep his emotions in check. "I was trained for those situations. If Ash hadn't talked me off the ledge…."

Calvin put his hand to Ethan's cheek. "Shultzon messed with you. He fucked up your meds."

"And what does that say about me, huh?" Ethan asked, agitated. "I'm so fucked-up I can't function without them anymore. I can't…. Without the meds I'm nothing. I can't do my job. I can't have fucking dinner with my family. Thanksgiving was a disaster. You got into a fight because of me. *Again. My whole life I've had someone fighting my battles for me because I've been too weak to do it myself.*"

"We talked about Thanksgiving. That wasn't your fault." Calvin's heart broke, but he did what he always did. He remained strong for Ethan, doing his best to soothe Ethan's fears. Calvin wiped the wetness from Ethan's reddened cheeks. "As for the rest, I will always fight for you. Not because you can't fight for yourself, but because you're my best friend. If some asshole has the balls to mess with you, he has to get through me first. I know you're bigger than me, and stronger, but that doesn't mean you're not allowed to lean on me, Ethan. That's what people do when they care about someone. Your fight becomes mine."

"I'm going to be on meds for the rest of my life. What if they stop working?"

"Then we'll find something else to help you."

Ethan sat up and shook his head. "I hate that I have no control of my own head. That I have to rely on stupid little pills. Everyone thinks I'm a fucking spaz."

"Hey, no one thinks that." Calvin sat up with a frown. "Are you telling me our friends, who woke up at four in the fucking morning after a twelve-hour shift and ran in here to make sure you were okay, that they think that?"

Ethan shook his head, and Calvin took hold of his hand.

"No, they don't. Look at your brother. How many prescriptions does Seb have? He can't function without those pills either, and he's the reason you wanted to become a THIRDS agent. You remember what he told you when you said you wanted to become an agent like him but couldn't because of your mutism?"

Ethan nodded.

"Tell me."

"He said my disabilities didn't define me. I define me."

"That's right." Calvin placed Ethan's hand to his lips for a kiss. "You define you, Ethan. Not your meds, not your mutism, not anyone else. You."

Ethan went quiet. He dropped his gaze to his hand in Calvin's before looking up at him, his expression softening. "I got out for you, you know."

"What do you mean?"

"In the cage, I couldn't move. I was so scared. Ash told me to do it for you. He said you didn't think I was broken."

Ethan searched his gaze, and Calvin made sure Ethan found what he was looking for.

"And he was right," Calvin replied with all the conviction he possessed. Twenty-four years they'd been inseparable, yet Ethan still needed to be reminded that Calvin was at his side because he wanted to be, *needed* to be, as much for himself as for Ethan. Calvin took Ethan's face in his hands. "You're not broken, Ethan. You're amazing, and that will never change." He stroked Ethan's cheek with his thumb and smiled. "Thank you for getting yourself out of there. I couldn't stop worrying about you."

"It scares me sometimes," Ethan said quietly.

"What's that?"

"How much I need you." Ethan pulled Calvin with him as he lay down. He snuggled up close and pressed his lips to Calvin's.

Calvin closed his eyes and parted his lips, allowing Ethan to slip his tongue in and deepen the kiss. He didn't question it or overthink it, just went with it. Whatever Ethan needed, Calvin would give.

Ethan's lips were soft, his mouth warm and tasting faintly of mint. Calvin loved how Ethan tasted, how he smelled, how he felt underneath his touch. He loved the way Ethan's strong hands caressed his skin.

This was uncharted territory for both of them, and despite knowing everything about each other, Calvin was eager to explore more of this side of Ethan. They'd seen each other naked more times than he could count. They argued and fought but always worked things out. When Ethan pulled back, Calvin missed his breath on him, the feel of his lips, but he smiled at his best friend and cuddled up to him. As long as they were together, they'd make it through anything. Them against the world.

Chapter Two

CALVIN TOOK a sip of his beer before letting out a happy sigh. After the last few months dealing with all the crazy of the Order, Coalition, Hogan, and Shultzon, he was relieved they'd gotten back to doing regular callouts. It was no less emotionally and physically exhausting, but it was a far cry from what they'd been up against recently. Though their first week back on callouts seemed determined to make up for lost time, he was glad things were back to normal. Well, as normal as was possible for their team.

Following another long rotation, Destructive Delta did what it had been doing since Dex joined the team—taking over Dekatria, their second base of operation. By now all the regulars knew who they were, welcoming them with open arms. There was no hostility toward them, and no one cared if they were Therian or Human. Whatever anti-Therian regulars had frequented the bar had jumped ship the moment Bradley bought the place.

He made it known real quick he wouldn't tolerate any of that crap. There were plenty of other bars in New York City for them to spread their stupid, but his place wouldn't be one of them.

The jaguar Therian himself dropped by the table, a big grin on his handsome face. He gave Dex a playful shove. "So what do you think of the new menu?"

Dex's eyes lit up as he scanned the trendy, newly designed menu. "I think I've died and gone to heaven. Except I know I haven't because Ash is here."

Ash gracefully flipped Dex off before resuming his conversation with Cael about sharing some loaded cheese fries.

They all laughed as Dex put in his ginormous order. Calvin had no idea how the guy put all that food away and managed to stay in shape. It was like he had cheetah Therian metabolism or something. Calvin noticed the black line art on the right side of Bradley's neck peeking out from under his T-shirt.

"Hey, is that new?" Calvin asked, pointing to the intricate swirls. It looked Japanese in style, possibly a koi fish.

Bradley touched his fingers to it. "Yeah. It's been a while since I had a new one. Started getting that itch." He laughed softly.

"Who designs your tattoos?" Dex asked curiously.

"Friend of mine. I love ink, but sadly I'm not much of an artist. Otherwise I'd probably have been doing that instead. Gonna have to find myself a new artist, though. My friend's getting himself hitched and moving to California."

Ethan pointed to Calvin, catching him off guard.

"You design?" Bradley looked as surprised as some of their teammates. It wasn't really something

Calvin talked about. His face grew warm as all eyes landed on him.

"Yeah. I've been drawing since I was a kid. In college I did a couple of designs for people. Word spread, and pretty soon I had enough commissions to pay for my books and supplies."

"Shit, that's right," Dex said, his grin widening. "Apparently he's awesome. Hobbs said he draws some kickass designs."

Calvin glanced over at Ethan, who had *guilty written all over his silly smiling face. Ethan nodded and held his thumbs up.*

"You still design?" Bradley asked.

Calvin shrugged. "I never really stopped. I didn't need to take any more commissions once I joined the THIRDS, and my schedule didn't leave a lot of time for it, but yeah, for fun."

"Maybe I can give you a call sometime. See your stuff."

"Sure." Calvin returned Bradley's smile. It had been a long time since he'd drawn anything for anyone. Bradley went off with their orders, and Dex was about to say something when Calvin felt someone step up behind him.

"Agent Summers?"

Calvin turned in his chair to see Felipe Bautista standing there, a shy smile on his face. "Hey." Calvin stood, smiling warmly. "I'm surprised to see you here."

"Agent Summers—"

"Calvin. Please," Calvin insisted. He held his hand out, and Felipe took it with a smile.

"Calvin. I'm sorry if I'm interrupting." Felipe greeted the rest of the table, some more warily than others.

"You're not," Calvin assured him. *"How have you been?"*

"Would you mind if we talked privately?"

"Not at all. I didn't think you'd want to talk to me after what happened."

"You were doing your job." Felipe motioned over to the bar and a couple of empty stools at the end of it.

Calvin excused himself, telling Ethan he'd be back. He slid his half-empty beer to Ethan to finish off. His best friend looked puzzled by Calvin's departure, but his attention was quickly commandeered by Dex. Leaving his teammates to their shenanigans—or rather, Dex's—Calvin joined Felipe at the bar, where they ordered a couple of beers. Calvin patiently waited for Felipe to say whatever was on his mind.

"When I heard Drew was dead...." Felipe swallowed hard and closed his eyes for a moment before seeming to get his emotions in check. He shook his head and let out a soft laugh. When he opened his eyes, they were filled with heartache and pain. *"What does it say about me that I miss him? That for the first few seconds when I wake up in the morning, I expect to see him there? I miss a murderer."*

"You miss the guy you fell in love with. The guy you thought he was. When Hogan approached Drew, he should have walked away, or at the very least asked for help. Instead he let Hogan twist him up inside and turn him into a killer. He risked his freedom, his life, you, to follow Hogan. He hadn't been your Drew for a long time, Felipe." Calvin put his hand on Felipe's arm in the hopes of offering him some comfort. *"What happened to Drew wasn't your fault."*

"I keep telling myself that I should have pushed harder. I suspected he was lying to me about where he went, but I didn't want to believe something was wrong. I was terrified he might be cheating on me." Felipe wiped a tear from his eye. "It was so much worse."

Calvin felt for the guy. He really did. "How have you been?"

"I've been seeing a therapist to help me work through all this. I feel guilty, thinking if I'd done more, he wouldn't have involved himself with Hogan. That he'd still be alive, and things might have gone back to how they were. I left the city for a few weeks, to get away from the reporters, the threats, the hate mail, everything. The way people looked at me...." Tears welled in his eyes again. *"Like I* had killed those people."

"Hey." Calvin pulled him into his arms. It wasn't Felipe's fault his boyfriend had done what he had. Felipe was a good guy, a Therian teacher who cared about his students and worked with local homeless Therian youth. He didn't deserve the shit he'd been thrown into. "Drew shut you out. If you'd suspected and gone after him, Hogan might have killed you."

Felipe nodded and pulled back with a sniff. He thanked Calvin for the tissue he offered, a small smile coming on his face. "Seems like whenever we meet, I end up crying on your shoulder."

Calvin smiled. He reached into his pocket and pulled out one of his THIRDS cards with his name and number on it. After flipping it over, he took one of the pens lying on the bar for signing credit card slips and scribbled his personal cell phone number. "Here." He handed the card to Felipe. "Anytime you need my shoulder, you call."

"Thank you. I'd like that." Felipe tucked the card into his pocket before wiping his eyes. "On a lighter note, how's your boyfriend?"

"Ah, that. He's not really my boyfriend. Sort of." Felipe arched an eyebrow at him, and Calvin laughed. "Yeah, we THIRDS agents don't do anything the easy way. Everything I told you about us was true, except the boyfriend part. Ethan and I have been best friends since we were kids. Things changed between us, and that night I left you in your apartment, things got a little heated."

Felipe's face went red. "Oh God, he knows about that night?"

There was no way to make it sound less awkward. "He was in the surveillance van listening."

"He's an agent as well?" The color in Felipe's face intensified.

"He's my partner at the THIRDS."

Realization seemed to dawn on Felipe. "Was he at the table?"

"Yeah, the tiger Therian sitting next to me."

Felipe's eyes went wide. "Oh my God, he must want to punch my lights out."

If Felipe had been close by that night, it's possible Ethan might have. Calvin had never seen his partner so pissed off. "Ethan knows the job. He doesn't hold it against you." Too much.

Felipe's expression softened. "From what you've told me about him, he sounds like a great guy."

"He is. We've been through everything together. Then, like I told you that night, things changed." Calvin took a sip of his beer. It wasn't just the change that had turned everything upside down. It was Ethan's inability to decide what to do about it.

"Does he feel the same about your relationship?" Felipe asked gently.

"He's got SM—selective mutism—and social anxiety. Change is really hard for him. Something as big as this…. It's been difficult for both of us. He hasn't told me he loves me, but the way he feels about me has definitely changed. I don't know if he's ready to put a name to whatever's going on between us or if he'll be ready to move forward. I don't want to push him, so we've been taking things slow. Really slow."

"I can understand how the SM would make things difficult for him. I have a student with SM, though he's responding well to the behavioral therapy. How long ago was Ethan diagnosed?"

"Late teens. Ethan was always a shy kid, and with everything going on at home, his parents assumed he was quiet. Ethan's doing better now than when we were kids, but he didn't take to the therapy as well as his parents had hoped. The therapy definitely helped, but he's never been able to work past the mutism. He has good days and not-so-good days. When his anxiety hits him hard, it tears me up. There's not much I can do for him on those days other than help him feel safe."

"He's lucky to have you."

"I'm lucky to have him too. He gave me something to fight for." It was hard, thinking about everything he and Ethan had endured. It wasn't something he usually brought up. There was something about Felipe that made him feel at ease.

"What do you mean?"

"Growing up, it was me and my mom. My mom had two jobs so she could pay the rent and buy food, so I was on my own a good deal of the time. We lived in whatever shithole we could afford, though sometimes we were barely able to pay for that much. There were a few months when we were living in my mom's car.

We moved around so Social Services wouldn't take me away from her. She did her best, and she was clean. No drugs, no booze, no string of deadbeat boyfriends. When my dad left, he took everything but the car. He would have taken that if she hadn't chased after him with a shotgun."

"I'm so sorry to hear that."

"Yeah, I wasn't always the shiny agent you see before you," Calvin said with a laugh. He moved his gaze to his fingers, feeling embarrassed. "Anyway, Ethan wasn't much better off. His dad lost his job after he was left paralyzed by the Melanoe virus. It slowly ate away at his immune system, affecting his leg muscles. Took years, working beneath the surface. You know what Therian medicine was like back then. Imagine being a little kid and hearing your dad screaming in pain day in and day out. No one could do anything about it. Ethan's doctors believed he was traumatized by the ordeal, bringing on the SM. The hospital bills bankrupted them. They lost the house and everything in it, forcing them to move into a shitty complex right next door to us. We met at school."

"And now?"

Calvin couldn't help his smile. "We got out. Together, we made a pact. We always wanted to help people, protect them. Ethan's older brothers worked for the THIRDS, and Ethan wanted to follow in their footsteps. I wanted to be someone my mom could be proud of. My dad had let her down. I wasn't going to do the same. Rafe, Seb, and Ethan worked to get their parents a new house, and I'd been saving every penny I could for years. With the THIRDS, I managed to buy my mom a nice little brownstone on the same block as Ethan's family. By then our moms had been through almost as much as we had. They're best friends, help each other out. We didn't want to separate them. We're family."

"Can I ask a favor?" Felipe leaned in close and placed his hand on Calvin's.

"Um, sure."

"Would you come to my youth center and talk to the kids?"

"Me?" Calvin couldn't help his surprise at the request.

"Yes. Your story is inspiring. Everything you and Ethan suffered, where you came from, it's not defined you. Look at you. You saved my life. These kids need to see that no matter where they are in life right now, it can get better. You're living proof of that."

"I, uh, sure. Of course. Call me and we'll set up a date." *Wow. Calvin didn't know what else to say. No one had ever looked at him as a role model before. He'd never pictured himself as anything other than a survivor. Though he often wondered if he would have ended up where he was now without Ethan at his side.*

There was a distinct clearing of the throat, and Calvin turned his head up at a disgruntled-looking Ethan. He narrowed his eyes at Calvin before he dropped his gaze to Calvin's hand. Felipe swiftly pulled away. Calvin had been so lost in thought he hadn't noticed Felipe's hand had still been on his. He hadn't felt Ethan approach either.

"Felipe, this is Ethan Hobbs. Ethan, you know Felipe Bautista."

Ethan looked Felipe over, his expression guarded.

"It's an absolute pleasure to meet you, Ethan. Calvin's told me so much about you."

Felipe smiled widely, and Ethan wrinkled his nose in response. This was going well. From somewhere close by, someone called over to Felipe.

"My friends have arrived. Please excuse me."

Calvin was pretty sure it wasn't just the arrival of his friends that had Felipe taking off in a hurry. Ethan stepped in front of Calvin, blocking his view of Felipe. Well, this was new.

"What?"

Ethan motioned behind him, where Calvin could just about make out Felipe hugging his friends and smiling brightly. They chatted before going off to find a table. When Calvin turned back to Ethan, his best friend put his hand on Calvin's as Felipe had done.

Wait, was Ethan jealous?

"We were talking. He's been having a hard time since the incident with Collins."

Ethan removed his hand and turned to the bar. His expression hadn't changed. He was jealous. At times Calvin had no idea what to do with Ethan in these types of situations. With a sigh, he got up.

"I'm going to the bathroom." He left Ethan at the bar and headed for the restroom. How was he supposed to process this information? Ethan was jealous. So he didn't want Calvin getting close to another guy, yet he was afraid to be with Calvin. Was it that big a step? They'd already kissed and fooled around. They had their friendship to keep them grounded. He wished he knew what Ethan wanted from him. Whatever it was, he hoped Ethan decided soon. Calvin didn't know how much more his heart could take.

"I see you two are getting nowhere fast."

Great. Just what Ethan didn't need. He let out a grunt in response to Ash's tease.

"Don't get pissy with me. If you don't make a move on your boy, someone else will. I got a feeling there's a certain wolf Therian who wouldn't think twice. Bautista's already sampled the goods. Guess he liked it."

Ethan hissed at him, and Ash chuckled. *Asshole.* Since when was Ash the expert on relationships anyway? Then again, he and Cael seemed to be settling into theirs. Ash was actually happy most days. It was weird. What did it say about him that Ash could get it right and he couldn't? God, he needed a drink. He tapped the bar and held up two fingers to Bradley. With a wink, Bradley brought him a double shot of whiskey.

"Wow, on the hard stuff already?"

Ethan rolled his eyes and snatched up his whiskey glass, giving Bradley a nod in thanks. Everyone else was moving forward in their relationships except for him and Calvin. Although Ash wasn't completely at ease with being open about him and Cael, he was doing his best and making the effort. The rumor of his relationship with a guy had spread through Unit Alpha, and instead of worrying about it, Ash went with it. He challenged anyone who tried to make something of his move from girls to guys, or rather one guy in particular. And of course he did so in typical charming Ash fashion—in other words, putting the fear of God in anyone dumb enough to make a joke at his expense.

Dex and Sloane were sweet together, even when Dex was driving his boyfriend crazy, which was the majority of the time. The two were in synch, their bond bringing them closer together, giving them the ability to sense each other in a way they hadn't before. Ethan still couldn't believe they'd bonded. He didn't know all that much about Therian bonds. It was one of those things not discussed out in the open, something that stemmed from deep within their feral side. Therians were always being accused of being animals. The last thing they needed was evidence suggesting there was some truth to the accusations. His dad had talked to him and his brothers about it when they'd been younger, stressing how serious it was, how dangerous for the parties involved. If there was ever a cautionary tale, it was Seb and Hudson. His big brother hadn't been the same since he'd lost his mate. Like a part of him was missing. He suffered daily, and Ethan hated seeing Seb in pain like that, but there wasn't anything he or Rafe could do about it. Not that Rafe gave a shit. When had his big brother become such a dick?

With a sigh, Ethan sat on the barstool Calvin had vacated and sipped his whiskey, when Ash took a seat beside him. He ordered a beer and took a few swigs after it arrived, sitting silently. Ethan arched an eyebrow at him. Maybe Cael's manners were rubbing off on him.

"You, me, Sloane, we've been through a lot of fucked-up shit. The last year and a half alone has been insane. Yet for some inexplicable reason, these guys have stuck by our side. We've put them through hell. We've hurt them bad. And they keep coming back. Now that means they're either fucked in the head, which in Daley's case is most likely, or they see something in us we don't. I know you got it rough, but you got a guy who's been bleeding for you since the day you met. He's had your back and taken on anyone stupid enough to cause you grief. I ain't ever seen anything like it. For a Human his size, he's one tough little son of a bitch."

Ethan swallowed hard. He couldn't deny Ash's words. Calvin had been at his side from the beginning, their friendship tested time and time again, but it never faltered. Calvin never faltered. While growing up, he'd taken on Humans and Therians, anyone who messed with Ethan. Here he was this huge tiger Therian, and his Human best friend had fearlessly defended him against all odds. He still did.

Cael cheerfully bounded over, his pink cheeks giving away how tipsy he was. He threw his arms around Ash's neck and planted a big kiss on his cheek, making Ash chuckle.

"Hey, Trouble." Ash gave Cael a kiss on the lips.

Ethan's brows shot up. He might never get used to seeing this side of Ash.

"Hi, Hobbs!" Cael gave Ethan a hug before pulling back and looking around. Ethan was used to it by now. Wherever he or Calvin went, everyone expected the other to be there at all times. It didn't annoy him. He just found it strange that everyone thought they did every single little thing together. Okay, maybe they did most things together, but not *everything*. He pointed behind him to the door that led to the restrooms.

"Ah, okay."

Cael turned back to Ash, and Ethan noted how at ease he was. He noticed the special way Cael smiled just for him, the sparkle in his bright gray eyes, and the subtle gestures that always had him touching some part of Ash, his arm, his chest, his shoulder or leg.

"So… Mr. Keeler…."

"Uh-oh." Ash laughed and received a playful punch in the arm. He winked at Cael and nudged his cheek. "What can I do for you, sweetheart?"

"Dex says that Sloane can totally beat you at arm wrestling. I told him he's been eating too many gummy bears and the sugar's gone to his head, because you can totally beat Sloane."

Ash eyed Cael. "You two made a bet, didn't you?"

Cael nodded, a big sweet smile spread across his face. It was clear to Ethan then how easily Cael wrapped Ash around his little finger. It was also clear Ash was fully aware and went along with it anyway.

"What are the stakes?" Ash asked before taking a swig of his beer.

"If he wins, you have to wear the T-shirts of his choice for a week."

Ash let out a low grunt. "And if you win?"

"Twenty-four hours of complete silence to distribute at the time of your choosing in whatever amount you choose."

Ash put a hand up. "Wait. You're saying if I beat Sloane, I get twenty-four hours' worth of silence to dish out on your brother whenever I want? So let's say, if he's annoying the fuck out of me during lunch, I can tell him to shut up for an hour?"

Cael nodded. "The only exception is if it's an emergency."

Ash jumped off his barstool. "Let's do this." Cael bounced off, and Ash leaned into Ethan, talking quietly. "Don't worry so much about fucking it up that you end up doing just that." Ash gave his back a hearty pat before strolling off, his arm around Cael, who'd stopped to wait for him.

Ethan finished off his drink, recalling the night in the surveillance van. Not their little show in front of Dex—he was still trying to forget Dex had been there—but what had come before that. He could still hear the soft gasps and moans in his ear as Calvin seduced Felipe. Ethan had watched Felipe kiss Calvin on the front steps of his house moments earlier. It had twisted Ethan up inside. Until then he'd been trying to figure things out, but when he saw Calvin being kissed and touched by another guy, when he heard Calvin's hoarse whispers and moans, Ethan had been ready to go feral. His inner Felid had been furious. No one was supposed to lay a hand on Calvin in that way or make him sound like that.

Ash was right about Felipe. All Calvin had to do was say the word, and the guy would make a move. Felipe might be a nice guy, but Ethan wasn't about to give Calvin up. It was time for him to get his act together and do what he had to for the both of them.

Ethan headed for the restroom and caught Calvin as he emerged. Before anyone could spot them, Ethan pulled him into the next room. It was a supply closet filled with storage equipment, trunks, microphones, the karaoke machine case, and loads of other gear. Ethan locked the door behind him before turning to Calvin. He took hold of Calvin's waist and lifted him onto the edge of a large speaker trunk so they were eye to eye.

"I was jealous," Ethan admitted. He put his finger to Calvin's lips so he could finish. "I don't want anyone taking you away from me."

Calvin gently moved Ethan's hand away, his features softening. "Ethan, no one's going to take me away from you. I love you. That's not something I give easily."

"I know." Ethan put his hand to Calvin's cheek, trying to find the right words. There was so much he wanted to say, but his thoughts got all jumbled in his head. Ever since Calvin kissed him at the hospital, Ethan had been trying to make sense of all these new and unsettling emotions. There was only one way he could approach this. The same way he approached everything with his best friend. Head-on. "When we were kids, I'd dream about you. About us. Together."

Calvin gaped at him. "You did?"

"Yes." Ethan felt his cheeks heat up. There wasn't much he kept from Calvin, but this was one of those instances where he'd believed keeping his thoughts to himself would be best for the both of them. "Lots of times."

"Why didn't you say anything?"

"I was scared. Scared you'd stop being my friend. If I lost you…." That earned him a scowl, and rightfully so. In his heart, Ethan knew Calvin would never stop being his best friend, but convincing his head was another matter.

"After everything we've been through together, did you really think I'd leave you, and over something like that?"

Ethan's mind fought against him like it did with so many other things, allowing his fear to paralyze him. Fear was one thing that had never factored into his relationship with Calvin until things started changing between them. Now he couldn't seem to shake those fears. Change was difficult for him. Always had been. One day, when he was little, they didn't have his favorite cereal in stock, and his mom brought home one he'd never had before. He'd cried for days. Despite being young, he knew his crying was irrational. No one had died. But to him, it felt like his world was crumbling around him. Seb helped him challenge those distorted thoughts, and soon Ethan could do it on his own. Didn't mean it was easy, but at least he hadn't cried over cereal since.

"One night, when you slept over, I watched you sleep. I wanted to kiss you, but my head wouldn't let me. I told myself I had to stop thinking about you that way. How I was lucky to have you there with me. You were my whole world. You still are. After a while, it worked. I loved you, just not the way I wanted to love you."

"Jesus, Ethan."

Calvin swallowed hard. A host of emotions seemed to flash through his eyes, and Ethan would have given anything to know what his best friend was thinking. His shy smile squeezed Ethan's heart.

"How did you want to love me?"

Ethan stroked Calvin's hand as he held his gaze. His eyes were so blue. Like the ocean. Ethan loved the ocean. Why couldn't he be more eloquent? The more he wanted to say something, the less he could say it. Like his vocal cords didn't work. He opened his mouth and his throat tightened. Closing his eyes, he took a deep breath and tried again. His pulse sped up, and he couldn't say a damn word. Calvin put his hand to Ethan's cheek.

"It's okay."

It wasn't okay. It was frustrating and embarrassing. This was important, too important to mess up, to leave to chance, or for the moment when he could relax enough to mumble a few words. It wasn't good enough. Not when it concerned the man who'd had his heart from the very first day they met. Who'd shed blood, sweat, and tears at his side.

Unable to draw sound for the words in his heart, Ethan kissed Calvin, intent on showing him what he meant to say. No one understood him better than Calvin. He prayed this time was no different.

Calvin blossomed at his touch, his lips parting so Ethan could slip his tongue inside his mouth to taste every crevice. Ethan lost himself in Calvin's scent, in their hungry kiss and the desperation flowing through him at wanting to feel more of Calvin's skin. He longed to kiss every faint freckle peppered across Calvin's nose and cheeks, over his shoulders and back. Calvin eagerly returned his kiss, a soft gasp escaping him when Ethan wrapped his arms around him and brought him up hard against Ethan. Their breaths grew ragged, their hands exploring, fingers digging into flesh. Ethan needed Calvin to understand how much he wanted him, even if at times he didn't know how to say so.

Ethan's tongue swirled around Calvin's before he pulled back. He trailed wet kisses down Calvin's chin, up his jawline to his neck. His hands slipped under Calvin's T-shirt, his fingers caressing soft skin before moving down to Calvin's waist. Ethan delved in for another hungry kiss, loving the taste of him. With every caress, Ethan craved so much more. He unbuttoned Calvin's jeans and tugged them down with his boxer briefs, groaning when Calvin lifted himself enough for Ethan to get his jeans and underwear down around his knees, releasing his leaking cock.

Ethan palmed Calvin's erection, a low growl rising up from his chest at his best friend's whimpers. No one would make Calvin sound like this but him. Never again. It had been different for Calvin with Felipe. Ethan's heart broke when he thought about how Calvin hadn't been completely faking it. Thankfully, Calvin had managed to get the information he needed from Felipe before things could go too far. Ethan knew Calvin well. It had been agonizing listening to them. At one point he'd been forced to remove his earpiece. It was different now. The sounds Calvin made, the gasps, pleas, and moans, the way his fingers dug into Ethan's shoulders as Ethan got down on his knees and wrapped his lips around Calvin's dick, were unlike any he'd heard come from his best friend before today. The sounds were new, his pleasure greater, like he couldn't get enough of Ethan. Job or no job, no one was going to be kissing Calvin's lips but him. His inner Felid roared at the thought.

"Oh God, Ethan." Calvin's fingers slipped into Ethan's short hair, holding on tight as Ethan sucked, licked, and nipped at Calvin's cock. His whimpers and pleas urged Ethan forward. He wanted to consume Calvin, wanted to hold him close and never let go. Calvin's hips lifted, and Ethan held him, his mouth taking Calvin down to the root. His best friend smelled faintly of soap and his own heady musk, the scent filling Ethan's nostrils and driving him crazy. He doubled his efforts, sucking at Calvin's head, then licking his slit, lapping up any precome on offer. Ethan's fingers squeezed at Calvin's asscheeks. They were round and firm and begging for Ethan to bury himself in between them.

"Ethan...." Calvin gasped his warning, his hips bucking. Ethan tightened his lips around Calvin and picked up his pace, his tongue pressed against the underside of Calvin's cock, his moan reverberating against Calvin and sending him over the edge. Ethan's warm mouth filled with the taste of Calvin, and he eagerly swallowed every drop. He continued to suck Calvin until Calvin hissed at the tenderness. Gently, Ethan pulled off him. He licked at the corner of his mouth, his gaze on Calvin, who shuddered, his eyes hooded and filled with lust. He tenderly pulled Ethan to his feet before pushing him away so he could hop down. His intense blue eyes remained on Ethan while he tucked himself away and sorted out his clothes. Then he stepped up to Ethan, his voice throaty and rough as his fingers stroked Ethan's arm and chest.

"Tell me what you want."

Ethan unzipped his jeans and pushed them down, his thick, hard cock jutting up against his stomach. He was painfully hard, and Calvin's low moan, along with the way he licked his bottom lip, didn't help. The sight of Calvin on his knees looking up at him from under long blond lashes had him letting out a low groan. Calvin's plump lips around Ethan's dick almost undid him. His face grew warm, and he wondered if his cheeks were as flushed as Calvin's. Probably not. Calvin's fair skin flushed easy, a sweet rosy hue that made Ethan smile. There were nights his imagination ran wild, and he'd dream of this, of Calvin's mouth on him. He'd wonder what his best friend tasted like, what his skin felt like. Usually it was followed by guilt. Now there was only the sheer pleasure brought on by Calvin's mouth and hands on him. Ethan's heart pounded fiercely, and his body was on fire, or at least that's what it felt like.

Ethan placed his hands on Calvin's soft blond hair, his fingers closing over fistfuls of it. He closed his eyes, losing himself to the sensation of Calvin's firm grip on the base of his cock as he sucked Ethan off, his full lips sliding up and down, his tongue pressing into his slit. When Ethan felt Calvin's free hand on his balls, he gasped, and his eyes flew open. He met Calvin's sparkling blue gaze, the heat and need in them hitting a very primal part of Ethan. He wanted to grab Calvin, bend him over the trunk, and plunge himself deep into his ass. Instead he let Calvin drive him crazy with his mouth. He wasn't going to last. It had been so long.

Calvin doubled his efforts, and Ethan's muscles tightened. He gave Calvin's hair a gentle tug, warning him he was about to come. Calvin moaned around Ethan in approval, allowing Ethan to do as he wanted.

Ethan thrust his hips and drove himself deep into Calvin's mouth. His best friend didn't flinch. He took all of Ethan's length deep into his throat. *Oh shit.*

Ethan wasn't small by any means, not in length or girth, but Calvin eagerly took him all in. Ethan's muscles tightened with his impending orgasm, and a strangled exhale escaped him. He doubled over, holding on tight to Calvin's head as he came. It seemed to go on forever until finally he was spent, his brow beaded with sweat. Carefully, Calvin pulled off him to stand. His face was flushed, his lips swollen from being kissed. He wrapped his arms around Ethan.

"I love you."

Ethan opened his mouth, when he heard a key being inserted and turned. The door burst open and a couple came barreling through, their hands tugging at each other's shirts while their mouths tried to devour each other. Ethan cupped himself, his eyes wide. Then he realized who it was.

"Holy shit!" Dex gave a start and flung a hand to his chest. Sloane looked just as alarmed. "You two scared the fuck out of me!"

Calvin threw a hand up. "Dude, seriously?"

Sloane closed the door behind them, his face as red as Ethan's felt. This was becoming a very disturbing habit.

Dex turned his face up to the ceiling. "Why me? Why's this keep happening to *me*?"

"I think the answer's pretty obvious," Calvin muttered.

"It is?" Dex frowned in thought.

"You attract crazy," Calvin replied sincerely. "Like bees to honey."

"Thanks."

Sloane turned to Dex, his expression wary. "I'm all for getting adventurous, but I gotta say, I'm a little concerned right now."

"Really?" Dex folded his arms over his chest, his expression uninspired.

Sloane shrugged. "Just saying. I mean, that's twice now."

"I'm not doing it on purpose!" Dex spun toward them. "Sorry, fellas, but you're going to have to find yourselves another utility closet. This one's spoken for." Dex frowned at Ethan. "Dude, pull your pants up."

Ethan nodded, then realized he'd need his hands to do that. His hands were kind of occupied at the moment. He motioned behind Dex.

"He wants you to turn around," Calvin said.

"Oh, so *now* you're feeling modest?" Dex shook his head in amusement as he turned, Sloane rolling his eyes as he did the same.

Ethan quickly pulled up his underwear and jeans, zipping himself up before straightening out his clothes. He cleared his throat, and their friends turned back to them.

"Good," Dex said cheerfully. "Now get lost. It's our turn."

Ethan did not need to know that.

They headed for the door when Calvin stopped to ask Dex, "How'd you get in here anyway? The door was locked."

"It's always locked."

"It wasn't when we came in here."

"Yeah, I know." Dex held up a key, his grin wide. "Because I unlocked it. We got caught up when Dimples the Firefighter showed up. We really need to ask

Letty what the dude's name is. I feel kinda weird calling him Dimples to his face."

"You could not call him that," Sloane suggested. "I have a feeling he would prefer you not call him that."

Calvin frowned. "Why do you have a key to the utility closet?"

Dex arched an eyebrow at him.

"Oh." Calvin scrunched up his nose. "Ew."

"Ew? It stinks of sex in here. Thanks for that."

Calvin's face went beet red, and he grabbed Ethan's wrist, pulling him out of the closet to the sound of Dex's laughter. "Dick," Calvin muttered as the door was shut behind them. He stopped in front of the exit that led out into the bar. "So, um, where does this leave us? Not that I'm complaining about what happened," Calvin said with a shy laugh.

Ethan didn't know how to respond. His expression must have said as much, because Calvin let out a heavy sigh, one that went straight to Ethan's heart.

"Don't worry about it, okay? I know you don't want me with anyone else. Not a problem, considering you're the one I want." He stepped up to Ethan and put a hand to his cheek. "I need to know what's going to happen with us, Ethan. I need to know where we stand, and I can't… wait in this limbo forever. I'm trying to be patient. I really am. It's getting too painful. Whatever you decide, I'll always be here." Calvin walked out the door before Ethan could respond.

Calvin was right. It wasn't fair to leave him hanging, wondering if they were more than friends with benefits. He needed to get his thoughts in order, to accept once and for all that Calvin was more than his best friend, and not just in secret, but out there.

Ethan left the back end of Dekatria and found Calvin at the bar ordering a drink. Ethan put his hand to the small of Calvin's back, earning him a warm smile. Calvin ordered him a beer, and they headed back to their table, where the rest of their team was gathered, minus Dex and Sloane. Bradley pulled a small square table next to them with a chair to each side of it. Looked like Ash and Sloane were actually going to arm wrestle. Ash took a seat on one side with Cael kneading his shoulders. Did they know Sloane was… busy?

"Where the hell is he?" Ash grumbled. As if summoned, Sloane materialized with Dex at his side. It was pretty obvious what they'd been doing.

"Jesus, really?" Ash shook his head in disgust. "Sit your ass down, Casanova." He thrust a finger at the chair opposite him, and Sloane sat with a wide grin on his face.

"All right, let's do this."

Ash faced Sloane, their hands flat against the table surface as Bradley went over the rules. The whole bar stopped to see what was going on.

Calvin leaned into Ethan, his voice low as Dex and Cael gave their boyfriends pep talks.

"Who's your money on?"

Ethan thought about it. Ash was stronger than Sloane, but Sloane was more focused. It was a tough call. Ash clamped Sloane's hand with his, a wicked grin coming onto his face as he shifted his gaze to Dex.

"You're going down, Daley."

Ash was definitely motivated. Twenty-four hours of silence from Dex? Ethan pointed at Ash.

"Really?" Calvin eyed him curiously. "You know something I don't?"

Ethan whispered in Calvin's ear, letting him know what the stakes were.

"Damn, you're right." Calvin reached into his wallet and pulled out a twenty. He handed it to Letty, who was taking bets. Ethan did the same. "Our money's on Ash," Calvin said, receiving a wink from Letty.

Bradley played referee, making sure Sloane and Ash were in position. Once the two were ready, Bradley gave the signal, and the match started, their faces quickly growing red as they tried to take each other down. The bar erupted into cheering. The bets had been placed, and everyone rooted for either Sloane or Ash. Dex and Cael encouraged their boyfriends and engaged in brotherly rivalry, teasing and taunting each other.

Ash's jaw muscles worked as sweat beaded his brow. His arm shook as Sloane gritted his teeth and inched Ash's hand closer to the table. Cael whispered something in Ash's ear, and for a moment Ethan thought Sloane was about to slam him down, when Ash growled and pushed at Sloane's hand. Sweat trailed down both their reddened faces before Ash slammed Sloane's hand against the table.

"Yes!" Ash jumped from his chair with a victory cry before grabbing Cael to swing him around and kiss him. Everyone burst into cheers or playful boos while Letty got to work distributing their winnings. Sloane stood with a chuckle, and Ash pulled him into his embrace, patting his back before ruffling his hair. He turned to Dex with a triumphant grin.

Dex groaned. "Shit."

"I am so going to enjoy this." Ash rubbed his hands together in glee. Ethan had never seen him so happy.

"Sorry, babe." Sloane kissed Dex's brow and pulled him against him for a hug.

"It's okay," Dex sighed. "You tried. Plus he has the forces of darkness behind him. Tough to beat that."

"Screw you, Justice."

Dex's glare could cut through rocks, but Ash ignored him to clap Sloane on the back again. "You did good, bud."

Sloane laughed. "Thanks. I think."

"Maybe next time you should save your strength instead of getting your boy off in the broom closet."

Sloane rolled his eyes and went back to comforting his pouting partner while Cael hugged Ash.

"I knew you could do it."

Ash wiped away an imaginary tear. "I don't think I've ever been this happy."

"I'm surprised you know the term," Dex grumbled. "You sure you don't mean grumpy? You might be getting them confused."

"You know what, Daley? Not even you can spoil this for me. Twenty-four hours of silence to distribute when I please." He let out a contented sigh. "It's like my birthday and Christmas all rolled into one."

Everyone laughed, and Ethan put his arm around Calvin's shoulders, smiling when Calvin subtly leaned into him. After the last few months, things were finally starting to settle down. It had been rough on all of them, but now as he watched his teammates' antics, a sense of peace washed over him. He had everything he needed right here.

Chapter Three

"TWO MINUTES, Agent Hobbs."

Damn it. *Just ignore her and get it done.*

"Two minutes, and the building will blow with your partner inside."

Yes, I know. Thanks. Ethan wiped the sweat from his brow with the back of his gloved hand. Three devices down, another three to go. So far each one had required a different method of deactivation. He concentrated on the mechanism and wires in front of him and not the red numbers counting down, bringing him ever closer to losing everything. Okay, no antihandling mechanism. Enough C-4 to blow the floor he was on, along with the floors above and below him. He had to get to Calvin.

Ethan swiftly but carefully checked each wire until he found the one he needed. Blue. He snipped it and shoved the cutters back into his kit before taking off down the hall. Three armed gunmen emerged from the door at the end, the door he needed to get through. Ethan dove into an alcove to his right as the first bullet whizzed by.

"One minute and forty-five seconds."

Ethan growled at the female voice. He did *not* need a countdown. Removing his Glock from his thigh rig, he sneaked a peek to get a visual on his targets. After a deep breath, he darted out and fired at the three Humans without hesitation, only allowing one shot per target, as he'd been instructed. He got one on the leg, one in the neck, the third in the arm. The third spun but didn't go down. Having used up his allotted shots, Ethan charged, and with a roar grabbed the guy, lifted him off his feet, and slammed him onto the concrete floor. The guy was out.

Almost there. Ethan rushed through the door at the end of the corridor and took the stairs up three at a time, sweat dripping down the side of his face. He rammed the fire door, thankful it wasn't locked. His heart caught in his throat at the sight of Calvin tied to the pillar in the center of the empty garage with the remaining two devices attached to the columns on either side of him. Ethan took off toward Calvin just as a pair of doors opened somewhere behind him. He spun and shot at the armed Therian who emerged.

Using the columns as cover, Ethan dispatched the hostiles as quickly as he could. When it was clear, he sprinted to Calvin. His partner was out and gagged. Ethan would have to carry him out. *I'll get you out of this, Cal. I swear.*

Ethan studied the device, his mind scanning through all the different schematics of the various explosives he'd dealt with over the years, along with some of the more obscure ones, until he found the one he needed. Each and every diagram was filed away in his mind. His head retained a hell of a lot of information, even if he wasn't so good at communicating it. He could remember the most minuscule of details, from the most rudimentary homemade bomb to the top high-end multifaceted devices.

"You don't have enough time, Agent Hobbs. Abort."

Like hell. He had less than two minutes to take care of this, or the place was going to blow with him and his best friend in it, because there was no way in hell he would leave Calvin behind.

"If you don't leave now, you won't make it out."

Didn't matter. He wasn't leaving Calvin. Ethan went to work on the first explosive. No antihandling device, but there was a trap. A thin, barely visible wire ran from the device in front of him to the one on the other side of the pillar. He'd have to disarm that one first. *Shit.*

Hang on, Cal. Ethan stepped in front of the second device, his fingers moving deftly as he inspected and found what needed before removing the cutters from a kit attached to his belt. The device wasn't a problem, the volume and time was. It took him ten seconds to disarm both explosives. He moved fast, removing the gag from Calvin's mouth before cutting through the ropes. Calvin crumpled into his arms. He knew what awaited him. Doing his best not to think about that, Ethan hoisted Calvin onto his shoulder, his best friend's words quiet in his ear.

"She's going to kick your ass."

Ethan patted Calvin's butt in response. *Yeah, I know.* He hurried down the stairs and out of the garage.

There was no big "boom." With a smile, he stopped in front of Sparks and placed Calvin on his feet.

Sparks's gaze remained on her tablet. She tapped away with her manicured fingernails before raising her head, her expression unreadable. "You failed, Agent Hobbs."

What? Ethan stared at her. He shook his head. With a glare, he thrust his finger at the building behind them. He'd disarmed all the bombs, eliminated every threat, and gotten his partner out.

"You missed the sniper."

Ethan's eyes widened. *Sniper?* He felt the back of his head. His hair was wet. When he brought his fingers in front of him, his glove was stained with red paint. He'd been hit. Not only had he missed the signs, he never felt the blow. *Fuck.*

"Congratulations. You defused the explosives with barely enough time to get you and your partner out. Unfortunately, had this been an actual mission, you would have been dead before you could execute the extraction. The building would have exploded next, killing your partner and any civilians which remained." She finished tapping away at her tablet and handed it to one of her suited operatives standing silently by. "Your skills are commendable, Agent Hobbs, but you can do better. I expect more from you next time. Dismissed."

Ethan gave her a somber nod and tried not to feel too disappointed. On the way to the BearCat, Calvin patted his back.

"You did great, buddy. Don't beat yourself up over it."

Ethan gave a noncommittal grunt. Despite his mutism, he was expected to perform at the highest of standards like any other agent, like any other tiger Therian.

Like his big brothers. He'd taken Seb's advice to heart
a long time ago, promising himself that his mutism
wouldn't define him. Not in life and not at his job. At
times he needed to remind himself of his oath, but it
was always there, permanently etched into his brain.
The THIRDS placed its trust in him, gave him a chance
to be exceptional on an elite team, despite his mutism
and social anxiety. He couldn't let them down. Couldn't
let his team down. He'd have to try harder.

"Hey." Calvin put a hand to Ethan's chest to stop
him in his tracks. "I know that look. Stop. You're too
hard on yourself. We're dealing with TIN now, remember? Whole other ballgame. Cut yourself some slack."

Ethan nodded, but the frown on Calvin's face said
he could see right through him. He looked like he wanted to say something, then decided against it. Silently,
they crossed the large empty indoor lot to where the
BearCat was parked. It was the only vehicle there.
Ethan had no idea where they were. Austen had driven
the BearCat from HQ to wherever this was. The ballistic windows on their vehicle had been shielded so they
couldn't see outside.

The back door opened after Calvin knocked, and
Ethan helped him climb in. From the looks of it, his
teammates hadn't fared any better. Cael was in his Therian form with almost as many red paint spots as black
spots. He was chirping angrily at his brother, who had
one big red paint splat in the middle of his forehead.
Ash was glaring at Dex, which wasn't really anything
new. There were red paint marks all over Ash. Letty
and Rosa had fewer paint marks. The only one who
didn't have paint on him was Sloane. Ethan cocked
his head to one side. He showed Sloane his red-stained
glove, then pointed to the back of his head. With an

unimpressed look, Sloane turned. There was a big red paint splat on his ass.

Ethan burst into laughter.

"Well, I'm glad someone finds this funny," Dex grumbled. He looked Calvin over. "You look nice and clean. Did you make it out?"

"We thought we had. Turns out there was a sniper." Calvin took a seat on the bench next to Rosa while Ethan showed Dex the back of his head. He turned with a frown and shook his head.

"Ethan didn't see it or feel the blow."

"Damn. You didn't feel it?" Dex pointed to his forehead. "This shit knocked me on my ass. Fucking hurt like a bitch. It still burns."

"You're going to have that for days," Ash said with a laugh.

The security console's speakers buzzed, and Sparks's voice came through. "Austen will get you back to HQ. I expect to see you all in the training bay. Clean yourselves off before you reach HQ. There are extra uniforms in the duffel bags."

Rosa got up to help Cael with his shift and PSTC, hitting the button to drop the privacy screen. As Cael shifted, Ash spoke quietly. As if Sparks couldn't hear them. Ethan wouldn't be surprised if she'd placed wiretaps in the showers at HQ. She seemed to know every move they made no matter where they were. It was unsettling.

"Why us? Sparks hasn't given us a reason why she's picked us for her so-called specialist training. My fucking bruises have bruises. It's not like we work for her. Them. Whoever the fuck they are." Ash jutted a thumb toward the front cabin of the truck. Ethan's frown deepened. He wasn't crazy about Austen driving his BearCat.

"I don't know, but it's good for us," Sloane replied, removing his boots so he could put on a clean pair of tac pants. Dex playfully smacked Sloane's ass.

"They shot your ass off," Ash reminded Sloane.

"Because someone decided he was going to be John McClane and thought the fire hose he'd tied around his waist would hold him as he jumped through a window," Sloane grumbled, buttoning up his clean tac pants.

Ethan shook his head at Dex, who blinked innocently. "Had that wall been real and made of concrete instead of shitty plaster, it would have worked."

"I had to save his ass and in return lost mine."

Calvin grinned wickedly at Dex. "Did you say the line?"

Dex looked affronted. "Dude. Of course I said the line."

"This is bullshit," Ash grumbled as he finished buttoning up a clean shirt. "We've been fucking training since this morning, and now she wants us back at HQ training some more? This was supposed to be our day off."

Sloane rolled his eyes. "We've been at this for weeks. Quit bitching. We agreed, remember?"

Ash's brow furrowed thoughtfully. "No. Nope. I'm pretty sure I didn't agree to jack shit. *You* agreed for us. The CQC and Muay Thai is one thing, but all that other shit? Why? We don't know who the hell these TIN guys are or what they do. What happens when the training is over? What are we even training *for*?"

Ash was kind of right. Technically, none of them had agreed to anything, but Sloane was also right. The extra training would be good for them. The last few months proved being better prepared wouldn't hurt. When he'd first joined the THIRDS, their callouts had been mostly disturbances, high-risk warrant cases, and providing backup for Recon with the occasional Therian gone feral. Nowadays it seemed like someone was always trying to blow them up or shoot them down. Ethan hated to admit it, but he also agreed with Ash. Were they supposed to blindly follow Sparks? Ethan trusted her, to an extent. Their training was intense, with some disciplines far more than they needed for the THIRDS. It was rare for them to come up against a perp who also happened to be a secret spy.

"You're right," Sloane said, "about all of it." He put his finger to his lips before tapping his ear. They were most likely being listened to. "You don't like it, you can tell Sparks."

Ash let out a snort. "Yeah, sure. I'll tell the fucking Black Widow what to do with her extra training. She'll probably snap my neck in my sleep."

"You think she'd do that?" Cael asked, eyes wide.

Dex folded his arms over his chest and pinned Ash with a glare. The two had developed some kind of weird method of telepathic communication where Cael was concerned. It was creepy. Ash let out a heavy sigh and patted the bench next to him. Cael took a seat, snuggling up close to him, his arm wrapping around Ash's waist.

"No, I don't think she'd do that, sweetheart. But let's face it, whoever we thought she was...."

"Pretty sure she can hear us," Dex murmured, scrubbing furiously at the paint on his forehead.

"Thank you, Justice, for your amazing insight."

Whoa, hold on. That was the second time Ash had referred to Dex as Justice. Ethan held a hand up before

Dex could tell Ash off. He pointed to Dex, who let out a groan as he dropped into the chair across the bench. "Yes, all right. Since Simba opened his big freakin' mouth—"

"Technically, your boyfriend spilled the beans first," Ash corrected, smiling broadly.

Sloane cringed. "Yeah, that was my bad."

"You're lucky you're damn sexy, Brodie," Dex grumbled before addressing Ethan. "That's my middle name. Justice."

Rosa and Letty broke off into laughter, and even Calvin seemed unable to keep himself from laughing. Ethan grinned broadly at Dex. That was so adorable. The look on Dex's face told him he didn't agree.

"Yeah, all right. Get it out of your systems. You can all bite me."

They laughed at Dex's grumbling. Ethan thought the name suited Dex, even if his friend didn't think so. According to Dex, he'd been named after his great-great-great grandfather, who'd been a Pinkerton detective back in the day.

They finished cleaning themselves off and changed into new uniforms before reaching HQ. Austen was outside the truck when Ethan hopped down. He really didn't like anyone driving his BearCat. Except for the sarge, obviously, and maybe someone from his team. *Occasionally.* But he really didn't like anyone else driving it.

"Don't worry. I didn't feel her up." Austen threw Ethan the keys before wriggling his eyebrows. "Too much."

Ethan growled and made a swipe for Austen, who darted behind Dex with a laugh. They were seeing a lot more of Austen these days, with him being their liaison to Sparks and anything TIN-related. The guy was exhausting. He was filled with boundless energy, never-ending innuendos, and loved to pop out of the shadows like some damn ninja. Austen gave Dex a sniff and purred. "I know Sparks gave you that arm thing, but you still smell good. Like Broodie Bear."

Sloane promptly clamped a hand on Austen's shoulder and removed him from Dex's person. "What have I told you about that?"

"Don't rub up against your boyfriend without you?" Austen asked hopefully.

"Nice try." Sloane released Austen before pulling Dex up against his side and nuzzling his hair. Dex no longer batted an eye at Sloane's Felid Therian needs, though Ethan had noticed Sloane was more possessive over Dex than he'd been before. He wasn't very vocal about it, but he didn't have to be. It showed in his actions. The way he always had to touch Dex in some way when another Therian was close by, whether it was a subtle gesture like a hand on the small of Dex's back or a clear message like him wrapping his arm around Dex.

"Speaking of bears," Dex said as they headed for the corridor leading to Sparta. "Have you talked to Zach lately?"

"Not cool, man." Austen narrowed his eyes at Dex, who looked puzzled by Austen's sudden change in mood.

"What? I was curious. Sloane said he asked about you the other day."

Austen peered at Dex before moving his gaze to Sloane, who nodded.

"He did. He asked me if I'd seen you around, if you were doing okay."

"Oh." Austen frowned.

"What? No cheesy comeback? No zingers?" Ash cocked his head to one side, his expression smug. "Looks like our pal Zach's managed to accomplish what no one else has. Leave you speechless. Wonder why that is?"

Austen's expression darkened, and for a moment Ethan wondered if the guy was going to plant one in Ash's face. Wouldn't be the first time someone on their team had managed it. Instead, an evil smile spread across Austen's face as he turned and walked backward ahead of them. "Have fun in training. Try not to get your asses kicked too badly. We'll be in touch." With a salute, he disappeared into the shadows at the end of the garage.

"By the way," Dex said to them, "don't forget tomorrow's moving day. Bright and early."

"Yeah, yeah. We'll be there, your majesty."

Ash held the large steel door open while everyone walked through. With a wide smile, Dex patted Ash's chest.

"Thank you, Jeeves. Next time perhaps a little less snarl."

"You know what? That's thirty minutes, Justice. Starting now."

Dex's jaw dropped, and Ash grinned smugly. When Dex made to open his mouth to speak, Ash held a hand up.

"Nope. Rules were clear. This isn't an emergency, so for the next half an hour I get blissful silence." Ash patted Dex's cheek none too gently and smiled widely. "That's a good boy." Ash ruffled Dex's hair, talking to him as if he were a puppy. "Who's a good boy? You're a good boy, that's who. Yeah, now get lost."

Dex's jaw muscles tightened, and he flipped Ash off before thundering down the corridor toward one of the larger training bays, much to everyone's amusement, especially Ash's.

"I'm so going to enjoy this."

Ethan was pretty sure they wouldn't be enjoying whatever Sparks had in store for them. They stood in formation, their hands clasped behind their backs while Sparks tapped away at her tablet with her bright red manicured nails. She was back in her signature white pantsuit and five-inch heels. Ethan was still getting used to the fact she was some kind of secret spy agent. According to Dex, Sparks had been with TIN since the THIRDS opened its doors, so Ethan had to wonder how long that had been. He had to give her credit. None of them had ever suspected a thing.

The room was empty except for their team, Sparks, and some random equipment, including tactical vests and a privacy screen. He noticed there were no mats. At the end of the room was a climbing wall, and at the top in the center a black case dangled from a rope. Between them and the case was a shitload of obstacles that included hurdles, tires, ramps, blockades, and scattered everywhere were a bunch of little disks with green lights.

"For this training sequence, make certain you pay attention and think about what you would do differently from your teammates. As you can see, there is a case at the end of the room. One of you will retrieve the case. Consider your opponent your enemy. I expect you to give it your all. Don't think of this as training. Think of it as you out in the field. There is no room for failure. The green lights are hostiles patrolling the area. Get too close, and the light will turn red, meaning you've lost precious time dealing with the problem. You lose ten points for each one you cause to go off." Sparks pointed to the table beside her, with fancy laser tag equipment. "You're to take one tactical vest and one laser gun. You may keep your standard equipment on you. Use the laser gun to disable the hostiles before the light changes. You have a limited number of shots. Agent Keeler and Agent Summers, you're up. The rest of you pick up a tactical vest and suit up. Not you, Keeler."

Shit. Calvin and Ash? Ethan didn't like this. And why did the rest of them have to wear tactical vests if they weren't involved in the training?

"Agent Keeler, please shift into your Therian form. Agent Summers, please pick up your equipment. I'll attach the sensor to Agent Keeler once he's shifted."

Ethan stared at her. Ash was going to be in his Therian form against Calvin? His best friend looked surprised, but he seemed to quickly snap himself out of it. He nodded and did as he was asked, though not before Ash gave him a wicked grin.

"I'll try not to ruin that pretty face of yours," Ash said, chuckling as he strolled off to the privacy screen. Sparks motioned for Letty to assist him before turning her attention to Calvin.

"You're to retrieve the case, Agent Summers. Agent Keeler will do his best to stop you."

Calvin frowned. "By his best, you mean…?"

"He *will* hurt you."

Ethan stepped forward, only to have Sparks stop him. She waited until Ash's pained cries stopped resonating through the training bay. A fierce roar followed, and once it was quiet again, Sparks addressed the team.

"Out in the field, you deal with feral Therians. They don't give a damn who you're sleeping with, and if they find out your lover is working beside you, they will do everything they can to destroy you. You stated your romantic relationships wouldn't impede your performance? We're going to start putting that to the test. Tactical vest on, Agent Hobbs."

Ethan swallowed hard. What exactly did that mean? He strapped himself into his vest, as did the rest of his teammates before resuming formation. What wasn't she telling them? He was coming to learn that Sparks held out on a lot, feeding them tiny morsels of information as they went along, and only when she deemed it necessary. Ethan hated being in the dark. As an explosives specialist, he relied on having as much information as possible in order to perform his duties. Without the necessary intel, an easily resolved problem could turn fatal.

Ash emerged from behind the screen, shaking his head and causing his massive furry mane to swish impressively. Ethan rolled his eyes. *Show-off.* The only one impressed was Cael, but then Ethan supposed that was to be expected. Cael always looked at Ash as if he was some big rock star, and Ash ate it up. Ash trotted over to Sparks and sat on his haunches, his tail thumping against the floor. Lion Therians were so smug. Calvin finished strapping himself into his vest and tucked the laser gun into the back of his waistband while Sparks clipped a sensor to Ash's mane. Ethan couldn't help but snicker, and the rest of his teammates soon joined him. Sparks had clipped it below his ear, making it look like he had a barrette in his mane.

Calvin walked over with a laugh. "Well, aren't you a pretty kitty."

Ash snarled, taking a swipe at Calvin, claws drawn. Ethan instinctively stepped forward, and Sparks arched an eyebrow at him. Damn it, he had to control himself. With a frown, he stepped back into line and gave Sparks a nod. He could do this. His partner was an experienced agent. Ethan took comfort in the fact Calvin wouldn't hesitate in planting one in Ash's face if he had to. Ash turned his amber eyes on Ethan, and Ethan could tell he was enjoying this. He narrowed his eyes at Ash. If he was in his Therian form he'd knock the smugness out of him. Ash might be fierce, but in his Therian form Ethan was bigger, his claws and fangs were sharper, his mass heavier, and his roar fiercer than any lion Therian. Of course, in a fight to the finish, Ash would kick his ass. Lion Therians were survivors. They would fight until their last breath with everything they had. Their mane also protected their necks. Ethan didn't have a mane to protect him. Still, he'd give it his best.

"All right." Sparks addressed Calvin. "You have a five-second head start, Agent Summers. Go."

Calvin took off, maneuvering through the tires as fast as he could. He climbed over one of the blockades. Not an easy task considering the added weight of his vest. At least his partner didn't have to worry about tactical equipment. That alone would have slowed him down a good deal.

Seconds later, Ash's roar resounded through the training bay, and Ethan balled his hands at his sides. He watched nervously as Ash sped after Calvin, who was running up one of the ramps to the swing rope ahead of it. Ash caught up in seconds, roaring and bounding onto the ramp. He had Calvin in his sights, and he had every intention of catching his prey. Ethan knew the feeling. His muscles tensed at the familiar call. Despite being in his Human form, the tiger inside him stirred, eager to join the chase, to protect what was his. His pulse picked up, his heart pounded fiercely, and his senses grew sharp. At this moment, nothing mattered to Ash other than getting his claws into the flesh of his quarry. Sparks met Ethan's gaze, her intense pale eyes knowing.

"Agent Hobbs, I suggest you keep a tight grip on your Therian half."

Ethan gritted his teeth and nodded. He turned his attention back to Calvin, his heart in his throat as Calvin dropped onto the ramp and rolled onto his back, kicking out as Ash leaped at him. He caught Ash on his belly with his boots and sent him tumbling down the ramp. Jumping to his feet, Calvin spun on his heels and took off, leaping when he reached the end of the ramp. He caught hold of the rope and swung to the other ramp, hitting the wood boards with a roll before popping up onto his feet.

Ash swiftly recovered, his snarl heard from where Ethan stood. Their lion Therian teammate was pissed, even more so than usual. *Come on, Cal. You can do this.* Calvin hurried through the obstacle course, making certain to stay clear of the sensors or shooting at them when there was no way around them. Ash was quick on his heels, but Calvin made sure to use the obstacle course to his advantage, anything that would take Ash longer to go around. *Way to go, Cal.*

As Calvin headed for one of the hurdles, Ash changed direction. Where the hell was he going? Ethan watched as Ash sped up one of the ramps. *What the—* Realization dawned on Ethan, and it took everything he had not to run off after Calvin. Ash leaped and slammed into Calvin, knocking him to the floor and sending them rolling. Three of the sensors went off around Calvin, his laser gun skidding across the floor and out of his reach.

His gun was hardly his partner's biggest concern at the moment. Ash roared and pounced, taking a swipe at Calvin's side and his claws snagging Calvin's tac vest. The move backfired as his claws got caught in the bulletproof fabric, giving Calvin enough time to pull back a fist and punch Ash across the muzzle.

Ethan cringed. Ash's fierce roar sent a chill up his spine, and he watched anxiously as Ash swatted at Calvin again, his claws tearing at Calvin's sleeve. Luckily his partner had moved away before Ash could draw blood. Using the end of his Glock, Calvin swung at Ash, forcing him to jump back. Calvin scrambled to his feet and ran to the climbing wall. He jabbed his gun into his thigh rig and climbed with Ash trying to claw at him. Calvin was fast on his feet and agile. He dodged Ash's blows and continued to climb. Ash jumped and swiped, but each time he was met with Calvin's boot. Lucky for Calvin, lion Therians weren't so good at climbing.

That's it. Annoy the living hell out of him!

Calvin reached the top and swiped the suitcase. The only problem was Ash was waiting for him at the bottom, pacing with fangs bare as he hissed. Ethan was on edge as he watched Calvin doing his best to hang on to the rope with both hands while holding on to the case. Ethan could read Calvin clearly. He was considering all his options. Then a familiar look Ethan knew all too well came onto his partner's face. He'd found the solution. Calvin tugged a Therian-strength zip tie from his belt and secured the case to his belt. Then he swiped up his Glock and fired two rounds in their direction. Right into Cael's vest.

The force of the bullets hitting Cael knocked him off his feet, and chaos quickly followed. Ash roared and took off toward Cael while Dex and Sloane rushed to

Cael's side. Ethan watched, stunned, as Calvin dropped to the ground and broke into a run, reaching Sparks just as Ash reached Cael. Calvin handed her the case as Cael was pulled to his feet.

"What the fuck, Cal?" Dex glared at Calvin. "You fucking shot him."

"He's wearing a vest," Calvin replied calmly. "I wouldn't have shot him otherwise."

Dex stared at him. "What if you'd missed? Jesus Christ, do you realize—"

"Are you saying I can't hit a fucking inanimate object?" Calvin challenged Dex. "Shooting is what I do. If he'd been running I still would have been able to hit him. Had I wanted to shoot him somewhere else I would have aimed there."

"Now I'm inanimate? Thanks, man." Cael groaned, removing his vest and tossing it to one side. He rubbed at his chest. "Fuck. That hurt." He was going to have a couple of nasty bruises.

"Sorry. It was my only option."

Ash turned with a hiss. He bounded toward Calvin, only to have Sparks step between them.

"Stand down, Agent Keeler! That's an order."

Ash growled and hissed, but he sat back on his haunches. Sparks pointed to the privacy screen. "Change. Now. Agent Guerrera, you'll find supplies in the duffel bag by the screen. Help your partner."

Letty silently did as ordered, and they all resumed formation, waiting as Ash shifted back into his Human form and Letty administered Post Shift Trauma Care. Ethan stood beside Calvin, and he couldn't help but sneak a glance at him. He refrained from smiling at the pleased look on his partner's face. He'd beat Ash, and did so by thinking outside the box. As Ethan studied

Sparks, he had a feeling she knew what might happen. Why else would she have issued them vests? As if reading his mind, Sloane spoke up.

"You knew this might happen. That's why we're wearing vests, even though we're not involved in the training."

"An exceptional agent makes do with what he has and always has an escape route."

A loud clatter caught their attention, and Ethan braced himself as the privacy screen skidded across the floor. Ash thundered toward Calvin, his amber eyes burning with anger. He ignored Letty's pleas to finish drinking the Gatorade. He wasn't fully recovered, and it was clear in his unsteady march. Letty ran to his side and threw an arm around his waist as he reached Calvin and jabbed a finger at him.

"You fucking cheated."

"Agent Summers did exceptionally well," Sparks declared.

"What?" Ash rounded on her, a mistake he realized too late. His knees gave out, but thankfully Sloane and Dex were there to catch him before he hit the floor. They helped Letty hold him up. Why was their friend so damned stubborn? He knew full well what would happen if he didn't receive the proper care.

"This test wasn't just about him, Agent Keeler. Your objective was to stop Agent Summers. You allowed yourself to not only become distracted, you allowed an enemy operative to escape with the package to check on your boyfriend. Your performance was commendable, until that point. Agent Summers discovered your weakness and exploited it. Then on top of that, you don't allow yourself to recover from post shift properly. You're no use to your boyfriend or anyone else in this state."

Ash frowned at her. "Wait, you didn't say anything about me being judged on my performance."

"I shouldn't have to. You had your mission, Agent Keeler. You failed to follow through and allowed an enemy operative to expose your weakness. I expect better results next time. You're all dismissed. Go home and rest. Agent Keeler, get something to eat and finish your PSTC, before I have the medical team drag you away."

There was no doubt in Ethan's mind that Sparks would follow through with her threat. They removed their vests and left them by the table where they'd picked them up earlier. Ethan followed Calvin to Sparta's male locker room while Cael and Letty headed for the canteen. Ethan could all but feel Ash's laser-beam stare boring into him and Calvin. It was probably best for all of them if they showered quickly and went home to give everyone time to cool down. Well, to give Ash time to cool down.

Of course, they had no such luck. Calvin seemed determined to take his sweet time. They had showered and dressed when Ash stomped into the locker room fully recovered and fully pissed. Whatever agents had been lingering around darted out like the place was on fire. Sometimes Ethan felt bad for their fellow agents. Destructive Delta had a habit of running everyone off with their drama.

"Summers," Ash growled, marching over to Calvin. Ethan subtly stepped up behind his partner. He wouldn't get involved, but he'd be there if his best friend needed him.

"Hey, you wanna lay one on me," Calvin said, opening his arms wide, "go ahead. You won't always be able to protect him, Ash."

"Fuck you!" Ash stepped forward, only to have Cael put a hand to his chest, stopping him in his tracks.

"He's right, Ash."

Ash's expression softened. "Cael...."

"We should have both been paying better attention to Calvin and not each other. I was worried about you. That's exactly what Sparks was talking about. I know it might be different out in the field, but we can't take that chance. I thought because I was on the sidelines that I was safe, and how well did that go with Hogan? He caught me by surprise. What if I hadn't gotten out from under him?"

"Wait, what do you mean 'out from under him'?" Ash's amber eyes clouded over.

Cael's eyes widened, and it was clear he hadn't meant for Ash to find out whatever happened inside the surveillance van that day.

"What did Hogan do?" Ash growled, his fists balled at his sides.

Ethan and Calvin backed up.

"Cael?" Dex dropped his duffel bag on the floor and turned to face his brother. "What happened in the van?"

Cael folded his arms over his chest. "What does it matter? Hogan's dead."

"It matters!" Ash snapped, making Cael flinch.

Ethan had no idea what was happening, but one minute Ash was about to go feral, the next he had Cael in his arms, his voice soft.

"I'm sorry."

"It's okay, Ash." Cael hugged Ash close and buried his face against Ash's T-shirt. After a few seconds of being in each other's arms, Cael pulled back, but he wouldn't meet anyone's gaze. "Before Hogan knocked me out, he managed to pin me on my stomach. He…." Cael shook his head and closed his eyes. "He felt me up, said maybe he should fuck me right there, that we should make a video for you. He said he would've loved to see your face when he defiled me. Then I head-butted him."

"That motherfucking son of a bitch!" Ash turned away from Cael, his fingers flexed at his sides. Sloane was going to say something when Ash slammed a fist into his locker, the force behind his punch denting the metal.

"Ash, please." Cael took hold of Ash's arm, turning him so he could cup Ash's face. "I'm okay. Hogan's dead."

"He's damn lucky he's dead, because if he wasn't, I'd beat the ever-living shit out of him until he joined Collins in hell for putting his fucking hands on you."

"Stop. Why do you think Sparks is so concerned about our training? We're not as prepared as we think we are. None of us are. We rely on our weapons, our partners, our proficiencies and Therian forms, everything that can quickly be used against us. What good is all our training if we let our emotions get the better of us?" Cael lowered his voice. "I'm willing to bet the kind of assholes TIN operatives face know how to discover and use those weaknesses."

"But we're not TIN operatives," Ash argued. "We have to be careful."

"The way we were a few minutes ago?" Cael shook his head. "I'm glad Sparks is training us. I don't want to ever feel helpless like I did in that van. I can't rely on you to protect me."

"I'd do anything to protect you."

"And when you don't have that choice? We've all got each other's backs, but we have to learn to be strong on our own." Cael took Ash's hand in his. "I love that you're always there for me, but that leaves you vulnerable. You've already taken a bullet for me once. I don't want you to be placed in that position again. Not if I can do something about it. If I lost you because I wasn't equipped to handle the situation, I'd never forgive myself."

Ash swallowed hard. He let out a resigned sigh and nodded. "I understand."

"Cael's right," Dex said, grabbing his bag off the floor. "We need to step up our game. If Sparks can help us do that, then I'm all for it. Pearce, the Coalition, Hogan? We're dealing with a whole new type of criminal. They're strong, smart, and will do whatever is necessary to take anyone down. We can't give them the means to do that."

"The only question is, what's Sparks's training going to cost us?" Sloane put his arm around Dex, taking the duffel bag from him. "We don't know what the end game is with Sparks. She's not putting in all this time and effort for nothing. At some point she's going to want something in return. On a lighter note, see you all at my apartment tomorrow morning."

Cael groaned before turning to glare at Calvin. "Thanks for shooting me the day before moving day."

Ash gave Cael's head a kiss. "That's okay, sweetheart, it means Calvin will have to do twice the lifting."

Calvin flipped Ash off before grabbing his jacket. The rest of their team said their good-byes and headed off, leaving Ethan and Calvin alone. Knowing there was no one in there for the time being, Ethan turned to

Calvin and drew him close to plant a soft kiss on his lips.

"You did great," he said quietly. His partner had been quick thinking, using whatever was available at the time to help him survive, because that's what Calvin did. Survive.

Calvin smiled up at him, his blue eyes filled with warmth. "Thank you. Now let's get out of here. I'm starving. Mom's invited us over for dinner."

Ethan's eyes lit up, and his stomach rumbled. "Did she...?"

"Of course she did. She made chicken-and-dumpling casserole, cornbread, fried green tomatoes, and her famous pecan pie. Like she doesn't know you," Calvin said with a chuckle.

A mew escaped Ethan, and his mouth watered. Calvin's mom made the best Southern food ever. Usually he ate so much he wouldn't be able to move for hours. She knew all his favorites and always cooked up Therian-sized portions, plus leftovers because she knew neither he nor her son liked to cook. Ethan could eat Darla's cooking every day, though it was probably a good thing he didn't or he'd never fit into his uniform. He grabbed Calvin's hand and pulled him along to hurry him up, making him laugh.

"I'm driving," Ethan declared before hurrying out of the locker room with Calvin in tow.

"Yeah, all right. Just don't get us pulled over. Again. I have a feeling the next cop might not see jambalaya as a good enough reason not to give you a speeding ticket."

They were headed for the elevator when Dex and Sloane showed up. Both were out of breath and flushed.

Dex's uniform shirt was half hanging out, and Sloane's collar was a mess.

"I don't even want to know," Calvin muttered.

"Hey, we're getting some dinner," Dex said as he tucked in his shirt. "You guys wanna come?"

Ethan shook his head and pointed to Calvin before patting his belly.

"Sorry, Mom's homemade chicken-and-dumpling casserole wins out over air itself. Seriously. There's no keeping Ethan from my mom's cooking."

Dex's eyes sparkled. "That's right. Your mom cooks real Southern food. Old-school recipes made from scratch, passed down for generations. Fried green tomatoes?"

Calvin sighed and took his phone out of his pocket. He tapped the screen before placing it to his ear. "Hey, Mom. We got enough for two more? One's a Therian, the other eats like one. Great. Thanks. Love you too. See you soon." Calvin hung up and grinned as the elevator pinged. He motioned to the open doors. "After you."

Dex and Ethan all but fell over each other trying to get in the elevator. Inside, Ethan gave Dex a shove. Calvin stepped in after Sloane.

"Yeah, a word of warning. Don't get between Ethan and my mom's dumplings."

Ethan narrowed his eyes at Dex. *I will bust your shit up.*

Dex held his hands up. "I apologize for any dis-respect caused while hungry. It's not me. It's my stomach."

Ethan patted Dex's shoulder, perhaps a little hard-er than necessary. Dex shook his head and chuckled. Good food and good company. Today was turning out to be a pretty good day after all.

Chapter Four

OH NO you don't.

Ethan smacked Dex across the ass with a throw pillow, causing him to give a start. He turned to gape at Ethan.

"What? Why are you attacking me?"

You know what you did, and you were about to do it again. Ethan pointed at Sloane, who was bent over a box, organizing its contents. *You were going to pounce, and then you'd both disappear to the bathroom for ages and leave me to move the heavy stuff.*

Dex gasped, a hand going to his chest. "I don't know what you're insinuating. I was merely checking to see if my partner needed help."

Ethan shook his head. *The only thing you were checking was your boyfriend's ass.* Ethan grabbed a box and shoved it at Dex. He pointed to the other end of Sloane's living room.

"But...." Dex pouted.

Yeah, nice try. That doesn't work on me. He folded his arms over his chest and arched an eyebrow at him. *Don't make me carry your ass over there.*

"Yeah, yeah. I'm going," Dex huffed before stomping over to the bookshelf to start packing it up. Ethan shook his head. It was like babysitting two horny teenagers. Sloane straightened, his gaze landing on Dex. He took a step forward, and Ethan cleared his throat.

"Oh hey. I didn't realize you were there," Sloane said, scratching his head. "Thought you, uh, left with the guys."

Ethan shook his head. *Nope.*

Sloane shoved his hands into his pockets. "We've been at this all morning. You sure you don't want something to eat? There's leftover pizza in the fridge."

Really? That's the best you got? Ethan smiled brightly and pointed to the box behind Sloane. *Get back to work.*

"What are you, our chaperone? His virtue is way past being salvaged, just so you know. I've pretty much annihilated it." Sloane wriggled his eyebrows before puffing up his chest, clearly proud of himself.

Ethan wrinkled his nose. *That was way more information than I needed to know, but thanks.*

"Hey," Dex protested from across the room. "You're as much of a slut for me as I am for you."

Sloane let out a resigned sigh. "That's true."

Ethan rolled his eyes. *Each of you is as bad as the other.* He pointed to the box behind Sloane. *Get to work, oh fearless leader.*

With a pout, Sloane returned to his box, giving it a pitiful kick. Dex did the same. Ethan had started putting a box together when the front door opened and Calvin walked in. *Oh thank God.*

"All right, guys. We need to load up the van. Ash is double-parked. Rosa and Letty already unpacked the last load at Dex's. They went for a coffee run."

Sloane and Dex each grabbed one of the packed boxes lining the left wall and headed for the door. Calvin turned to Ethan with a smile.

"I see the supervising is going well."

The door closed, and Ethan threw his hands up. "Seriously. I can't let my guard down for a minute. Those two can't keep their hands off each other. It's amazing they leave the house every morning."

Calvin shrugged before heading over to the wall of boxes. "It's kind of sweet, though. I mean, being that in love with someone you can't help but touch them when they're near you, wanting to always be in their arms. Like being away from each other is painful. They're lucky."

Ethan frowned. Was that what Calvin wanted? Ethan walked over and took hold of his arm as his partner reached for a box. He worried his bottom lip. He wanted to say something, but he wasn't sure what. Calvin cocked his head to one side and studied him.

"What's on your mind?"

"Is that how you feel?"

Calvin averted his gaze. "I wasn't implying that... I mean, I don't want to make things uncomfortable for you."

Ethan couldn't help his surprise. Did Calvin hold back from showing affection so Ethan wouldn't feel uncomfortable? He took hold of Calvin's face and kissed him. *I'm sorry.* There was nothing he wanted more than to give Calvin everything he wanted. He needed a little more time. *Please don't stop loving me, wanting me. God, I do want you so bad. I need—*

"Are you kidding me?"

Ethan gave a start. He turned to find Ash, Cael, Dex, and Sloane standing there frowning at him. He gave them a sheepish smile.

"No, you know what? If there's no sexy times for me and Sloane, then none of you are getting any either." Dex jumped on the couch and addressed the room, pointing to everyone one by one, starting with Ethan. "No sexy times for you." Then Calvin. "None for you." He pointed to Ash. "None for you." He pointed at Cael. "Definitely none for you." He ignored Cael rolling his eyes and moved to Sloane. "Sorry, babe, none for you either. We're all chaste until moving is over."

Ash let out a laugh. "You and Sloane, chaste? That's the funniest shit I've heard all year! You two can't go one day without boning each other. All Sloane has to do is look at you, and you drop your pants."

"Hey, I have self-control," Dex said with a sniff.

Ash and Cael looked at each other before bursting into laughter. Yeah, Ethan didn't buy it either. Sloane took a sudden interest in a piece of tape stuck to his shirt.

"What? You're saying I don't?"

Ash reached into his back pocket and pulled out a bill. "Fifty bucks says you two can't go forty-eight hours without getting off."

Dex eyed Ash warily. "What are the rules?"

"What I said. No getting off. Kissing is fine. Nothing else. Who wants in on this? Easiest money you'll ever make."

Calvin pulled out his wallet and handed Ash a fifty. Cael followed suit. Ash smiled sweetly. "I'm gonna put in for Rosa and Letty, because we all know they're going to jump in on this." Sloane handed Ash fifty bucks. Dex gaped at his boyfriend.

"Dude, you're betting *against* us? What the hell?"

Sloane shrugged. "I'm being realistic."

"That's it. We're doing this." Dex jumped off the couch and marched over to Sloane. He poked him in the chest. "It's on now."

Ethan gave Ash his fifty, smiling apologetically when Dex gaped at him.

"You too? I thought we were bros?"

Ethan shrugged. *We are, just, let's face it, you're going to lose.*

"All right. Let's get the van filled up. You can collect your winnings from me on Monday." Ash laughed as Dex flipped him off. "Oh, and just for shits and giggles, that's thirty minutes of silence."

Dex stared at him. He spun on his heels and stormed over to the wall to pick up a box. On the way to the door, he stopped next to Ash and glared at him some more. It was more likely Dex was cursing him out in his head. Then he marched off.

Ash sighed. "I have a feeling this is going to be a great weekend."

They all laughed and grabbed boxes to take downstairs. Cael stayed in the truck to organize, and in no time they had the whole thing full. Ethan thanked his lucky stars Sloane was moving into Dex's and not the other way around. He'd been to Dex's basement. It was scary. Dex had used his Tetris skills to fill it to capacity. Who knew what was down there? The guy was a pack rat. He'd deny it until his dying breath, but he was definitely a pack rat. The fact that the majority of what was in his basement belonged in the eighties didn't change a thing.

Soon they were on their way to Dex's house. Rosa had called Cael to let them know she and Letty had picked up everyone's coffee order along with some pastries. There was still the bedroom and living room to finish packing up, but they'd done the kitchen, dining room, hall, closets, and bathroom. While they packed, Rosa and Letty moved the boxes they dropped off into the right rooms in Dex's house and helped unpack, organizing and even putting stuff away. It was like a military operation with how smoothly and quickly everything went on their end. Now that he thought about it, there was probably a reason they chose to be where the rest of their team wasn't.

While their coffees cooled down, they all unpacked the van. By the time they were done, Ethan had worked up quite a sweat. Luckily the cool air kept him from getting too hot. They left the van parked outside and decided to take a little rest. The living room was filled with boxes, some unpacked and a few empty and waiting to be tossed into the back of the van to be reused. Ethan was definitely ready for a little caffeine boost.

Dex checked his watch for the umpteenth time, his big smile telling Ethan his thirty minutes of induced silence was about up. "Yes!" He shouted, startling Rosa.

"*Me cago en diez*! Really, Dex?"

Dex opened his mouth to reply, then looked at Ash warily. When Ash chuckled and continued to unpack, Dex let out a sigh of relief.

"I'm so enjoying this," Ash said to no one in particular. Ethan couldn't remember the last time he'd seen Ash this happy. It didn't take much, did it.

Dex took a sip of his drink and frowned. "This isn't my triple shot mochaccino. This is hot chocolate."

"It's not there?" Letty asked, checking the cup labels. "I know I definitely picked it up. It was bucket-sized, with enough whip cream to give me diabetes."

Calvin checked the other cups on the island counter that hadn't been picked up yet. "These are all coffees. Who ordered the hot chocolate? Maybe they got them mixed up."

Sloane went pensive. "Is there anyone who doesn't drink coffee?"

"Oh shit." Dex's eyes went wide.

"What's wrong?" Calvin asked worriedly.

"Cael. He's the only one who can't drink coffee."

"Why's that again?" Letty asked.

"Cheetah Therian metabolism and his general Cael-ness. That shit makes him—"

"Dex! Dex, look! Deeex, you're not looking! Looook at meee! Dex!"

They all turned toward the dining room, and Ethan couldn't help his laugh. Dex, on the other hand, looked horrified. Cael stood on top of the dinner table wrapped in bubble wrap from his shoulders to his ankles. Ethan cocked his head to one side. How the heck had he managed that without any help?

"It's like being in a big squishy bubble!"

"How much of the coffee did you drink?" Dex asked, hurrying over to his brother.

"You know I don't drink coffee. I had hot chocolate. All of it! Oh my God, there was *so* much whip cream!" Cael bent his knees, and Dex gasped.

"Don't you dare! Cael, no!"

"Dex, I think I can hear colors," Cael whispered loudly, his pupils dilated. "Your T-shirt sounds like Journey."

"Oh dear God. Ash, help me out here."

Ash made his way over just as Cael launched himself off the table. Ethan was enthralled. It was like watching a weird action movie in slow motion. Ash dove for Cael, catching him before he could hit the floor. Cael landed on him and bounced off, rolling slowly across the wood floor with a frown on his face.

"Ash," Cael huffed, "I was fine. The bubbles were going to break my fall."

Ash crawled over to Cael and helped him sit up. "The floor was going to break your fall, and your head, you monkey."

"Nuh-uh." Cael squirmed and tried to wriggle away. He paused and giggled. "Your T-shirt sounds like the Spice Girls."

"Thank you. I'm officially horrified. No more jumping off furniture." Ash kissed the top of Cael's head, then tore the bubble wrap off him. Before he had a chance to get up, Cael was already sprinting into the living room.

"Oh my God, Ash! Look at this huge box!"

Ash swore under his breath before chasing after him. Ethan paused to look around. Why was no one recording this? Cael tried to strip while Ash did his best to stop him, but Cael was determined to shift into his Therian form to play in the giant box. Ethan had to admit he was tempted. There was enough room in there for at least two of them in their Therian forms. Maybe. Okay, maybe one of them. It was so big and cardboard-y. He did love a good box….

"Don't even think about it," Calvin murmured, bursting his bubble. "You wouldn't fit in there."

I don't have to fit in there. The fun part is trying to fit. Ethan huffed and folded his arms over his chest. *Party pooper.* Humans were walking contradictions.

When they were little they loved boxes as much as Felid Therians. Then they grew up, and suddenly they were too mature to play in boxes, yet many of them spent their lives working inside cubes.

For every piece of clothing Ash attempted to keep on Cael, another piece came off. Until Cael's attention was seized by a rustling sound. He gasped.

"Packing peanuts!"

Calvin took a sip of his cappuccino. "So that's what happens when he has coffee. I always wondered."

Dex went to the fridge and grabbed three bottles of water. "It hasn't even fully kicked in yet. If we don't move quickly, he's going to shift, pounce all over the place, climb the freakin' walls, and scratch the shit out of whatever he can get his little cheetah Therian claws on before he passes out from exhaustion." Dex turned to Sloane with a somber expression. "Babe, your pouf is about to become a casualty of war."

"Not my pouf!" Sloane darted off to save the round pouf that resembled the Death Star. Ethan had thought it was Dex's. Apparently there was a lot they still didn't know about their team leader.

Dex let out a dreamy sigh. "One day I'm gonna marry that man." With a chuckle, he headed off in Ash and Cael's direction. Cael was emptying all the packing peanuts into the giant box. *How come Cael gets to have all the fun?* Dex handed Ash a bottle of water.

Ash took it and tried to get it into Cael's hand. "Sweetheart, you need to have some water. Lots of water."

"But I'm not thirsty. What should we do with all the peanuts?" Cael continued to pour packing peanuts into the box while Letty and Rosa snickered in amusement at their partners from their perch on the love seat. They sipped their coffees and munched on their donuts.

"Let's build a peanut pit! Like a ball pit but with packing peanuts!" Cael said excitedly. He was actually bouncing. Ethan gave him five minutes before he was stripping again.

Dex returned and leaned against the counter, shaking his head in amusement.

"So you're going to leave Ash to it?" Calvin asked. "What about all the furniture you were worried about? Also, I've never seen Sloane move that fast. Has he always been a closet nerd, or was it all your doing?"

Ethan would have put his money on it being Dex's influence. It would also explain the gallons of coffee Sloane now consumed on a daily basis or the occasional eighties song Ethan heard Sloane humming.

"Nope. He's always been a closet nerd. Speaking of, he's got a cardboard cutout of Han Solo in his bedroom closet. It's on the left side to the back. I didn't tell you. Pretend you stumbled across it. And yes, I'm going to let Ash take care of it. He has to learn how to handle these types of Cael-mergencies."

"Cael, sweetheart, please get out of the box." Ash held a bottle of water out to him. "Or at least drink this."

Ethan pointed to the box and Cael, who was already nestled in the packing peanuts. *I think Ash needs more training in that department.*

Cael smiled sweetly up at Ash. "I'll take the water if you join me."

"No."

"Why?"

Ash let out a heavy sigh. "Because I don't fit."

"Get your phone ready." Dex dug into his pocket and pulled out his smartphone. At that moment Sloane reappeared.

"What's going on?"

"Cael's asked Ash to join him in the box," Calvin replied with a chuckle.

Sloane wrapped his arms around Dex. "You think he'll do it?"

"Are you kidding me? Cael's about to bust out the sad puppy face. Not even my dad's immune to that shit. Ash is finished, and he knows it."

"Please, Ash?" Cael jutted out his bottom lip. "It's not fun if you're not with me."

Damn, he's good. Ethan turned to Calvin, his bottom lip jutted out. *Please can I play in the box?*

Calvin didn't hesitate. "Still no. If I let you shift now, you'd never get out of the box, and we both know it."

Well, it was worth a try.

"Cael…."

"It's okay," Cael sighed. "I can have fun on my own." Cael flicked a Styrofoam peanut. It fluttered pathetically down in front of him.

"Really? You're really going to make me get in there?"

Ash looked pained, like the thought of getting into the box physically hurt him. How could Ash resist? Ethan had spotted Sloane eyeing the box earlier. As if sensing his thoughts, Sloane met his gaze. They peered at each other.

No box for you, Brodie. Sloane looked like he might challenge him on that. With a wicked smile, Ethan petted Dex's cheek. Sloane straightened.

"Um, that was weird," Dex murmured. "Did you pet me?"

Ethan grinned.

Sloane narrowed his eyes at Ethan. "Did you just leave your scent on my boyfriend?"

"I'm not sure what's happening here," Dex murmured. He took hold of Calvin. "Help me."

"Sloane was eyeing the box, and Ethan knows you'd let him shift and play, so he's trying to wind Sloane up." Calvin shook his head. "Besides, the box is about to become a little crowded."

Calvin pointed to Ash, who was climbing into the box, the packing peanuts fluttering around him as his heavy mass took a seat, his expression less than impressed. At least until Cael started tossing up handfuls of packing peanuts.

"It's like snow, except you don't freeze your ass off!" Cael stated cheerfully, tossing a handful at Ash, who grabbed a handful and tossed it back. The two proceeded to have a packing peanut fight.

"This is perfection," Dex said quietly. "Ooh, look at this one." He showed them a shot of Ash half-buried in packing peanuts. "This one's going in next month's newsletter."

"He will murder you," Calvin said with a laugh.

"He's always threatening to murder me, but I have an insurance policy in the form of an adorable cheetah Therian brother."

"Hey, Hobbs!" Letty called out to him, and he turned, smiling when she waved him over. "Come here, big guy. I got a question for you."

Rosa shook her head. "Tell her she can't use explosives to unclog the kitchen sink."

Ethan beamed brightly. He cracked his fingers and gleefully went over, then deposited himself between Letty and Rosa. *Oh, Rosa. Sweet Rosa. You have no idea.*

"SO HAS Hobbs always liked blowing things up?" Dex asked, swatting Sloane's hand away from his ass.

They were so going to lose that bet.

Calvin couldn't help but smile at Ethan's dopey grin as he showed Letty his phone. "His favorite holiday was the Fourth of July because of the fireworks. Seb showed us how to be safe, especially since Ethan was so fascinated. He'd take the fireworks apart to see how they were put together, then reassembled them. Sometimes it didn't work out so well. He burned his eyebrow off once." Calvin's phone went off. It was his mom. "Hey, Mom." The moment he heard the screaming, he straightened. *Shit.*

"Can you and Ethan come home? We can't get ahold of Seb or Rafe."

"We're on our way." Calvin hung up and turned to Sloane. *"Hey, sorry, man, we gotta go. Ethan's mom needs help with his dad, and she hasn't been able to get ahold of Seb or Rafe."*

Dex looked worried. "Shit, everything okay?"

"Yeah, it's his Therian Acheron Syndrome. Some-times the pain gets so bad he needs to be sedated, but Julia can't subdue him and administer the injection, and certainly not on her own. When it hits, Thomas's strength peaks, and he can be dangerous. The doctors didn't think he'd last this long. That shit's fucked up his immune system, his joints, everything." Calvin shook his head. "It's heartbreaking to see."

"Go, and if you need anything, let me know."

"Thanks." Calvin looked over at Ethan laughing at something Rosa said. "We won't be able to come back, though. This is going to set off his anxiety really bad." Calvin hated that he had to bring Ethan into this. If he was a Therian and could handle it, he wouldn't even tell Ethan. "Thomas's condition is difficult enough for Ethan at the best of times. Seeing his dad in pain like that, it'll hit Ethan hard. That's why his mom usually calls Seb or Rafe."

"I'll go," Sloane said.

Calvin snapped his head up, his eyes wide. "What?"

"You don't really need Hobbs to be there, right? I mean, you just need a Therian to help subdue Thomas?"

"Yeah."

"So spare him the pain." Sloane put his hand on Calvin's shoulder. "Don't tell him, and I'll come with you."

Calvin didn't hesitate. "Okay." He walked over to Ethan and smiled, hoping his best friend wouldn't want to come with him. Ethan seemed comfortable nestled between Letty and Rosa, his right arm hooked with Letty's as she teased Rosa. "Hey, I'm going to pop out with Sloane for a few minutes. We'll be back soon."

Ethan nodded, a wide, dopey smile on his face. He put his thumbs up, and it took everything Calvin had not to let his own smile falter. That smile meant everything to Calvin. With a wink, he turned and left, with Sloane following quietly. When they were sitting inside Sloane's Impala, Calvin let out an unsteady breath.

"You okay?" Sloane asked as he turned on the ignition.

"Yeah, sorry." He blinked away his tears and laughed at himself. "God, look at me. I'm such a dork." He wiped his eyes and drew in a deep breath. Sloane put a hand to his shoulder, giving it a squeeze.

"Hey, whatever it is, you can talk to me."

"It's fine. I'm fine. Really. Thanks."

Sloane didn't look too convinced, but he nodded. "Okay."

Calvin was grateful Sloane didn't push him. He didn't want Sloane knowing about his selfish thoughts. About how sometimes he wished he could hide Ethan away from the world so it was the two of them, nothing to set off Ethan's anxieties. Just *one* day where his best friend could be happy without the threat of fear. Where some asshole wasn't screaming at him on the street for not ordering his food fast enough, where someone wasn't looking at him like he was some kind of freak, with pity or disgust because he was having a panic attack. Where looking at his own father was painful enough to bring him nightmares.

"Thank you. I really appreciate this, Sloane."

"No problem."

In twenty minutes they were pulling up in front of Julia Hobbs's brownstone. His mom's house was a couple of doors down, but she spent most of her time around Julia's. The two had been best friends as long as Calvin and Ethan. Calvin had paid far more than asking price for his mom's house so she could live on the same block as Julia. His mom and Julia's happiness had been priceless. After years of shitty—and at times dangerous—jobs, his mom was able to retire and get the break she deserved in a house all her own. No crackhead neighbors, no drunks in the stairwell, and no scumbag landlord making inappropriate offers in exchange for skipping a month's rent.

"Will Julia be okay with me there? I can imagine that sort of thing is pretty personal, and with what happened with Seb and the team...."

"It's fine. Julia never held it against you," Calvin assured Sloane. "She understood Seb had a choice, and he chose to save the man he loved. Don't for a second think she doesn't know that it was thanks to you and Dex that Seb got promoted to team leader."

Sloane held his hands up. "That was all Seb's doing. He worked his ass off for that promotion." As soon as they stepped out onto the sidewalk, they could hear the screams. "Jesus." Sloane stared up at the house. "Poor guy. No one's called the cops?"

Calvin shook his head. "Everyone on the block knows what the Hobbses have been through. They're really good about it. It doesn't happen as often as it used to." He pulled out his keys to the Hobbs residence and quickly went inside. Calvin's mom came running and gave him a kiss.

"Hello, darling. Thank you so much for coming."

"I brought Sloane. I couldn't...."

She placed her hand to his cheek. "You did good, baby. Ethan doesn't need to see this." She turned to Sloane and gave him a big hug. "Thank you, Sloane. This means so much to us."

"Of course, Darla. Anytime."

"They're upstairs in the bedroom."

Calvin and Sloane followed her upstairs, the screaming getting louder as they neared Julia and Thomas's bedroom. No matter how much he was used to hearing Thomas's screams, it still sent a chill through him. Calvin stepped into the room and couldn't stop himself from turning away. Jesus Christ. Thomas was thrashing around on the bed, his cries turning Calvin's blood to ice. He looked as if he was possessed, his body and limbs contorting, his muscles strained, his black hair soaked in sweat from the exertion.

"Cal." Julia ran over and hugged him. "Thank you so much." She looked up at Sloane and smiled. "Sloane, it's been too long."

Sloane hugged her close. "Julia. It's good to see you again."

"Okay." Calvin turned to Sloane. "We need to hold him down and keep him from lashing out. It's going to take three injections. The one to his spine is always the worst."

Sloane nodded and took a deep breath. They went over to the bed, and Calvin spoke to Thomas, his voice loud yet gentle.

"Thomas, it's Cal. Sloane's here with me. We're going to help Julia."

Thomas nodded as he gritted his teeth. His skin was red, his veins bulging as he struggled fiercely to keep himself in control. If they weren't careful, he could shift before they administered the sedative.

"You hold down his arms. I'll hold down his legs," Calvin told Sloane. He wrapped his arms around Thomas's legs and held on tight while Sloane managed to get a good grip on Thomas's arms. Julia got to it, taking the injector and placing it to her husband's neck.

It wasn't so much the holding Thomas down that was difficult. It was the screams of agony. They were heart-wrenching and terrifying. Calvin held on to Thomas, waiting on Julia's signal to turn him onto his stomach. This was going to be rough.

After the injection to Thomas's arm, Julia gave them a nod. It was time. Calvin and Sloane struggled to turn Thomas over. Despite his condition, Thomas was still a tiger Therian. He wasn't as strong as his sons, but he was still stronger than Calvin, which meant Sloane had to do most of the heavy lifting. At one point Sloane's hand slipped, and Thomas managed to elbow him in the face. Sloane cursed under his breath and grabbed hold of Thomas as blood trailed down from his nose. They flipped Thomas over and held on as Julia placed the injector to Thomas's spine. Darla quickly wiped the blood from Sloane's nose and mouth with a wet towel. As soon as she stepped back, Julia pulled the trigger.

Thomas's scream shook the windows. He arched his back violently, and his body went into horrific spasms, followed by what resembled an epileptic fit. Except it wasn't, because if they released Thomas now, he'd shift into his Therian form and have no control until the medication set in.

As they held on for dear life, Julia did her best to calm her husband, talking to him softly and running her hands over his face and head. She kissed his brow and smiled warmly. The love they had for each other shone in their eyes, and Calvin was forced to look away. He'd always thought it so unfair that Thomas suffered the way he did. He'd given so much for his country, and what did he get in return? A virus that didn't kill him yet tortured him every day of his life. Still, Thomas fought it with everything he had, for his wife and his boys. Maybe what hurt Calvin most of all was how much Ethan looked like Thomas.

When Thomas settled down enough not to pull at them, they turned him onto his back. It seemed like forever, but he finally calmed, and soon he was out. Darla returned from the bathroom with a damp hand towel and fussed over Sloane, who obviously had no experience with that sort of thing. Poor guy didn't know what to do with himself. It suddenly occurred to him that several of his friends had spent only a little time with their moms before losing them. The thought saddened Calvin. As far as he was concerned, he didn't miss his dad. His dad had been a royal dick. If he hadn't been, maybe Calvin would have felt the same loss. In Cael's case, he couldn't even remember his biological parents.

Julia's voice snapped Calvin from his thoughts.

"Thank you." She took hold of Sloane's hand, her eyes filling with unshed tears. She was flushed and a little shaky, but her relief was evident in her smile. "Thank you for sparing Ethan. This would have been difficult for him. And I'm so sorry about your nose."

Sloane waved a hand in dismissal. "I've had much worse. Don't you worry about it."

Darla ushered them outside and left the door slightly ajar. They headed downstairs into the living room, where she left to make some coffee. Julia took a seat on the couch with a weary sigh. "Thomas didn't want me to call. He didn't want to put Ethan through that."

"I'm glad you called," Calvin said. "Thomas might have hurt you or Mom, and the pain would have gotten worse until he passed out, if he didn't shift first."

"Mom? Are you okay? I got your message." Rafe rushed into the room in full tactical gear. He came to an abrupt halt when he saw Calvin and Sloane. "What are you two doing here?"

"I asked Darla to call them," Julia said gently, standing to greet her eldest. Darla returned from the kitchen and quietly took a seat beside Calvin, her hand going to his knee. She knew him too well. Encounters with Rafe rarely went well for him these days.

Calvin would say Rafe looked pissed, but he always looked that way. Ash had nothing on Rafe Hobbs. Even Ash was known to smile and laugh every once in a while. Calvin had never heard Rafe laugh in all the years he'd known him. Smirk, maybe. Look not as angry, definitely. Smile? Calvin couldn't remember. Laugh, definitely not.

Rafe turned to his mother. "How's Dad?"

"He's sleeping. The boys helped me."

"Where's Ethan?"

"I told Calvin not to tell him," Sloane said. "I came instead."

Rafe shook his head. "You can't keep your nose out of my family's business, can you?"

Sloane stood, and Calvin tensed. He kept an eye on the two, hoping there wouldn't be a repeat performance of the epic fight they'd had after the shooting incident that had cost Seb his place on Destructive Delta. Rafe had punched Sloane, and Sloane's retaliation had been just as brutal. Tension had been high enough without Rafe making things worse. It had taken several Therian agents from Unit Alpha to break up the fight. Both had walked away with bruises and split lips.

"I was helping," Sloane said steadily.

"You're enabling. You're as bad as the rest of them, babying him. He's never going to be normal if everyone keeps treating him like a spaz."

"Watch your mouth," Calvin growled, jumping to his feet. He got up in Rafe's face, not caring that Rafe towered over him by nearly a foot and a half. "Maybe you don't give a shit about your brother's health, but the rest of us do."

Julia took hold of her son's arm. "Please, honey. You know your dad doesn't want Ethan to see him like that. He feels guilty enough."

"Well, he shouldn't. Ethan's an adult. He should have grown out of this by now."

Calvin couldn't believe the arrogance. "Grow out of it? Do you go around telling people in wheelchairs to walk it off? Or tell people with disabilities to grow out of it? What the fuck is wrong with you?"

"Baby," Darla warned gently. She put her hand on Calvin's shoulder, and he told himself to calm down before he planted one in Rafe's face. His mom was right.

The last thing they needed was another fight. There was enough pain in this house.

"Forget it. Like you give a shit." Calvin side-stepped Rafe and kissed Julia's cheek. "Take care. If you need anything at all, you call me."

"Thank you, sweetheart."

Calvin turned and kissed his mom. "Talk to you later. Love you."

Darla hugged him close. "I love you too. Take care, baby."

Julia and Darla said their good-byes to Sloane and thanked him again before they headed off. They climbed into Sloane's car, and Calvin was surprised when Sloane popped on an eighties music station. Calvin arched an eyebrow at him, and Sloane gave him a guilty smile.

"It helps calm me down."

Calvin laughed. He buckled up as they drove off, listening to some eighties ballad. Was Sloane aware of all the quirks he'd picked up from his boyfriend? It was probably best he not mention it. Dex, on the other hand, hadn't changed one bit. No, wait, he was eating healthier, though some of that was down to Sloane sneaking healthy options into Dex's meals without him knowing.

"Has Rafe always been such a dick? When you were growing up, I mean."

Calvin shrugged. "The guy was hardly ever there. No one knew where he'd disappear to. Seb was the one who looked after Ethan. Seb and Rafe argued so much that Rafe kind of stopped coming home after a while, but then again, it was up to the two of them to keep the family afloat. Between Thomas's medical bills and Ethan's, I really don't know how they managed. I try to remind myself of that every time something infuriating comes out of Rafe's mouth."

Sloane went pensive. "I wonder if the whole thing with their dad hits him harder than he's let on. Rafe's not exactly the sharing type, but he cares about his family. He has a fucked-up way of showing it, but you remember the shitstorm that hit after the shooting? Rafe was out for blood. He was pissed with Seb, but he went after anyone remotely involved. When Ethan got hurt in the youth center bombing, Rafe got there before Seb and turned the hospital upside down. I had to warn him off because he kept getting in my face about it. I told him if he wanted to go at it off the clock, fine, but he had to stop that behavior at work. It was unprofessional and unacceptable, especially for a team leader. I understood his concern, but he went about it the wrong way. The guy's always so pissed."

"Yeah, most of the time we all stay out of his way." Sloane was right about Rafe always being pissed, and especially about him not being the sharing type. Calvin wouldn't be surprised if his anger was rooted in something, but it'd be a cold day in hell before Rafe told anyone what that would be, and lashing out at everyone wasn't going to help him any.

On the ride back to Dex's house, Calvin thought about what excuse he might give Ethan if he asked. He didn't want to lie. It wasn't something they did, and even if he felt he had no other choice, he'd feel shitty about it. When they arrived, no excuse was needed. There was little chance Ethan would grow suspicious or wonder where they'd been because what they walked into at Dex's house was nothing short of chaos.

Ash, Cael, and Ethan were in their Therian forms, and they'd turned the living room into their personal

Felid playground. Ethan was nestled inside the huge box, though he hardly fit. His big tiger butt was sticking up in the air while Ash chased Cael around the box, packing peanuts flying every which way. Dex, Letty, and Rosa were on the couch. Letty was painting Dex's toenails, and Rosa was styling Dex's hair.

Sloane's jaw went slack. When he regained his powers of speech, he planted his hands on his hips. "What the hell is going on here?"

Everyone came to a screeching halt.

"Seriously? I step out and suddenly we've got Felids Gone Wild?" He walked over to Dex with a deep frown. "What happened?"

"Check it out, babe." Dex lifted a foot. "Blazing Blue Bombshell. Letty says it matches my eyes."

Sloane closed his eyes and pinched the bridge of his nose, which was a bad move on his part. Clearly, he'd forgotten about what had happened a little while ago, and his nose started bleeding again.

"Shit." Dex carefully scrambled to his feet. "What happened?"

"It's fine. You want to help me out in the kitchen?"

"Yeah, of course." Dex glanced over at Calvin and gave him a nod. He smiled before leading Sloane into the kitchen. It was hard to believe that at one point Ethan had been Calvin's only friend. He'd never trusted anyone else, and those who'd tried to get close to them always ended up bailing, unable to stick by them when things got rough. Now they had a whole team of friends willing to walk through fire to help them. A mew caught his attention, and he walked over to the box. Ethan was sitting serenely, his innocent furry face watching Calvin.

"Look at you. You look like a big loaf of striped bread with a tail."

Ethan chuffed and closed his eyes, making Calvin laugh. He scratched Ethan behind his ears and under his chin, smiling at his friend's mews and chuffs. He was so happy sitting there in that box, surrounded by people who loved him. Rafe was wrong. They weren't enabling Ethan. Their team treated him like any other guy, but the fact remained that Ethan needed support sometimes. Sparing him pain and hardship was what loved ones did for each other. Calvin let his head rest against Ethan's and hugged him close, his heart ready to burst from the love he felt for Ethan. As long as Calvin was at Ethan's side, he would always do everything he could to protect him.

Chapter Five

"HOLY SHIT."

Ethan looked up at Calvin sitting at his desk interface, his jaw all but hitting his desk's surface. Had Dex sent out another memo with Ash's picture? Ethan listened intently. Nope. No cursing or chaos.

"What is it?" Ethan asked.

"Have you checked your inbox?" Calvin glanced up at him, eyes wide. Whatever it was, it was big. Ethan shook his head. He tended to leave his emails for when he needed a break from his reports and invoices. They always had *so* many emails, and the ones from Intel made his head hurt. He needed Google to help him decipher the text. It was THIRDS policy for Intel to explain every upgrade, every change to Themis, every tiny detail of anything and everything they did that affected all the other departments. The problem was that Intel agents seemed to speak a different language that no one understood. Except for Cael.

Calvin swiped his hand across his desk interface, sending the email onto Ethan's desk.

"She did it. Sparks amended the no-fraternizing rule."

Ethan couldn't believe it. Sparks had kept her word.

"She's added a shitload of subclauses, but she did it."

Ethan read through the amended rule, which had been sent out to everyone at THIRDS HQ. Agents were instructed to be discreet and professional, but relationships were no longer subject to discipline or transfer unless it resulted in an agent being unable to perform their duty to the best of their ability. The new amendment was extensive, but the gist of it was they were no longer subject to disciplinary measures simply for conducting a romantic relationship with a teammate. He wondered if Dex and Sloane had seen this.

The alarms blared, and Ethan sat up. They listened intently as Dispatch called in Destructive Delta. Suspicious device found off Times Square at the Deimos Tower. Calvin cursed under his breath as they both jumped to their feet and rushed out of the office, joining the rest of their team in formation as they hurried out of Unit Alpha to the elevator. Their sergeant took up the rear.

As they descended to the armory, Dispatch called in Theta Destructive and Beta Ambush. Looked like Seb would be joining them. Ever since Seb was promoted, Ethan noticed that Theta Destructive was often called on to assist Destructive Delta. Not that Ethan was complaining. Having his big brother near was comforting, but it meant there was a greater chance of

Seb and Hudson running into each other. In fact, it was pretty likely they'd be working the same scene.

Downstairs, Ethan grabbed his EOD Packbot from his weapons locker and two EOD X-Ray kits, then handed one to Calvin. Anything else he might need he could pick up from the BearCat. They hurried to their tactical vehicle, parked in the garage next to Theta Destructive's. Before Ethan could climb up into their vehicle with the rest of his team, Seb pulled him aside.

"You be careful out there, little brother."

Ethan gave him a big smile. He playfully poked his brother in the chest. *You be careful too.* He didn't have to say the words. Seb knew. His brother chuckled and knocked their helmets together.

"Yeah, all right. Get going."

With a nod, Ethan turned and climbed into the truck. He secured his equipment in the weapons cage before heading into the front cabin. Calvin was already buckled up in the passenger seat.

"Everything okay?"

Ethan gave him a wink and buckled up before starting the truck. Time to get his baby moving. And boy could she move. Dex was always teasing him that he drove the BearCat like he was at NASCAR, and maybe he did, but he had years of maneuvering her through the streets of New York City. The BearCat might be an oversized beast of armored steel, rubber, and bulletproof glass, but Ethan had quickly tamed her wild ways. Her engine purred like a kitten, and she vibrated under his touch, her every move graceful and flawless.

"Seriously, I think you've got a kink for this truck," Calvin muttered, his blue eyes narrowed.

Ethan laughed. He threw Calvin a suggestive look. *Don't worry, baby, your engine's the only one I love to rev.*

"By that look, I'm gonna assume you just gave me a cheesy pickup line."

The fun and games quickly came to an end when they reached their destination and the chaos that surrounded it. Ethan parked the BearCat at the end of the block, maneuvering it so it blocked the street and any possible oncoming traffic. One would think a bunch of flashing lights and law-enforcement vehicles might deter motorists from entering that particular street, but nope. Unless the street was on fire, citizens would try to drive through, and even then there were always exceptions.

Ethan waited for Calvin to exit the cabin first, then joined their team in the back. He tossed the keys to Maddock and removed his Packbot from the weapons cage. Calvin helped him secure it to his vest before handing Ethan one of the EOD X-Ray kits.

Maddock gave Ethan's shoulder a pat. "All right, Hobbs, you get in there and check it out. The device is said to have been found in the server room on the twenty-third floor. Calvin, you're his backup. Assess the situation. I want you giving Sloane updates as soon as you have them. Destructive Delta, clear the building. Let's get these people out of here." Maddock opened the back doors, and they all jumped out. Taylor and Seb were organizing their teams when Sloane joined them.

Seb presented a map of the area on his tablet, and with a swipe of his finger, Sloane circled the perimeter. "Four-block radius. Get your teams to clear the area. As soon as we get word on the device, we'll reassess."

Ethan was about to head to the building when Taylor grabbed Dex by the arm and jerked him against him. Dex made to shove Taylor away, but the guy wasn't budging. What the hell was he doing?

"What the fuck, Taylor?" Dex tried pulling his arm out of Taylor's grip, but Taylor held on. He sniffed at Dex, a low rumble of a growl coming up from his chest. *Shit.* Was it the mark? It had to be. They all knew Taylor had a thing for Dex. He'd been sniffing around Dex since he joined the THIRDS, but Ethan thought they'd reached an understanding. With a feral growl, Sloane jerked Taylor away from Dex. He got up in Taylor's face, his larger stature imposing as he loomed over Taylor's smaller leopard Therian size.

"There are people's lives at risk. We don't have time for this posturing bullshit. Get your team in gear, Taylor, and do it *now*!"

Taylor looked like he might take a swing at Sloane, but instead he thundered off, hissing and shouting orders at his team. Sloane gave Dex's arm a squeeze, and the two seemed to exchange unspoken words before Dex gave him a nod.

"All right, everyone, move out."

Ethan hurried down the street and into the building with Calvin close behind him. THIRDS agents were already clearing the building, but it would take time, considering how many floors and offices there were. Ethan took the emergency exit, rushing up the stairs as fast as he could. The elevators were out of order due to the evacuation procedures put in place. Calvin was a few steps behind, but he did his best to keep up with Ethan. They were both sweating by the time they reached the twenty-third floor. Toward the end of the hall, he spotted the door marking the server room. As soon as they reached the room, Calvin held up two fingers and switched his earpiece to channel two. Ethan did the same.

After they'd been hired, Ethan had been surprised by the speed and length to which the THIRDS had accommodated his mutism. Sparks set up a line of communication for him, a special frequency on channel two reserved for him and Calvin. With the simple click of a button on their earpieces, Calvin could switch between their channel and the main channel used by their team. Ethan's com was specially programmed. He could still hear the rest of their teammates through his channel. However, they wouldn't hear him unless he specifically set his earpiece to do so. Only Calvin would hear him.

"Let's see what we've got." Calvin opened the door for Ethan, and they began to search the large server room. He tapped his earpiece. "Sarge, what are we looking for?"

"According to security, the network went down this morning, so they called in tech support. A technician came and repaired the network, only to have it go down again an hour later. Just when they were going to call tech support again, one of the techs showed up. Apparently they were answering the first call. Whoever came in earlier wasn't one of theirs. That's when the real tech found a box that shouldn't be there. I'm getting word now. Unit Twelve-B."

"Got it."

Ethan checked the servers and went through the numbers until he found the one they were looking for. He scanned the outside of the unit. All the lights were on, and the wires were where they were supposed to be. Moving lower, he found a shelf in the center of the unit. His pulse sped up at the sight of the large cardboard box. Inside the box was a large roll of brand-new, unused Ethernet wires. Upon further inspection, he noticed the shelf rolled out. Carefully, he pulled it toward him and studied the roll of wires, checking to make sure they weren't attached to anything. Underneath it, he could see a blue glow, but the whole thing was under a black lid.

"I have a visual on the device," Ethan said as he gingerly removed the roll of cables.

"Affirmative." Calvin spoke into his earpiece. "Sloane, Sarge, Ethan has a visual."

"Keep me posted," Sloane replied.

"Got it."

The door burst open, and Ethan stared at the couple in expensive suits as they sucked face and grabbed at each other's clothes. *Are you fucking kidding me?* Ethan ignored the two and went back to work inspecting the device in front of him while Calvin tried to get the couple to leave.

"Folks, I need you to evacuate the building," Calvin told them.

"You scared the shit out of me, man."

"Sir, miss, you need to leave right now. There's a possible incendiary device in the building."

The yuppie in the thousand-dollar suit sneered at Calvin. "It's a drill. We get these all the time."

"Sir, please, I need you to head for the exit as quick as you can. This is not a drill."

"Yeah, give me five minutes."

"Sir—"

"Hey, you work for the government, right? Which means I pretty much pay your salary. So you can wait a minute."

Uh-oh. Ethan smiled to himself as he removed the Packbot from his vest so he felt less constricted. From the corner of his eye, he saw Calvin's nostrils flare.

"Get out of the building *now*!" Calvin barked, his hand going to his rifle.

The guy nearly shit himself as he took off. His girlfriend swiftly followed.

"Un-fucking-believable." Calvin shook his head before joining Ethan. "What have we got?"

"Let's find out." Ethan removed his knife from his belt and inspected the edges of the lid before slowly inserting the blade underneath one corner. The lid wasn't wired, simply an outer casing. Carefully he removed it and cursed under his breath. The explosive was nestled inside a shitload of C-4. He removed his smartphone to snap a few pictures of it just in case. His phone would send the images to his desk interface, where he could analyze them later for more information on who put this together.

"It has antihandling measures. A mercury tilt switch. I need to lower the temperature. It'll take a few seconds," Ethan said, grabbing his kit containing the dry ice. "You need to go."

"Fuck. Okay. How long do you have?"

"Four minutes and thirteen seconds."

Calvin relayed the information to Sloane before turning to Ethan. "Get it done and be safe." Calvin kissed his cheek before running off.

As quickly as he could without compromising himself, Ethan removed the dry ice rocks with his tweezers and one by one placed them on the tilt switch, watching as the temperature steadily dropped. With each degree, seconds ticked by.

"Come on." As soon as it hit the temperature he needed, he used his knife to lift the clock, revealing the wires underneath. He was familiar with this device. Carefully he snipped the blue wire, and the clock turned off. With a sigh, he tapped his earpiece when he heard a faint beep.

Calvin's voice came over his earpiece. "Ethan, what's your status?"

"The device has been disarmed." He quickly walked down the wall of servers, listening to the beep. Something was wrong.

"That's great. We'll send in Disposal."

"Wait." Ethan rounded the corner. He scanned every server, and then he saw it. One of the servers had a disconnected wire. The light was flashing to indicate the loss in connection. Someone had tampered with it. "Shit."

"Ethan?"

"There's another device." Ethan pulled out the shelf and inspected the box. It was identical to the other one. He slipped his knife under the lid and gently pulled it off.

"How much time?"

Ethan took off around the corner and grabbed his bag. He removed the dry ice and hurried back to the second box. There was no time for him to take a picture. Hell, he was lucky if he had time to disarm it. The two devices had been set to go off at completely different times, with this one meant to explode first.

"Ethan," Calvin demanded.

"Forty-three seconds." Ethan plucked the dry ice rocks from his container and dropped them one by one on the tilt switch.

"Ethan, you need to get out of there. That's not enough time."

"Is the building clear?" *Come on. Hurry up.* He willed the dry ice to work faster, but the clock seemed determined to beat him.

"Negative."

"I can do this." Ethan added another piece of dry ice. That was it. He couldn't add any more or he'd risk the stability of the switch. It wasn't enough.

"Please, you can't do this to me again."

Calvin's frantic plea was followed by Maddock's growl.

"Hobbs, you get your ass out of there right now. That's an order."

Ethan considered ignoring his sergeant, but he knew better. There was no time. He dropped his equipment and broke into a run, rounding the servers and bolting out of the room. He sped down the hall, skidding when he reached the corner and almost running into the wall when he turned. *Shit. Shit. Shit.* He was running as fast as he could when the bomb exploded, the force of it blowing through the corridor until it hit him in the back, propelling him forward. Then everything went black.

WITH A groan, Ethan stirred. His ears were ringing. The muffled sounds grew louder until he realized they were voices, one laced with fear. Air rushed into his burning lungs, and he gasped. Everything was murky and gray around him. His eyes stung, and his muscles protested his every movement. At least nothing was broken. Pushing himself to his feet, he leaned against the wall for support, coughing at the smoke that burned his lungs. Giving himself a quick once-over, he was grateful to find no puncture wounds or blood. When he could manage it, he tapped his earpiece, his voice hoarse.

"Cal? I'm okay."

"Oh thank God!"

Calvin's voice came on the line, and Ethan got himself moving. The corridor was filling with smoke, and the sprinklers were going off. By the time he made it down to the lobby, he was soaked. His hair was plastered to his brow, and the water had made a streaky, muddy mess of his face despite how many times he tried to wipe it.

Downstairs, Calvin ran into his arms. He hugged Ethan tight, and Ethan held him, the rest of his team rushing over to make sure he was okay. The disposal team arrived and headed to what was left of the twenty-third floor. Ethan was lucky the bomb hadn't been powerful enough to take out the whole floor, or it would have taken him with it. If he'd known there was a second device from the beginning, he would have been able to disarm both in time.

Maddock approached and motioned toward the ambulance. "Get yourself checked out. Everyone else, let's clear this mess and start asking questions. Cael, start on the surveillance feeds. Dex, Letty, Rosa, start with the employees. Sloane, coordinate with Seb and Taylor. I want to find out who would want to blow this place up." Maddock looked to Ethan. "What kind of threat are we talking about here? Professional?"

Ethan shook his head. Anyone could have put those bombs together. He removed his phone and pressed his thumb to the screen, signing him into Themis. A few taps and he showed Sarge the device, along with a diagram and the materials needed to construct it.

"All right. Get yourself checked out and start on your report. I want to know everything about this device, along with a list of places that have sold supplies in the last six months, and I want it all cross-referenced with potential suspects. Calvin, I want you cross-referencing suspects with any and all personnel in this building. Intel's already started the algorithms. Oh, and Hobbs, I want to see you in my office after this."

Damn it. Ethan nodded and headed for the ambulance waiting by the curb. He really didn't need it, but it was better than facing Sloane, who looked pissed at him, though not nearly as pissed as Calvin was going to be. And now he had to face Maddock. *Great.*

After the EMT told Ethan what he already knew—that he was fine and lucky—Ethan went back to his truck. He climbed in and went to the medical station to grab some wipes for his face. His pulse was finally steadying and his adrenaline dropping. It always took him some time after an incident to calm down, and that was without a device going off mere feet away from him. He hoped this wasn't about to become a thing.

Ethan cleaned himself up as best he could and changed into a clean uniform, balling up the one covered in debris, dust, and grime. Once he'd stuffed it into one of the black laundry bags, he clipped his thigh rig back into place. Damn it, he'd lost his Packbot and both EOD X-Ray kits in the explosion. On the bright side, he'd made it out in one piece. That made two close calls in one year. He cringed at the impending argument with his best friend.

Feeling somewhat better despite not having been able to prevent the last device from going off, he took a seat on the bench. Even though he'd been cleared by the EMT's, Maddock wouldn't let him drive the truck back to HQ. With a sigh, he removed his tablet from his tac pants. He might as well get a head start on his reports. As Themis logged him in, Ethan took a moment to observe the chaos outside the truck's ballistic window. Lights flashed from the dozens of service vehicles, THIRDS and HPF tape everywhere, a couple of strips flapping in the crisp air like streamers at a Fourth of July picnic. Human and Therian service people ran around, momentarily united by the greater good of helping their citizens.

Ethan was on the fourth page of his report when the back door opened and his partner climbed up. Calvin took a seat on the bench, and Ethan opened his mouth to speak when his partner narrowed his eyes. Ethan promptly shut his mouth. Cal was pissed. Whether at him or someone else, he'd soon find out. If it was with someone else, Calvin would go off on a rant. If it was with him, his partner would stew in his anger and explode later. Calvin buckled up and stared at the floor, his arms crossed over his chest. *Damn. It was with him.*

Locating his backbone, Ethan turned in his seat and put his hand to Calvin's shoulder.

"Don't," Calvin replied. *He was seething.*

Got it. Ethan turned back to his tablet and put it away. At that moment the rest of their team was returning, including their sergeant. Recon agents arrived to take over the investigation. Any and all information they collected would be sent in to Maddock, who'd review it and pass it on to Intel for more algorithms. Defense was done here for the moment.

While Maddock drove them through the barricade toward HQ, Ethan occasionally glanced in Calvin's direction. His partner was a statue. He didn't move from his spot, barely even blinked. His team discussed the information they'd collected after questioning employees. After a recent downsizing resulting in the loss of over two dozen jobs, there were a lot of disgruntled employees. A few had been having financial problems long before losing their only income. The decision had come from the company's executives, which meant those who'd lost their livelihoods were just numbers to be cut off the payroll. The floor the devices had been planted on also happened to be where the offices of said executives were. Ethan had been doing this job long enough to have seen it all before. Now it was a matter of narrowing down the list of suspects.

Traffic was a nightmare, and it seemed to take forever to get back to HQ. Maddock hadn't even put the BearCat in its parking space before Calvin was jumping out. Ethan was almost grateful he was heading straight to the sarge's office. Calvin needed time on his own to cool off. Maybe by then he wouldn't look at Ethan with those big blue eyes filled with anger and disappointment. Ethan hated disappointing Calvin most of all. He'd known there wasn't enough time to disarm the bomb, yet he'd pushed his luck. It had been a stupid move, and now he had to answer for it. In his position, a few seconds meant the difference between walking away or having his name end up on a plaque on THIRDS headquarters' wall of fallen agents.

The team headed upstairs, with Dex and Sloane getting off on the fifteenth floor to get some lunch and Dex's third cappuccino that day. By now he was normally on his fifth. Ethan hoped Dex didn't find out Sloane had convinced Debbie the barista to make Dex's every other cappuccino caffeine-free. He could imagine the pandemonium it would cause.

Ethan reached Maddock's office in Unit Alpha. His sergeant had somehow beaten him to it. He was typing away at his desk's interface. Finishing up, he tapped the surface before raising his head to study Ethan, his lips pursed. Ethan knew that look. It was the Sergeant

Maddock "What's the best way to make you suffer without physically strangling you" expression. Usually Dex was the one at the end of that look.

"I was going to chew you out, but I decided against it."

Ethan cocked his head to one side. *Oh? Okay. That sounds good to me.... Wait.* Ethan narrowed his eyes. *There was a catch. He could see it in Maddock's eyes. Oh boy. Was he going to be on equipment duty for the foreseeable future? Surely what he'd done couldn't be worse than any of the dozens of harebrained schemes Dex had involved himself in over the last year and a half. Okay, maybe it was a tad worse.*

"I'm not going to chew you out because your boyfriend is going to do it for me." A smug smile spread across Maddock's face. "And that will be much, much worse."

Ethan wrinkled his nose. Yeah, it would be. Cal was going to—Wait, boyfriend? Ethan's expression must have said it all, because the sarge sat back in his chair with a sigh. He laced his fingers over his stomach and shook his head.

"Which part are you surprised about more, the word *boyfriend* or the fact I know about you two?"

Ethan held up two fingers together. *Both. Definitely both.*

"So, you're not there yet on the first one, okay. That's none of my business. But the second one is. Did you really think I wouldn't notice? That I don't know what goes on with my team?" A deep frown came onto Maddock's face. "Eight thousand agents in HQ, and you boys gotta date each other. I blame Dex."

Ethan arched an eyebrow at him.

"If there's crazy going on, that boy's never far from it. It spreads. But damn, I love him. Even if he's turned my team into some big hippie lovefest. Can I offer you some advice? From a guy who's got two sons with emotionally stunted boyfriends? The longer you try to ignore it, the more you'll hurt him. Things have changed. You can't go back to the way things were. And you sure as hell can't let it impede your performance, or Sparks will have your asses."

Ethan nodded his agreement. He knew that. He put a hand to his chest and patted it.

"Okay, so you're trying. Calvin knows you're trying. He needs more than that. You both do."

The door to Maddock's office opened, and Sparks hurried in, looking flustered. "Tony, we need to discuss—" Sparks stopped short when she noticed Ethan standing there. "My apologies, I didn't know you were busy."

"It's fine. We're done here," Maddock replied with a smile before turning his attention back to Ethan and giving him a pointed look. "Remember what I told you. And don't forget those reports. I want them ASAP. Close the door behind you."

Ethan nodded. He gave Sparks a nod in greeting before leaving and closing the door. He'd never seen the lieutenant flustered before. It was a strange sight. When he reached his office, Calvin was nowhere to be found. Where was his partner? Ethan tapped away at his desk and pressed his hand to the security panel, logging him in. Entering his security clearance, he searched for his partner's earpiece signal. He was in Dex and Sloane's office. Maybe he should stop by and check on Calvin. He was about to get up when Dex ran in.

"Hide me!" Dex dropped to his knees by Ethan's feet and crawled under his desk.

Okay. Just another day at the office. Ethan arched an eyebrow at Dex. *What have you done now?*

"I may or may not have Photoshopped Ash's face onto an image of Aslan and sent it out to the whole of Unit Alpha with this morning's PR memo. They really should have known better than to give me access to their template, so technically it's their fault."

How have I not seen this? Ethan swiftly tapped his desk and opened the memo sitting unread in his inbox. The moment he saw the photo of Ash's growly face on the CGI lion body, Ethan burst out into laughter. It was the most amazing thing he'd ever seen.

"Daley, you little sack of shit! Get out here so I can kick your ass!"

Ethan swiped his hand across his desk and got rid of the memo just as Ash stepped into the office. It took everything Ethan had not to laugh in Ash's reddened face. The guy was practically spitting fire.

"Have you seen Daley?"

Ethan shook his head, his lips pressed tightly together. *Don't laugh. Don't laugh.* Ash narrowed his eyes, and Ethan couldn't hold it in anymore. He held his hands up in apology but couldn't get himself to stop laughing. It especially didn't help that Ash had the same expression on his face now that he did in the image.

"Fuck you." Ash spun on his heels and marched off, bellowing down the corridor as he searched for Dex, leaving casualties in his wake. Poor Herrera. Ash was never going to forget or forgive him for taking a piss on his fern. Ethan held his palm out, and Dex slapped him five. He was so going to print out the memo. Something told him there would be plenty of copies circulating the department. Dex inched closer to Ethan, his voice a whisper.

"Is he gone?"

Ethan listened carefully. From the sounds of it, Ash had left Unit Alpha. He was most likely heading to the canteen. That's where Ethan would check if he was looking for Dex. He gave Dex a nod and was going to roll away from his desk so he could get out, when the chair got snagged on something. Dex tried to push at Ethan's knees and seemed to forget how low the desk was. He hit his head, cursing up a storm as he fell forward, his hands gripping hold of Ethan's thighs and his face landing on the chair between Ethan's legs.

Sloane and Calvin chose that exact moment to walk in.

"It's not what it looks like," Dex said, trying to push Ethan away.

It did *not* look good. *Oh my God, stop moving. You're making it look worse!* Ethan felt his face going up in flames. Why did every encounter with Dex end up with someone in a compromising position?

"I don't even have words." Sloane shook his head, clearly at a loss.

"I fell!" Dex squawked.

Ethan finally got his chair unstuck, and Dex hit the carpet face-first. He scrambled to his feet and ran over to Sloane. With his most charming smile, he took Sloane's hand in his.

"Babe. Darling. Snookums. I can explain."

Sloane eyed him dubiously. "You know, if this is your way of saying you want a foursome, I gotta say I'm not really the sharing type."

"It was an accident."

"Awful lot of 'accidents' lately."

At Dex's unimpressed expression, Sloane held his hands up.

"Just saying."

"Not funny," Dex muttered.

Sloane smiled and gave Dex's ear a tug. "It is a little." He chuckled at his boyfriend's pout and pulled at his arm. "Come on. Let's go home before Ash finds you and we have another Running of the Agents on our hands. Your dad's still pissed about having to replace the water cooler near the archive room. It also didn't help he was standing there when it exploded. I would have thought the water would have missed him, like the parting of the Red Sea, on account of how pissed he was, but nope. Soaked him completely."

"Okay, that one wasn't my fault. How was I supposed to know Ash was having a bad day?"

Calvin took a seat behind his desk with a scoff. "That's like saying I didn't know cats had claws."

"He's improving," Sloane replied just as Herrera whizzed by, leaving behind a trail of panicked apologies and promises to buy Ash a truckload of ferns. "Shit. Looks like Ash is back." Sloane took hold of Dex's arm and peered out. "Let's go. It's your turn to cook dinner, and I'm hungry."

"Gee, thanks, partner."

Sloane waited until the coast was clear before he took off with Dex in tow. Ethan watched them go, dodging and ducking through the bullpen like they were on a secret mission. Dex rolled behind a desk as Ash approached to ask one of their coworkers if they'd seen him. As soon as Ash turned, Sloane gave Dex the signal, and they scurried away. Ethan chuckled. *Those two. He turned his attention to Calvin, and the smile*

*fell off his face. His best friend was staring down at his
blank desk.*

"Cal?" Ethan said softly.

"I'm going home." Calvin stood, his hands balled
into fists at his sides.

Fine. Then I'm coming too. He got up and ignored
Calvin's deep frown. There was no point in prolonging
the inevitable. As much as Ethan knew Calvin was telling himself he wouldn't blow up, he always did. Why
did his best friend hold everything in?

As expected, Calvin waited until they got home to
explode. He preferred to lose it in private. Unfortunately it meant he got to stew over it all day until he was
ready to burst. He paced the living room before rounding on Ethan.

"I can't believe you!"

"I was doing my job," Ethan replied calmly. He sat
on the couch as Calvin paced.

"No, you were taking a stupid risk. Getting hurt to
save Dex was one thing, but what you did back there
was—" Calvin let out a frustrated growl before he spun
on his heels and threw his arms up. "What were you
thinking?"

"I was thinking about defusing the bomb."

"Don't," Calvin warned. "My God, Ethan."

His eyes grew glassy, and Ethan deflated. He knew
Calvin would be mad, but he hadn't expected this.

"When you got caught in the explosion at the Therian Youth Center, I'd never been more terrified in my
life. I thought I'd lost my best friend. Then I realized
you were more than that. Everything changed for me
during that Fourth of July party when I saw you fucking that guy, and I know it took me a while to figure it
all out, but seeing you lying in that hospital bed.... All

I could think about was that I'd never get the chance to tell you how I felt about you. I love you, Ethan. I know you might not be ready to accept it, but it doesn't change how I feel. And for you to disregard your safety like that…." Calvin walked off down the hall, the sound of his slamming bedroom door making Ethan flinch. There was no point in arguing or trying to talk to Calvin when he was pissed off like this.

Ethan spent the next few hours attempting to keep himself occupied. He tried napping, watching TV, listening to music, reading. Nothing helped. He felt miserable for hurting Calvin. It had been happening too often lately. For a moment he thought they'd been making progress, but every time they took one step forward, they ended up taking two steps back. How long could they keep this up?

After a cool shower, he dressed in loose pajama bottoms and a T-shirt. He headed for his bedroom. Calvin's door was closed. Ethan didn't like seeing it closed. It was only ever like that when Calvin was really mad at him about something. Ethan stepped in front of it, his frown deepening. The closed door was a stark reminder of the pain he'd caused. Calvin would be fine come morning. He always was.

Then why was he still standing there?

What if Calvin wasn't all right in the morning? What if he'd had enough?

He shouldn't go in. Calvin wanted to be on his own. He needed time. When Calvin got mad, he walked away. That's how it had always been. It occurred to Ethan that not once in all their years of knowing each other had he tried to stop Calvin from walking away. He'd never gone after him either, thinking it's what Calvin wanted. What if his best friend walked away in the hopes Ethan would follow? The thought hurt his heart.

Following his gut, Ethan opened the door with care. Inside, the room was dimly lit, not that it was a problem for him. The curtains were parted on the window across the room, the moonlight filtering in and landing on the bed where Calvin was asleep. He was on his stomach, one arm under his pillow, the other at his side, and his hair sticking up all over. Ethan stood by the bed watching him sleep. His black T-shirt had ridden up, and the waistband of his pajama bottoms sat low on his hips. The soft cotton jersey accentuated the curve of his ass, and it caused a stirring in Ethan's abdomen. When had he gone from seeing Calvin as his cute best friend to his sexy lover? His thoughts went back to that night in the utility closet at Dekatria. The way Calvin had tasted on his tongue, the soft moans and sweet gasps.

As much as he wanted to feel Calvin's skin, setting things right and making sure Calvin was okay was more important. He climbed onto the Therian-sized bed, mindful not to jostle his partner too much. Calvin was a heavy sleeper, so he barely stirred when the bed dipped under Ethan's weight. Ethan snuggled close, allowing himself a moment to study Calvin's face. His jaw was stubbly from having skipped a shave, yet his face remained boyish. Ethan had teased him when Bradley carded him their first time at Dekatria. His blond eyebrows and lashes only added to his sweetness.

Ethan could see it now, that whole "boy next door" vibe Austen kept going on about. Calvin could pull off an innocence he'd never been allowed to have. They'd both been forced to grow up pretty quick in their neighborhood. It seemed like a lifetime ago. The two of them huddled together, hiding from the gangs and bigger kids out to recruit them, use them, or beat them. For a long time making it to school and back in one piece had been a struggle. Once they got to school, a different kind of battle began. Yet throughout all that, Calvin never stopped fighting. The majority of his battles he could have avoided by simply not being friends with a messed-up tiger Therian kid who couldn't talk.

A lump formed in Ethan's throat. Unlike most people he'd met in his life, Ethan had managed to talk to Calvin. He'd felt drawn to him, comfortable and safe. When he was a kid, he'd pray every night that Calvin would always be with him. He loved Calvin, always had. Only now it was different. The softness of his skin, the plumpness of his lips, the blue of his eyes, his laugh, and his smile stirred emotions inside him he hadn't felt before. Tentatively, Ethan ran his fingers down Calvin's jaw. *You're amazing.* Calvin's lids fluttered open, his gaze landing on Ethan.

"Hi." Ethan's voice was barely a whisper, but it was enough to bring a slow smile to Calvin's face. That smile took hold of something inside him and shook it loose. Was he really going to risk losing this? Ethan slipped his hand over Calvin's and drew it to his chest, holding it close. "I'm sorry."

"Me too." Calvin's smile dimmed. "I'm sorry I got so angry."

"I'd like to make a pact."

"Okay." Calvin looked puzzled, but he waited patiently for Ethan to continue. He was always so patient.

"I won't take stupid risks, and you won't walk away from me when you're mad. I don't like going to bed with you mad at me. I'll give you your space until you cool down, but then we talk."

"You know what a miserable shit I can be when I'm pissed."

Ethan brought Calvin's hand to his lips for a kiss, his heart fluttering at the sweet blush that crept into Calvin's cheeks. "Things between us, they're the same, but not quite. We have to do some things differently. Work through it like… a couple."

"A couple of what?" Calvin asked, genuinely perplexed. Ethan chuckled.

"You're cute." He kissed the tip of Calvin's nose. "You know. A couple, in a relationship. Boyfriends."

Calvin opened his mouth to respond, then closed it when nothing came out. He swallowed hard, his eyes searching Ethan's. When he spoke, his voice was shaky. "Is that what you want? Because you know I'll wait. However long it takes, I can wait. You know I'd never push you to do something you weren't comfortable with."

"It's what I want. No more waiting. Though I might not always know what to do."

"Who does? You really think Sloane knows what to do with Dex the majority of the time?"

Ethan chuckled. "Good point."

"We'll help each other. Like we've always done. You're right. Some things have changed, but our friendship, having each other's back, that'll never change. You're still my best friend."

Ethan leaned into Calvin and kissed him, warmth spreading through him at the taste of his partner. A shiver replaced that warmth when Calvin parted his lips, inviting Ethan's tongue inside. Kissing Calvin was still so new, touching him even more so. With every caress, with every touch of their lips, Ethan grew bolder. He wanted more, wanted to experience every inch of Calvin. He loved the noises he made, the way he shivered under Ethan's touch, the way his skin flushed and made his freckles stand out. Ethan loved Calvin's freckles. He planted kisses down Calvin's neck and pushed his T-shirt to one side to kiss his shoulder. His skin was so soft and smooth. Ethan moved his hands down to caress Calvin's arm before slipping his hands under Calvin's T-shirt.

On Valentine's Day they'd bathed together. Ethan had wanted to make the night special. He'd been romantic, leaving pink rose petals on the floor leading to the bathroom, where he'd been waiting for Calvin in a bubble bath surrounded by illuminated candles. It was his way of showing Calvin he was serious about being more than friends. He'd gotten Calvin off in the tub that evening, and Calvin had returned the favor after they'd gotten out. Since then, they'd gotten each other off, kissed and cuddled, slept in each other's beds, but they'd been hesitant to take things further.

Ethan gently pushed Calvin onto his back and rolled over him, mindful of his weight as he pressed Calvin into the mattress. He'd dreamed of having Calvin beneath him, writhing, begging him to fuck him. Ethan remembered the way Calvin had trembled when Ethan had softly ordered him to come that Valentine's Day in the tub. He'd have to remember that. Ethan kissed Calvin, a deep, hungry kiss that showed his partner how much he wanted him. Ethan thrust his hard erection against Calvin's thigh, making him moan. With a smile, he whispered in Calvin's ear.

"I'd like to fuck you."

Calvin's soft gasp was music to Ethan's ears. His partner nodded, gently pushing at Ethan's chest so he could sit up. Ethan sat back on his heels, and they made quick work of their clothes, throwing them to the floor before they brought their lips back together in a frenzied kiss. Ethan wanted to taste all of him. This was a whole other side to his best friend, one he was eager to explore. Ethan nipped at Calvin's neck as he palmed Calvin's hard erection.

Calvin gasped, arching his back. "Please." He pointed to the nightstand. Foreplay might have to wait for another night when they were both a little less impatient. Ethan quickly found the bottle of lube inside the drawer. He didn't bother with the condoms. Neither of them had been with anyone since the Fourth of July that had changed everything, and they had always been safe. Both were tested regularly at work, and their most recent tests once again came back clean. Calvin didn't even question it.

Ethan's heart was racing, his pulse going at full speed. There were butterflies in his stomach, and he swore he'd never seen anything more beautiful than the man lying naked before him, exposed and begging for his touch. Ethan lubed up his cock as he knelt between Calvin's legs. He bent to kiss Calvin's lips and took hold of Calvin's cock, stroking him as Ethan pulled at his own dick. Calvin moaned and writhed, his cheeks flushed pink in the dim lighting. Ethan released Calvin and lined himself up with one hand while taking hold of Calvin's leg with the other. He slowly pushed himself in, groaning at the sweet pressure of Calvin's tight hole.

Ethan hadn't expected Calvin to be so tight. It felt incredible and raw at the same time. He paused when his partner hissed at the pain of being stretched by Ethan's girth. Calvin took a deep breath and nodded. Being as gentle as he could, Ethan pushed in little by little until he was settled inside Calvin to the root.

Sweat beaded his brow, but he took it slow. He hooked his elbows under Calvin's knees and gingerly pulled out before pushing back in.

Oh fuck, Cal.

Ethan started to move his hips, his fingers tight around Calvin's legs. Calvin grabbed fistfuls of the bedsheets as Ethan began to move a little quicker. He watched himself pulling out almost to the tip before plunging back in, forcing a surprised cry from Calvin. The sound sent a shiver through Ethan, and he felt his feral half stir. Calvin had made similar sounds with Felipe Bautista. Ethan let out a deep, feral growl. He lowered himself onto Calvin and grabbed his wrists. With a hard thrust that made Calvin gasp, Ethan pinned Calvin's wrists above his head.

"You're mine," Ethan hissed, his thrusts growing deep and fast. "I don't want him to ever lay a hand on you again. You spread your legs and your ass only for me."

Calvin arched his back, his whole body trembling with need. His lips were parted, and his breath came out ragged as Ethan pumped himself into him, the sound of skin slapping skin urging Ethan on. He wanted Calvin to feel him for days, a reminder of who he belonged to. The feral beast inside Ethan roared and clawed at him, enraged by the thought that someone else might make Calvin come.

"Say it," Ethan ordered, pulling out and then plunging himself deep into Calvin's ass.

"Oh God! I'm yours, Ethan. That's all I've ever wanted."

Ethan sucked on Calvin's neck, leaving his mark before moving his lips up to Calvin's jaw. He nipped at his stubble, then Calvin's ear. He fucked Calvin hard, the bed rocking beneath them and Calvin's wrists tight in his grip.

"Ethan, please. I need you to touch me."

Ethan obliged. He released Calvin's wrists and took hold of his cock, his other hand buried in Calvin's hair and holding on. Ethan's stroke matched his pace as he fucked Calvin. Nothing had ever felt so damn good. He could feel himself tumbling down the abyss, falling into this addiction, and he welcomed it. He grabbed one of Calvin's hands so he could take over the task of getting himself off. Ethan took a pillow and stuffed it under Calvin's hips before pushing both of Calvin's legs up against his chest. Calvin let out a soft cry as Ethan held his legs in place and pounded into him. He rotated his hips and changed his angle. Calvin cried out, ribbons of come shooting out onto his stomach.

Damn, he was gorgeous. Ethan felt his orgasm building inside him. His hips lost their rhythm, and his thrusts became short and hard, his muscles straining and the sweat dripping down the side of his face as he chased after his release. It slammed into him, and Ethan folded himself over Calvin, slipping his arms under Calvin's shoulders and taking hold of him. He brought Calvin down hard against him as he thrust in, Calvin's sharp cry sending Ethan over the edge. He gasped as he came inside Calvin, thrusting deep a couple of more times before slowing down. His muscles relaxed, and a heavenly haze washed over him as he gently pulled out. He collapsed onto his side as he tried to catch his breath.

Calvin let out a breathless laugh. "Fuck, man."

"Yeah," Ethan replied, feeling a little giddy as well. He lay on his back staring at the ceiling with Calvin next to him doing the same. His skin cooled, and he rolled over with a groan. Calvin wasn't going to be the only one sore in the morning. Ethan was disarmed by his partner's beautiful smile. "I didn't hurt you, did I?"

Calvin's cheeks went even redder, and Ethan sat up. "Cal?"

Calvin sat up and bit down on his bottom lip. He looked embarrassed.

"What's wrong?"

"I liked it. You being rough. In control. Demanding."

Ethan couldn't help his dopey grin. "Yeah?"

"Yeah."

Calvin lay down, and Ethan joined him, wrapping him up in his arms.

"Is that okay?"

"Of course it is. Whatever turns you on turns me on. And fuck, you turn me on."

Calvin looked up at him, his smile shy. "You think maybe we can research a few things? You don't have to do anything that makes you uncomfortable. I want it to be good for the both of us."

Ethan thought about the way Calvin responded to him, the way Ethan had relished Calvin's response. It had been easy for him, to be in control. He realized then that in here with Calvin, it was the only part of his life where he felt he had any control at all.

"You want to give up control to me?"

"Every day, the decisions I make on the job affect someone's life. When I'm looking through the cross-hairs of my scope, the whole world comes to a stand-still, waiting. I have to be in complete control of everything. Of my emotions, my thoughts, my actions. I don't want that in here with us. I don't want to be the one who takes action, who decides. I want you to do that." He looked up at him, hopeful. "Do you think you can do that?"

Ethan put his hand to Calvin's cheek. "Yes." Whatever Calvin wanted, Ethan would do his very best. Without Calvin at his side, he was only half of a whole. He couldn't imagine his life without the man in his arms, nor did he want to. He needed Calvin the way he needed air to breathe. He put his lips to Calvin's and kissed him. Out there the world was a terrifying place, but in here, feeling Calvin's lips on his, everything was perfect.

Chapter Six

WHERE DID he even start?

Ethan didn't know the first thing about bondage. The closest he'd ever come to tying anyone up was when he apprehended perps. From the looks of things, he'd have to do some research. The last thing he wanted was to hurt Calvin. He also wanted it to be good for his partner. Seeing as how said partner was in the canteen, Ethan decided to take a moment to look some stuff up and get a general idea about how much research would be involved. He put his browser in privacy mode and started typing. The amount of websites out there on the subject was staggering. How did he know which ones he could trust? He came across something called shibari, and it immediately piqued his interest. Tapping on one of the images of a blond man tied up very elegantly with red rope stirred something inside Ethan, not to mention in his pants.

Oh my. He could see his partner tied up like this, the ropes a sharp contrast to his fair skin. It was artistic, which suited Calvin.

"The Art of Shibari?"

Ethan nearly jumped out of his skin. He'd been so absorbed in the images in front of him that he hadn't seen or heard Dex approaching. "What's wrong with you?" Ethan growled quietly.

"According to some, *lots*, but let's talk about more exciting things, like bondage." Dex leaned his elbows on Ethan's desk and wriggled his eyebrows. "You're just full of surprises. So, I take it you and Cal have been getting jiggy with it? Doing the horizontal mambo. Playing hide the sausage."

Ethan groaned. "Please stop." His face was burning, and he quickly swiped his hand on the desk to close the image of the tied-up blond man.

"I'm gonna go out on a limb here and say this is for Cal. I knew he had a freaky side."

Ethan arched an eyebrow at his friend.

"The quiet ones always do," Dex replied with a wink.

Ash walked into the room, and Ethan didn't have time to minimize the shibari website before Ash saw it. *Damn it!*

"You guys are finally banging. Good for you. Cal likes it kinky, huh?" Ash leaned over to study the open website. "Fuck, man. You need a goddamn engineering and medical degree to figure that shit out. Your boy couldn't be into something simpler, like blindfolding or something?"

Oh my God, was Ash talking to him about sex? Did someone put something in the water? Had Dex finally cracked him? What was going on around here?

Ethan was about to reply when Cael popped his head into the office.

"Hey, what's going on?" He squeezed in between Dex and Ash, giving Ash a poke on his side and making him chuckle. "Whatcha all looking at?"

Really? Anyone else?

"Should I even ask?" Sloane mumbled as he stepped up beside Dex.

And now his day was complete. Ethan covered his face with his hands. This couldn't be happening. Maybe he should signal Letty and Rosa, get the whole team in here. They could help him take notes.

"It's like an Avon party but with sex toys," Dex stated cheerfully. "Do they have those? I bet they do."

Cael shoved Dex to one side and tapped away at Ethan's desk interface. "Actually, check this website out. They have top-quality stuff. It's a little pricier than some of the other websites but worth every penny. Trust me. They've also got experts on hand to answer any questions you might have. I think one's a shibari expert. If you sign up for their rewards program, you get a free pair of handcuffs. If they can hold Ash, they can hold Calvin."

Ash and Dex protested simultaneously. "Cael!"

Cael blinked innocently. "What? You should get a pair, Dex. They're Therian-strength. Oh, and they have body paint that tastes like Fruit Roll-Ups."

Dex looked horrified. "I do *not* want to hear about what this fiend gets up to in the bedroom with my innocent little brother."

"Innocent?" Ash laughed, receiving a glower from Cael. He cleared his throat. "No, you're right. It's all me."

Cael rolled his eyes. "It's just sex."

He opened up different product windows, and Ethan was ready to hide under his desk. Were those dildos? *Oh my God. Really, Cael? Really?*

"At home in my drawer I have this huge d—"

Ash clamped a hand over Cael's mouth, his face crimson. "Dictionary. A huge dictionary. Cael's teaching me new words, such as... delitescent. Adjective. This entire conversation should have remained delitescent."

"I'm a little scared right now," Dex whispered hoarsely, turning to Sloane. "Hold me."

Sloane put his arm around Dex and patted his head. "There, there." He turned his attention to the website. "Hey, check if they sell black leather chaps."

Dex perked up. "Ooh, assless please."

Ethan jumped to his feet and started pushing whoever he got his hands on. *Out, everybody out! You weirdos. Get out of my office.*

"Yeah, all right. Don't get your panties in a bunch," Ash grumbled. "Wait." He stopped abruptly and reached into one of his pockets. "I have your winnings. Cal's too."

Ethan shook his head at Dex in disbelief. *Wow. Couldn't even make it forty-eight hours.*

Dex didn't bother to hide it. "I'm big enough to admit when I have a problem. Well, it's not really a problem. I enjoy it too much for it to be a problem. I like having sex with my boyfriend. All kinds of awesome, sweaty man-sex."

Sloane groaned and covered his face with his hand.

Ash handed Ethan his and Calvin's money. "Yeah, they lost the moment we left the house."

Ethan gaped at Dex.

"Pretty much the second we closed the door," Dex admitted. "I tried to resist, but someone wasn't playing fair." He narrowed his eyes at Sloane.

"All I did was ask if he wanted to use the shower first."

"Which is sexspeak for 'let's do it in the shower,'" Dex insisted.

"No. It's regularspeak for 'do you want to use the shower first?'"

His team walked off with Sloane and Dex debating what Sloane had really meant, leaving Ethan once again on his own. With a sigh of relief, he returned to his desk. His butt had just hit the chair when Dex poked his head back in.

"Dude, no, seriously, let me know if they have the chaps. Sloane's a Therian thirty-four long. Make sure they're assless."

"Make sure what's assless?" Calvin asked as he walked into the office. He dropped his gaze to Ethan's desk. "Did you have to bring the whole team in on this?"

What? Ethan shook his head vigorously.

Dex held a hand up. "Actually, it was my bad. I walked in and caught him off guard, and then everyone else showed up and, well, you've been around us long enough to know nothing ever goes the way you want it to with Destructive Delta."

"Duly noted. Now you can get lost. Anyone breathes a word about this, and I swear I will snipe you."

"Got it." Dex saluted and spun on his heels, running into Ash. He peered at him. "What?"

Uh-oh. Ash looks happy. This can only mean one thing.

"One hour of complete and utter silence."

"But you'll be in your office. What's the point?" Dex whined.

Ash's expression turned wicked. "Actually, I'll be bringing my tablet and sitting in your office while I do my reports. That way I can bask in your silence."

"What?" Dex opened his mouth to reply, and Ash held a finger up.

"Starting now."

Dex flipped Ash off with both hands repeatedly before heading off with Ash sauntering after him while whistling a jaunty tune. Man, his team was weird. As soon as they were gone, Calvin came over to Ethan's desk.

"So what were you looking at?"

Ethan motioned to the website. "Cael recommended it. They have experts."

Calvin removed his smartphone from his pocket and placed it on the desk. He tapped his phone's screen, and the website popped up. "I'll check this out later."

Their desks blinked, and a little pair of ruby slippers appeared on the bottom right.

"Uh, God. The Black Widow's at it again." Calvin tapped the icon, and Sparks's face appeared on their board. She didn't look impressed.

"I suppose I've been called worse things, Agent Summers."

Ethan's face felt as red as Calvin's. *Wait, if she'd heard that....*

"Agent Hobbs, if you're looking for a shibari expert, I have several I can recommend. I'll forward them to your personal email account. Now, it's time for training. I'd like Destructive Delta to report to Sparta immediately. Sparks out."

The screen went blank, and Ethan turned to Calvin, who looked equally stricken.

"Can we, uh, forget that happened?"

Ethan nodded.

"Good. Let's go before anyone else shows up to give us sex tips."

Calvin hurried out with Ethan close behind. He wished he could say this day couldn't get any worse, but he was certain it could. Maybe Maddock was right. Maybe Dex was a magnet for weird. Nothing like this ever happened before Dex joined. The elevator doors closed with him and Calvin inside. His partner grinned wickedly before standing on his toes and kissing him, leaving Ethan breathless. Who the hell needed normal anyway? It was totally overrated.

TODAY WAS definitely not a day to be sore. From the moment they reached Sparta, Sparks had them training. There had been sparring, cardio, weight lifting, jiujitsu, and now more sparring.

"All right. Agent Summers, you were able to use Agent Keeler's weakness against him. Let's see how you do against yours. Unarmed."

Sparks tapped away at her tablet and motioned for Calvin to step onto the mat. He didn't like the sound of this.

"Agent Summers, pin Agent Hobbs to the mat. Agent Hobbs, prevent your partner from doing so. Take him out." She looked up from her tablet. "No holding back. I'll know if you are."

Calvin stared at her. "So you want him to kill me?"

"That depends, Agent Summers. Are you going to let him kill you?"

Calvin pressed his lips together to keep himself from saying something she'd undoubtedly make him regret. She couldn't be serious. No holding back?

"Take your stances."

This was insane. Calvin was no match physically, especially without weapons. He stepped onto the mat and took his fighting stance as Ethan hesitantly did the same. Calvin was reminded of all the times they'd roughhoused. He would jump on Ethan's back, and his best friend would walk around with him latched on like some spider monkey, as if nothing out of the ordinary was going on. Then he'd drop onto the couch or bed and playfully squish Calvin before pinning him. All Ethan had to do was get his arms around Calvin, and he was fucked, and not in the amazingly sexy way he'd been fucked last night. *Okay, now is not the time to be thinking about that.* He had to keep out of Ethan's reach. Easier said than done. Ash was probably going to enjoy the hell out of this.

"You may commence."

Calvin kept an eye on Ethan, watching his every move, paying attention to the little signs he'd picked up over the years. Ethan was worried, hesitant. It was written all over his face. Calvin slowly circled Ethan, subtly inching close as he did, but Ethan was onto him. There was no way Calvin would attack head-on. That would be stupid. He wasn't as small and graceful as Cael. Nor did he have Cael's cheetah Therian speed or flexibility. Ash had taught Cael how to use his size and build to his advantage. Calvin's skills lay elsewhere. At least he knew he could take a beating.

"Sometime today, agents."

At Sparks's comment, Ethan charged. Calvin dropped under Ethan's fist and rolled. He hopped to his

feet and did his best to remain out of Ethan's grasp.
Ethan only had to take a few steps to reach Calvin,
where Calvin had to dodge, parry, duck, and roll to
keep away. He managed to get close enough to land a
hit against Ethan's ribs, making Ethan growl and lash
out, his hand slapping Calvin across the cheek.

Motherfuck! Calvin was able to keep his balance,
but his cheek stung like hell. Okay, finally they were
getting somewhere. Calvin made to deliver a wide
hook, but at the last minute stepped left and deliv-
ered an uppercut to Ethan's side, cursing when Ethan
blocked it. Calvin swiftly retreated, managing to get
out of Ethan's reach before he could grab him. He was
getting nowhere fast.

"Agent Summers, you know what his weakness is.
This could be over in minutes."

"No," Calvin replied through his teeth. He knew
perfectly well what Sparks was implying, and there was
no way in hell he would use Ethan's fears against him.
If he was out in the field and he was facing a threat,
he'd use whatever was necessary, but not here and not
with Ethan. Ash's weakness had been easy. Get to Cael,
and he'd rid himself of Ash. With Ethan, it meant hurting him psychologically.

"And you really think someone else will give him
the same consideration? Do you think they'll worry
about your feelings, Agent Hobbs?"

Ethan shook his head, his expression growing dark
and a low growl rising up from his chest. If there was
one thing Ethan hated, it was someone fucking with
him on purpose. Calvin eyed his partner. They both
knew what Sparks was trying to do, and it wouldn't
work. Not with them. Anyone who tried to put the fear
in Ethan wouldn't give a shit about him, and Ethan

would be well aware. Coming from Calvin, the words could destroy him. Even if they didn't shut him down, they would linger. It didn't matter that Calvin wouldn't mean what he said. The words would trigger some deep-rooted fear in Ethan. Calvin would hand in his badge before he hurt Ethan like that. His partner turned to him and nodded, pupils dilated.

Calvin grinned. *That's right. Show her you're not scared. We can do this.* Calvin had his own way of getting results from Ethan, and none involved psychologically crushing the love of his life and partner. With Ethan, all he ever had to do was ask.

"Come on," Calvin ordered.

Ethan let out a roar as he charged. Before reaching him, Calvin dropped and rolled under Ethan. He jumped to his feet and spun, delivering a kick to Ethan's back. Ethan stumbled forward but quickly regained his balance. He turned and narrowed his eyes. With a growl, he came at Calvin, and Calvin did his best to avoid Ethan's fists. Of course, eventually he wouldn't be quick enough. Calvin sidestepped; Ethan anticipated it. He jabbed Calvin in the face, almost knocking him off his feet, but Calvin managed to regain his balance.

"Fuck." Calvin wiped the blood from his mouth and ran his tongue over his teeth to make sure nothing was loose. Ethan had gotten him good.

Calvin charged, blocking Ethan's fists while trying to deliver his own punches. He tried to remember everything they'd been taught over the last few weeks, concentrating on the force behind his blows and where to land them. He slipped behind Ethan and kicked at the back of Ethan's leg, sending him down onto his knees. Not allowing him time to get up, Calvin charged and slammed into Ethan, knocking him over onto his side.

He straddled Ethan and punched him square across the jaw. His victory didn't last long. Ethan hooked his arms through Calvin's, locked their legs together, and rolled until he was straddling Calvin.

Shit. Ethan had him pinned. He grabbed Calvin's wrists and pulled his arms over his head, his iron grip not budging as Calvin struggled. Ethan sat on Calvin's thighs, preventing him from moving his legs. Calvin cursed under his breath. He arched his back and pulled at his wrists, but it was like trying to move a fucking mountain. He would have tried head butting him, but Ethan kept himself out of reach.

"Well done, Agent Hobbs. You can let your partner up." Sparks tapped away at her tablet and motioned for them to join the rest of the team standing in formation. "Despite your defeat, you did well, Agent Summers. You're all dismissed."

That's it? A part of Calvin wished they could have another go. He'd expected the session to last longer. As they headed for the showers, Calvin was having trouble coming down from the fight. His adrenaline was still pumping. The sting on his lip felt good. Even after a quick shower in the locker room, he was still wired. Ethan was quiet on the ride home, and Calvin was fidgety. They got in, and Calvin threw his backpack on the couch.

Shit. This was bad.

Calvin tongued the inside of his lip where Ethan had gotten him good. He could still taste the blood. They'd never sparred like that, but they'd shown Sparks they were willing to do what they had to. They could function as a partnership and still be lovers. His heart was pounding again. All he could think about was Ethan holding him down, pinning him against the mat with his hard body, his larger hands gripping Calvin's wrists, restraining him....

Fuck, he was hard.

He looked up, his gaze meeting Ethan's. His pupils were dilated, leaving nothing but thin sparkling green rims around the edges, but it was the fire burning in his lust-filled eyes that had Calvin ready to come in his pants. A slow, feral grin crept onto Ethan's face, and his hand moved to his belt. Calvin followed the movement, swallowing hard when Ethan fingered one of the Therian-strength zip ties dangling there.

Calvin slowly knelt to unlace his boots. When he was done, he stood to gingerly kick them off. He'd become the prey, his every move scrutinized by the near three-hundred-pound apex predator before him. Ethan was still, waiting for the right moment to pounce. His eyes promised a night Calvin wouldn't soon forget. Calvin pulled his uniform shirt off and dropped it to the floor so it wouldn't get torn. He glanced down the hall to Ethan's bedroom before moving his gaze back to Ethan. A small smile tugged at his partner's lips.

It was on.

Calvin bolted down the hall. He didn't see or hear Ethan, but he didn't have to. He could feel him. Being hunted by a Therian was cause to lose your shit, unless that Therian happened to be your sexy-as-fuck partner who was about to pound you into the mattress. Calvin was hauled off his feet. His back came up hard against the wall with Ethan's knee pressed up against Calvin's painfully hard dick.

"Fuck," Calvin groaned. A low moan escaped him as Ethan brought their lips together in a searing, desperate kiss. He grabbed a fistful of Ethan's hair and tugged his head back, his voice low. "You really think I'm going to make it that easy for you?"

Ethan's eyes narrowed before his lips curled up. The tiger inside him was awake. Calvin could all but see him looking out from behind Ethan's blazing green eyes. This was going to be fun. Calvin brought his knees up between them and pushed, catching Ethan off guard and giving Calvin enough room to drop to his feet. He ducked as Ethan made a swipe for him. As suspected, Calvin didn't make it very far. Just inside the bedroom, Ethan grabbed his arm and spun him around before bringing their lips together in a scorching kiss. When they came up for air, Ethan grabbed Calvin by the waist and tossed him onto the bed. Before Calvin had stopped bouncing, Ethan was making quick work of Calvin's uniform, tugging his pants off and chucking them to one side.

Calvin put up a token struggle, enjoying the way Ethan assumed control of him, the way he swiftly and none too gently divested Calvin of his clothes until he was completely naked before him. Calvin turned, getting on his hands and knees to reach for the lube in the nightstand when Ethan dragged him back down before flipping him over. Ethan straddled him, took hold of his wrists, and pinned them above his head. The fire in his eyes as he leaned in threatened to consume Calvin.

"Don't move," Ethan ordered in a low growl. A shiver went up Calvin's spine, and he tugged at his wrists. He nipped at Ethan's bottom lip, then sucked on it before giving it a lick.

"And if I do?"

Ethan released him and sat back on his heels. He unhooked a zip tie from his belt, his chest bare and his stance begging for Calvin to challenge him. Fuck, he was hot. Calvin was rock hard, his cock leaking pre-come onto his stomach. He considered his next move. The wicked gleam in Ethan's gaze told Calvin he welcomed the challenge. Calvin bolted upright and threw a hand out, snatching ahold of the dog tag chain hanging from Ethan's neck.

Ethan twisted Calvin's arm and pushed him onto his stomach, then restrained his wrists behind his back with the zip tie. He pushed Calvin's head down into the pillow and pulled him onto his knees so his ass was in the air. Calvin groaned, feeling the bed move as Ethan got up. He turned his head, watching his partner shed his pants and boxer briefs. Calvin had never felt more exposed or more turned on. His mouth watered at the sight of Ethan's naked body. Man, he was fucking gorgeous. Strong arms and thighs, flat abs, a slim waist and rounded ass. Calvin wanted to run his tongue over every inch of Ethan's skin.

Ethan found the lube, then shoved several pillows under Calvin before climbing back on the bed. He leaned in, his soft words drawing a whimper from Calvin.

"I'm going to fuck you so hard right now."

Calvin all but unraveled. He didn't bother looking over his shoulder. He trusted Ethan completely. Ethan kneaded Calvin's ass, a low moan escaping him before he parted Calvin's cheeks. Calvin gasped at the feel of Ethan's tongue on his hole. The move was unexpected, and Calvin's body trembled with anticipation. He was surprised he didn't come right then and there.

"Oh God, Ethan."

Ethan alternated between using his tongue and his fingers, driving Calvin crazy. The heat spread through his body, and he thought he might pass out from his desperation. He wanted to touch himself so badly, but all he could do was kneel there and take whatever Ethan gave him, and right now, Ethan was making a meal out of Calvin's ass. He had no idea how much longer he could take this. Calvin's breath came out ragged as Ethan replaced his fingers with his cock. He went slowly, the burn drawing a hiss out of Calvin as he was stretched. Inch by inch, Ethan pushed himself inside of Calvin, until soon the pain gave way, and Calvin let out a low groan. Damn, that felt so good, but he wanted more, *needed* more.

"Please, Ethan, fuck me."

Ethan took hold of the zip tie securing Calvin's wrists and gave them a tug. "Is this what you want?" Ethan pulled out and slowly pushed himself in. Calvin nodded, and Ethan snapped his hips, causing Calvin to cry out. "Or is *that* what you want?"

"That," Calvin pleaded. "I want to feel you. I want to hurt and burn from the feel of you."

Ethan obliged, holding on to Calvin's wrists as he drove himself into him, plunging deep. The sound of skin slapping skin, moans, groans, and gasps resounded through the otherwise silent room. Ethan's thrusts hurt so damn good. It was as if every gasp, every whimper Calvin released urged Ethan on. Ethan changed his angle, hitting Calvin's prostate.

Calvin's body shook. "Oh fuck yeah. Ethan. Fuck." Ethan held him in place as he pounded into Calvin's ass, his soft groans the sweetest sounds Calvin had ever heard. The more Ethan fucked him, the more Calvin wanted. Ethan would slow down, torturing him before speeding up again. "Ethan…."

Ethan's hips lost their rhythm as he pounded Calvin's ass, pushing him down into the mattress. Calvin's muscles strained. His arms were killing him, but he didn't care.

"Come," Ethan growled.

"I need you to touch me." He'd never needed anything so bad.

Ethan folded himself over Calvin as he continued to fuck him, his words whispered in Calvin's ears. "You're going to come because I tell you to."

He flicked the tip of Calvin's dick, and Calvin yelped. His orgasm hit him hard, and he cried out as he came. He buried his head against the pillow, Ethan draped over his back as he thrust several times before Calvin felt Ethan coming inside him, the warmth spreading through his body. Slowly Ethan pushed himself down to the root, where he remained still and buried inside Calvin, a shuddered breath escaping him. He kissed Calvin's temple before he pulled out and removed the pillows from under Calvin. He slipped onto his belly as he tried to catch his breath, the blood in his wrists once again circulating properly when Ethan cut the zip ties.

Calvin lay on his stomach, smiling when Ethan cuddled up close. Ethan didn't say anything, just stroked Calvin's hair before trailing his fingers down Calvin's back, following the curve of his spine to his ass. The smack to his left buttcheek caught Calvin unaware, and he let out a surprised cry. He rolled onto his side to face Ethan, who smiled wickedly.

"Sorry, couldn't help it. I love the way your skin gets all rosy."

Calvin felt his checks burn. "Don't be sorry. I kind of liked it."

"Ooh, looks like I'll have to do some more research."

Ethan kissed Calvin, his lips soft and warm. Calvin loved kissing Ethan. He could spend hours tasting his lips. Ethan drew Calvin against him and deepened the kiss, his thumb stroking Calvin's wrist. He seemed to remember something, and he pulled back. He looked down at Calvin's wrists with a frown.

"You're going to be bruised. Did it hurt too much?"

"It was fine. High pain tolerance."

Ethan frowned. "That's not the kind of pain I want to give you."

Calvin gave Ethan's lips a kiss. "I'm fine. Cael recommended a good rope from that website of his, and I placed an order. It arrives next week. We can use that safely until we work the rest out."

Ethan smiled broadly. "Okay."

He sat up, and when he stretched, Calvin couldn't help but run his fingers down Ethan's back.

"You're amazing, you know that?"

Ethan turned to look at him, his gorgeous smile taking Calvin's breath away.

"I'm not. You, on the other hand...." He kissed Calvin and took his hand, pulling him along with him. "Come on. Let's make dinner and watch some TV."

"We should probably put on some pants."

"Don't need pants to make a sandwich. But we should clean up first." Ethan laced his fingers with Calvin's, and they headed to the bathroom to wash up before heading to the kitchen. Ethan popped on the radio as he removed ingredients from the fridge while Calvin grabbed the fresh bread. They might not be the best cooks, but when it came to hoagies and sandwiches, they ruled the school. A slow romantic ballad came on the radio, and Calvin went to change the station for something a little more upbeat when Ethan wrapped his arms around Calvin's waist from behind. He planted a kiss on Calvin's shoulders and began to sway with the music. Calvin didn't quite know what to do with himself. None of his sorry-ass boyfriends had ever been very romantic. Mostly it had been about the sex. He shouldn't be surprised. Ethan wasn't like anyone he'd ever known. He was kind, gentle, and the sweetest guy.

Calvin closed his eyes, his stomach filling with butterflies as Ethan let his chin rest on his shoulder. They swayed slowly, their fingers laced together. Ethan's soft voice sang in his ear. It was tragic that someone who couldn't speak could sing so beautifully. Ethan didn't do it often, and Calvin considered himself blessed when he heard him. He was the only one who'd ever heard Ethan sing. His voice had rhythm and soul. It changed pitch naturally, the words rolling off his tongue as if they came up from the very depths of his core, drawing from a lifetime of pain, fear, courage, and love.

Love…. Calvin had never put too much stock in love, and now he was in it so deep he never wanted to know anything else.

THE NEXT day, Calvin couldn't stop himself from smiling. That morning in the canteen Dex had given him a knowing look from across the table while they all had coffee—or in Cael's case hot chocolate—and Ash told Calvin he was freaking him out with his smiling. Calvin thought the day couldn't have started any better. He was sore as hell, but he didn't care. Ethan had fucked him into the mattress last night. They'd slow danced in the kitchen, and Ethan sang to him. They ate, watched TV while cuddled together on the couch. Then later that night Ethan woke him up and made his toes curl once again. The best part was every time Calvin looked up at Ethan, his boyfriend smiled shyly, and his face flushed. Calvin thought it was adorable.

At least they'd be spared one of Sparks's insane training sessions this morning. They were on their way to the training bay for their usual cardio workout when a call came through. Hostage situation down at Deimos Tower. Calvin met Ethan's gaze.

"Shit. That's the same building the bombs were planted in."

Ethan nodded somberly. They hurried down the hall outside Unit Alpha and met up with the rest of their team at the elevator. Calvin turned to Sloane.

"You think it's the same person? Recon having any luck locating the perpetrator?"

"I'd be pretty surprised if it wasn't the same suspect." Sloane looked over at Cael. "Any leads since the last time we spoke?"

Cael shook his head. "Themis has helped us narrow down the list of suspects, but none of the algorithms Intel programmed has yielded the kind of hits we were hoping for. Whoever it is is either unregistered or has no priors. There were far too many hits on the supplies used to construct the bomb, because there wasn't one single place which had sold all or most of the items, so it's likely whoever put it together made sure to purchase the items from several locations. Obviously the less reputable, the harder to find. Rosa and I were heading out for some more questioning when Dispatch called us."

"Okay. Hopefully Maddock will have something for us. Negotiators from Theta Destructive are already out there."

They all rushed down the corridor leading to the armory, Ash catching up to Sloane.

"Maybe our bomber found out no one was killed by his little gift, and now he's taking matters into his own hands."

"That's not unlikely. Okay, everyone. Suit up."

They went to their designated weapons locker and got into their full tactical gear. Hostage situations meant Calvin would be bringing along his sniper rifle. Not that he ever left HQ without it, but he'd been doing this job long enough to know what the likely outcome would be. If it was the bomber returning to finish what he started, and if there was no reasoning with him, Calvin would end up having to take care of it. He really hoped whoever they were dealing with would listen to reason, or that his team could get close enough to take the bomber down without any casualties.

Calvin lowered the visor on his helmet and grabbed the black bag containing his equipment. He locked up and followed his team through the hall leading to the garage and their tactical vehicle, where Maddock was waiting for them. Calvin climbed into the passenger seat and buckled up while the rest of his team swiftly secured themselves on the bench. Ethan hit the gas, and they sped out of the garage and into the street behind HQ. They listened as Maddock briefed them.

"Themis found our bomber. Problem is when Beta Ambush answered the call and went to pick him up, the guy wasn't there. A few minutes later Dispatch received a call about gunshots being fired inside the Deimos Tower. Our shooter is Mr. Fernando Ruiz, a bear Therian. He was fired three months ago from his security job for being late. The head of security said it was by five minutes, and Ruiz had called in, but it was out of his hands. The decision came from up top. Ruiz was a model employee, never sick, hardly ever late, a hard worker. They think Ruiz got screwed along with some of the other low-level employees. To make things worse, Ruiz had a loan taken out on his 401(k)."

"Let me guess," Ash grumbled. "As soon as he was let go, the loan had to be paid back in full."

"Yep. Within sixty days. Ruiz was already falling behind on his bills. The company owed him a shit-ton of overtime too. He tried to sue them for his dismissal and overtime pay, but the attorney he hired was no match for the company's team of lawyers. It ate away at whatever savings Ruiz had left. According to Mrs. Ruiz, they received a letter two weeks ago saying the bank was foreclosing on the house."

Shit. Calvin knew where this was heading, and it was all kinds of fucked-up.

"It gets worse," Maddock continued. "Ruiz went in last week to plead with the head of the department and found out the executives were all awarded hefty bonuses."

"What about the cutbacks?" Dex asked.

"It was either lose their bonus or make budget cuts."

Dex let out a sound of disgust. "So rather than lose out on a new condo in Miami, they get rid of their employees. Bunch of dicks."

"Welcome to corporate America," Ash muttered.

Maddock agreed. "It was too much for Ruiz. He planted the bomb, but he must have seen the news footage. Everyone made it out okay. Probably decided to take care of it himself. We're pretty sure one of the hostages is the guy who reported Ruiz for being late and got him fired. I'm guessing the executive that did the firing is also up there with him."

The BearCat sped through Manhattan, sirens blaring and lights flashing. Ethan did his thing, maneuvering through traffic, dodging, zigzagging, taking shortcuts that would probably get them fined, and doing everything he could to get them there as quickly as possible without running into anyone. It was like playing Snake at full speed with landmines.

They arrived on scene, and Ethan parked the BearCat at the end of the block. The media was already there and reporting. News choppers soared over the skyline along with police helicopters. It was pandemonium. Reporters tried to get their attention as they got out of the BearCat, but the team quickly put as much distance between themselves and the reporters as possible. There were agents posted everywhere, making sure no one tried to sneak onto the scene.

Seb and Taylor joined them, informing them of their teams' positions. Theta Destructive and Beta Ambush had evacuated the building, with the exception of the twenty-first floor where Ruiz was.

Maddock turned to Seb. "Where are we?"

"There are eight employees unaccounted for. We believe those are the ones Ruiz is holding hostage. The negotiator had been making progress, and Ruiz was going to let her in the building when he received a phone call from his wife. She'd been advised against trying to make contact with her husband and to let the negotiator handle things. She told the agents on-site she was going to the bathroom and made the call. Whatever she said to him, it set him off. Things started going downhill from there. Ruiz has threatened to shoot the hostages if anyone goes near the building. The negotiator's trying to calm him down and get him to let her in the building to talk to him face-to-face."

"Any demands?" Sloane asked.

Taylor shook his head. "This was clearly an act of desperation. He's distraught, doesn't know what he wants. He's rambling, shouting, and getting more pissed by the minute. He's unraveling."

Sloane turned to Calvin. He knew what Sloane was going to say. "Cal, we're gonna need you to take position. If things go south...."

"I got it." No explanation or further information was needed. Calvin headed back to the BearCat and climbed in. He placed his thumb to the lock on the weapons cage and pulled out the long black bag with his rifle in it. He hoped the negotiator would be able to get through to Ruiz. Calvin pushed up his visor and pulled on his black tac gloves before shouldering his bag. It weighed a fucking ton, but he was used to it by now. Was the weight of it all in his head? There were instances where it seemed to double in heft, while other times it appeared lighter. When he reached the end, Ethan was standing there looking worried. Calvin gave him a wink.

"Don't worry, big guy. You be safe, okay?"

Ethan nodded, his expression saying more than any words could. He was aware of what came next, what Ruiz's chances were of walking out of this alive. Shots had been fired. There was no telling how many were hurt or if anyone was dead. Calvin would be finding out soon enough. Ethan knew what would happen if Calvin pulled that trigger. How with one finger he'd be shattering a family. Calvin couldn't think about that. He gave Ethan's arm a squeeze before hopping down.

Quickly, he walked to the building across the street from Deimos Tower. It was still being cleared out, which meant he had to pass by employees on the way up the stairs. He made sure not to make eye contact. Most wouldn't know why he was there, but in the event someone did, he didn't need them challenging him. As if he got some kind of sick joy from what he did. Like it was easy to take someone's life.

Calvin had volunteered to be a sniper. The THIRDS never appointed an agent because they were good at shooting. That was the easy part. There was a list a mile long of prerequisites an agent had to meet before he was even considered for the position, and being a good shooter was near the bottom of the list. Calvin had a natural talent, but he also had the required discipline. The position was physically and emotionally demanding, and the responsibility placed on his shoulders could be overwhelming for some.

The safety of the hostages, his team, and the whole damn outcome could hinge on his observations and the intel he relayed, all while under pressure. At times he was his team's eyes and ears. He needed to be meticulous, articulate, and have a keen eye for details. And then there was the part where he had to be willing to kill someone.

Calvin reached the twenty-first floor and found the empty office that would place him directly across from the twenty-first floor of the Deimos Tower. He quickly pulled the zip down on his bag and deftly went about assembling his rifle. As officers, there were times when they were forced to draw their weapons and, in life-threatening situations, fire and possibly kill someone. As a sniper, he would have to sit and watch his target for perhaps hours. From his perch, it was plausible to develop a strange type of intimacy with his target, something that was unlikely to happen when, as a last resort, forced to fire on a threat.

With his rifle assembled, Calvin secured it to the tripod and adjusted his position. He looked through his scope. Getting a clear shot of the interior of Deimos Tower was going to be a challenge. Indoors he was dealing with blinds, shutters, furniture, equipment, and a dozen other things that could obstruct his view. He took a steady breath and focused. Not everyone was capable of detaching themselves emotionally. For every THIRDS sniper, there were legal, moral, and ethical issues to work through. Calvin tapped his earpiece.

"Sloane, I'm in position."

"Do you have a visual?"

"Affirmative." Calvin scanned the waiting area behind the reception desk of the floor. Ruiz was pacing in the center, surrounded by terrified Therian and Human hostages huddled together. One lay on the floor in a pool of blood, unmoving. Another was clutching her bloodied shoulder. "Sloane, we've got one hostage down. He's not moving, and there's a large amount of blood underneath his head." Calvin quickly but carefully swept his gaze over the victim. Shit. "I've got an entry wound to the head. He's gone. There's another hostage injured. Shot to the shoulder. We've got a third hostage on the floor, but she's breathing. Eight hostages total. Suspect has a gun." Ruiz shouted into the phone, and Calvin cursed under his breath. "His fangs are elongated. He's agitated enough to shift."

"Shit. Okay. Negotiator's managed to convince him to let her in to talk to him, but he's not letting anyone else near the building. It's all you now."

"Affirmative."

With Sloane unavailable to make the call, it fell to Calvin. The moment it looked like Ruiz was going to pull that trigger, Calvin would take the shot. It seemed

*like forever before the negotiator reached the floor.
The dark-haired wolf Therian agent walked in with her
hands held up in front of her to show Ruiz she wasn't
hiding any weapons. Through her com, Calvin could
hear everything going on. Ruiz demanded she stay
where she was by the elevator. Calvin remained stock-
still, his breathing steady as he focused on the scene before him. As everyone waited with bated breath, Calvin
listened to Ruiz screaming at the negotiator, telling her
how the disgraceful people on the floor had destroyed
his life, his family. How they'd robbed his children
of their home. There were tears streaming down his
reddened face, and he switched between Spanish and
English.*

*The minutes ticked by, and Calvin barely blinked.
His muscles strained, but he didn't dare move. He simply waited. The conversation between Ruiz and the negotiator got heated when one of the suits moved. Shit.
What are you doing, you idiot? Stay down.* In the blink
of an eye, it all went to hell. Ruiz spat in indignation at
the man in the suit, the guy arguing with him. The negotiator ordered the guy to stand down, but the hostility escalated beyond her control, growing volatile until
Ruiz swung his arm up to fire at the suit.

Calvin pulled the trigger. Mr. Ruiz crumpled to the
ground.

It was over.

Letting out a slow breath, Calvin straightened.
He tapped his earpiece. "Sloane, the threat has been
neutralized."

"Affirmative. Get back to the BearCat."

Calvin quickly went to work taking his rifle apart.
His mind was clear as he returned the pieces to his
black bag, followed by the tripod. When everything

was packed away, he grabbed his bag and left the room. It was like he'd never been there.

He descended the stairs and walked out of the building toward the BearCat. A reporter approached him from behind the truck. *What the fuck? Why was the press out here?*

"Agent Summers, you're the sniper officer for Destructive Delta. Did you kill Mr. Ruiz?"

Calvin gritted his teeth and made to go around the reporter, when the assistant pushed a camera in his face. Just what he fucking needed. Someone was going to get their ass kicked over this. Calvin turned away as a group of THIRDS agents rushed the news team. He climbed into the BearCat, then slammed the back doors shut.

"Son of a bitch!" Calvin dropped his bag on the floor. He paced before tapping his earpiece. "Sloane, we have a problem."

Sloane's voice came in over his earpiece. "What is it?"

"I just got a camera shoved in my face." The more he thought about it, the more pissed off he got. "What the fuck were they doing by the truck? They were waiting for me. The reporter called me by name and knew my position on the team. He asked me if I'd killed Mr. Ruiz."

"Shit. Who was it?"

"You know who. The same assholes who are always making shit up and calling it news."

"Sit tight. I'm going to look into it."

"Okay." Calvin snatched up his bag and returned it to the weapons locker. That fucking reporter had caught him off guard. Whether he was right or not about him being the one who pulled the trigger wouldn't matter to

the public. If they saw the footage of him being asked if he'd killed Ruiz, they'd assume he had. They'd seen his face. Calvin slammed the weapons locker door closed and pulled his tablet from his tac pants pocket. He went online to the news station's website. There it was in full-color, front-page headlines: "Human THIRDS sniper kills Therian during hostage negotiation."

"Son of a motherfucking bitch!" And then the press wondered why they were so goddamn hated by THIRDS agents. *Kills Therian?* They purposefully left out that the Therian was the hostage taker. Calvin had stopped the guy from killing a second hostage. Two others were badly injured. And why the hell did they have to bring up that he was Human? Would it have mattered if it had been a Therian sniper? As if the rest of that damned headline wasn't volatile enough. They hadn't even bothered to confirm their information. Under the headline, they had a photograph of him in his ceremonial uniform, his expression hard and his eyes red. He looked like shit. They'd gone out and found the worst picture of him. His anger threatened to bubble over. It was a picture of him at Gabe's funeral. Next to his image was a photograph of a smiling Ruiz with his family, and beside it, one of him being rolled away on a gurney in a body bag by Hudson and Nina.

There was nothing Calvin wanted more than to hunt down the bastard who'd had the fucking audacity to use that image of him in this sorry excuse for a news article. It was blatantly biased against the THIRDS, using manipulative language to paint him as some kind of trigger-happy dickbag. They'd all but called him a Therian hater.

By the time the team returned to the truck, Calvin was seething. According to Sloane, the PR department was running damage control. The image of him at Gabe's funeral had been removed, but unfortunately there was little they could do about the article until the investigation was finished. Back at HQ, Calvin turned in his rifle for investigation as per protocol. He put his equipment away and prepared for his session with Dr. Benedict Winters. Then he'd start on his report, which would be read by his superiors, administrators, lawyers, and everyone else on God's green earth that might question whether his decision to shoot Ruiz had been the right one.

Calvin understood the need to see the THIRDS-appointed psychologist. He was used to it by now. He'd have to see Dr. Winters for however many sessions was necessary until Dr. Winters signed him off. It wasn't often Calvin found himself looking through his scope. The last time had been during the exchange between the Coalition when Ash was shot, but this case was different. To Calvin, it didn't matter who was in his crosshairs, whether it was a deranged murderer like Isaac Pearce or a father pushed too far like Fernando Ruiz. To him, he was doing his job keeping the public safe. For many, they could justify a kill when it was someone like Pearce or Hogan, and depending who was reporting the news, they were either victims of unfortunate circumstance or villains. In today's scenario, no matter which way anyone looked at it, Calvin would be painted as the villain. Well, except maybe to the victims, but then he'd heard it all before, how the rich guys had brought it on themselves for being assholes. Did that mean they deserved to die?

"Cal?"

Ethan's soft word snapped him out of it, and he realized they were alone in the locker room. He didn't even remember walking in there. Calvin finished changing and shut his locker.

"I'm fine. I'll see you later." The heartbroken expression Calvin managed to catch a glimpse of as he turned away from Ethan had him adding the man he loved to the long list of people he'd hurt today. He walked off, needing to be alone. It was best he be on his own right now. He'd caused enough pain.

Chapter Seven

I'LL WAIT for you.

Ethan hated this part more than anything. This was
where Calvin shut down and shut him out. Ethan was
terrified one of these days Calvin would get lost for
good. The team stayed clear, knowing it was what his
partner needed. They'd finished up quick and left the
locker room. Calvin had gone through the motions, his
head somewhere else. It broke Ethan's heart to see him
like that. Even if it didn't last long, it was there, dim-
ming the brightness in his partner's blue eyes. Ethan
followed Calvin out, though he kept his distance. His
partner didn't know he was there. Calvin had changed
out of his uniform. He'd have the rest of the day off,
but first he'd be up to see Dr. Winters. Tomorrow he'd
spend the day filling out his report, finding the right
words to paint a picture and show why it was necessary
for him to do what he did.

I wish you would let me in.

Ethan yearned to reach out and take Calvin's hand, to pull him into his embrace and not let go, but he didn't. A thought struck him. He had a few minutes before Calvin went upstairs to meet with Dr. Winters. Ethan hurried to the elevator and went up to the seventeenth floor. He briskly walked through the corridor of offices and suites until he found the frosted-glass door with Dr. Winters's name on it. He walked into the reception area, where a young Human woman smiled at him. Ethan pointed behind her to the office.

"One moment. I'll check." The receptionist put in the call, and seconds later the doctor emerged. He smiled widely.

"Agent Hobbs. How good to see you. Please, come in. I have a few minutes before my next session."

Ethan walked into the doctor's office and waited while the tall wolf Therian closed the door.

"What can I do for you, Ethan? Have you thought about my proposal to learn ASL?"

Ethan was embarrassed. He shook his head. *I will, though.* The last few months had been so crazy, he'd completely forgotten about Dr. Winters's suggestion for him to learn American Sign Language. Ethan wasn't sure it would help. ASL was communication, and no matter what format he was using, whether it was spoken words or sign language, it didn't stop him from growing too anxious to communicate with someone.

"Well, you think about it and let me know. I have a wonderful program that can help. If it's what you want. No one's forcing you."

Ethan nodded his thanks. He placed his hand out around his chest level before moving his hand over his hair and making spike motions.

"Agent Summers?"

Ethan nodded. *I'm worried about him.* He swiped a hand in front of his face.

The doctor's expression softened. "Yes, I know. It's rather difficult to get through to him after an incident."

No, you don't understand. Ethan put his hand to his heart, then motioned between him and the door.

"Oh." Dr. Winters blinked at him. "You and Agent Summers are involved romantically?"

Ethan nodded. He waved his hand in front of his face again before putting it to his heart. *Every time he shuts down, it breaks my heart.* He pushed with his hands.

"He pushes you away."

Ethan nodded.

"Your partner carries the weight of the world on his shoulders, even when no one has asked him to, and that's when he's not carrying the responsibility of his duties. I'll see what I can do, but I'm sure you know better than anyone how willful your partner can be."

Ethan wasn't surprised. Calvin wasn't one to share his feelings. He had no problem expressing himself, but when it came down to the core of what was eating away at him, he never let anyone in, not even Ethan. All Ethan could do was hope for the best.

"CALVIN, THANK you for seeing me."

"I don't really have a choice," Calvin muttered as he entered the doctor's pristine office and headed for the couch. The room was furnished to resemble a living room more than a psychologist's office. Apparently it made agents feel more open and at ease. Didn't matter how you dressed it up, it was still a shrink's office.

"There's always a choice, Calvin."

Here we go. Calvin took a seat on the floral couch. At least it was comfortable. He sat back against the plush throw pillows, his fingers laced and resting on his lap. He waited for the doctor to finish setting up the recording application on his tablet. Once he placed it on the coffee table beside him, he crossed one knee over the other and placed his laced fingers on his lap. Now the usual questions began.

"How are you feeling?"

Calvin shrugged. "I'm fine."

"How are you feeling about what happened today?"

"I did my job."

Dr. Winters smiled warmly. "That's what you did, not how you feel."

"I had to kill someone. Someone with a family who loved them. How do you think I feel?"

"I can't answer that for you," Dr. Winters replied gently.

"I feel shitty." Like that was big news. What agent wouldn't?

"You know, Calvin, whenever we have a session, you sit here in my office, I ask you the same questions, and you give me the same answers. That you're fine. You were doing your job. That you understand what's required of you, and that you need some time, but you can handle it because you always have."

"Right." At least they were on the same page. "That hasn't changed."

"Let's try something different." Dr. Winters cocked his head to one side, his sharp amber eyes studying Calvin. He smiled. He was always smiling. "Tell me about Ethan. How is your relationship with him progressing?"

Calvin sat up and narrowed his eyes. He eyed Dr. Winters warily. Not that it did much good. The wolf Therian barely blinked.

"Things are good. Was he here? Did he come here?"

"Does that concern you?"

Why would Ethan come up here? Not that Ethan hadn't been up here before. Ethan had plenty of sessions with Dr. Winters before today, the most recent in connection to Shultzon taking him, Sloane, and Ash. "What did you say to him? Did he say anything?"

"He's worried about you."

"Why? It's not the first time this has happened. He knows how these things go. How is this different to any other time?" *It was a sad fact, but Calvin had done this a number of times.*

"You push him away."

Calvin swallowed hard. He was finding it difficult to meet Dr. Winters's gaze all of a sudden. "I need time. He understands that."

"He does, but it still hurts him. When you're in pain, he's in pain."

It was strange, hearing Dr. Winters talking about Ethan during one of their sessions. "I don't mean to hurt him. I need to deal with this on my own."

"Why?"

"Because he has enough to deal with. I won't lay my shit on him too." *On any given day, Ethan was struggling with his mutism, his anxiety, his family, and anything else determined to keep him up at night or fuck with his attempt to remain fully functional. Calvin's job was to protect Ethan, not bring him more heartache.*

"So you're protecting him?"

"Yes. Like I said, he has enough to deal with. His dad, his older brother, his job, the assholes who get in his face because he doesn't answer them or because he has to move when they sit next to him. They get offended. You know what it's like for him. I won't put my shit on him too."

"What about your mother? Do you speak to her about how you feel?"

Calvin frowned. "Of course not."

Winters nodded. His expression turned thoughtful. "You're protecting her as well."

"Of course I am. She's my mom. After all the shit she went through, she's finally happy. She worries enough about me being out in the field. What is she going to do with the information I give her? Nothing. She'll worry about me more. I can handle my job, Doctor."

"I have no doubt that you can. Otherwise I wouldn't continue to clear you for duty." Winters watched him silently before seeming to come to some sort of conclusion. "Tell me about Mr. Ruiz. How do you feel about what you had to do today?"

"I'm pissed."

"Why?"

"Because he gave me no choice. Because instead of asking for help, he took a bunch of people hostage. He shot someone dead and injured two others. He left me no choice."

"All right. Let's try a little exercise. Pretend I'm Fernando Ruiz. What would you like to say to me?"

Calvin shook his head. He hated this type of role-playing strategy. It never worked, and he always felt stupid doing them. "Doc, come on."

"Take your time. I'll wait."

Fuck. All right, fine. Calvin got to his feet. He looked at Dr. Winters and shook his head. *This wasn't going to work.*

"Why did you kill me?"

Calvin swallowed hard. He started to pace in front of the couch. "Because it was my job. He—*you* left me no choice. You were going to shoot that man." He felt like such an idiot doing this. What difference would it make? He didn't feel anything. That was the whole point. He wasn't going to go into his moral beliefs, what it meant that he was capable of killing someone, that he could detach. It would lead him to places he didn't want to end up in. "I did what had to be done. Someone was dead, and someone else's life was already in danger. If I'd gotten there sooner, there might have been injuries but no dead bodies."

"Do you care?" Winters asked as Ruiz.

"Do I care? That he's—*you're* dead? Of course I fucking care." Calvin continued to pace. He wasn't a heartless monster. Just because he could detach didn't mean he didn't care. Maybe they were targets to him at first while he had them in his crosshairs, but in the back of his mind, it was always someone's life. There had been plenty of times when he'd had nightmares about a shooting, reliving the moment. Sometimes it went exactly as it had during the incident; sometimes the details changed. The worst ones were when the target changed to someone he cared about, like his mom or Ethan, someone on his team. Those nights he'd wake up in a cold sweat, his face wet from the tears he'd cried unknowingly.

The more he thought about Ruiz, the more pissed off he got. Ruiz had no idea Calvin had been there. He was completely unaware of the sniper aiming at his head. Yet what did he think would happen if he killed that second hostage? That they'd let him keep killing people? What did he hope to accomplish? He wasn't the only one in the city in pain. The only one suffering. Calvin's mom had been through hell. They'd lost everything. He'd practically grown up in a goddamn car. His mom had gotten fired plenty of times for choosing to be with him when he was sick rather than serving at a roach-infested shithole for fifty-cent tips, if that. She spent more time fighting off the advances of lowlife scumbags than she did waiting tables in those hellholes.

"You think I don't know fucking hardship? You think my mom didn't know it? Fucked-up shit happens. We didn't go out and kill people. We didn't take it out on the fuckers determined to crush us under their Italian loafers. So you know what? Fuck you. Fuck you for making me pull the trigger. We're the ones left to pick up the pieces because *you* couldn't ask for help. How could you do that to your family? To your wife, your kid! Do you think they won't find out about this when they're old enough? Do you think your wife will be able to hide this from them? *You* chose to walk in there, yet I'm the asshole in this for doing my fucking job, for stopping you from hurting anyone else. I'm the one who has to tell your wife why you're dead. Do you know what that's like? Do you know what it feels like to watch someone's world come undone? No, because you fucking bailed! You bailed on your kid, you son of a bitch!" Calvin wiped the tears from his cheeks. He dropped down on the couch, his throat too choked up to go on. It was hard to breathe, and his eyes hurt.

"You're angry."

"Angry?" Calvin let out a harsh laugh. "I'm not angry. I'm fucking furious. Did you even think about what you were doing? When you picked up that gun and got in your car? When you stopped at a traffic light on the way there, did you stop to think about your kid? About what you were about to do to your family? Did you not give a shit? Did you give up? Everything is shit, so fuck the world. I'm going down in a blaze of fucking glory. Well it wasn't glory, was it? It was one fucking bullet. Mine."

"Kids."

Calvin blinked. "Excuse me?"

"You keep saying kid. Mr. Ruiz had two children."

The sudden change had Calvin confused. "Oh."

"Calvin, I believe this particular case is different. It's far more personal. You feel Mr. Ruiz abandoned his children because of the bad choices he made, like your father abandoned you."

"My dad has nothing to do with this." Where the hell had that come from?

"He was killed, wasn't he? By the police. He robbed a gas station and took the clerk hostage."

Calvin swallowed hard. It took him a moment to digest and believe what Dr. Winters said. He'd spent so long telling everyone, including himself, how his father abandoned him, how his mom chased him off after he tried to take her car, that he'd fallen for his own lies. Ethan was the only one who knew, and he'd promised Calvin a long time ago to keep his secret.

Shame and anger clogged his throat like thick smoke polluting his lungs. The THIRDS had overlooked his father's criminal record and given him a chance because of Seb and Rafe. His father had been a piece of shit who'd been so disgusted with himself and his life that he took his anger out on his wife and kid whenever he got a chance. Calvin flinched at the

memory of a belt hitting him across the face, split-
ting his lip. He'd been four years old and accidently
knocked over his dad's beer can.

"My mom cried the night he was killed." He wiped
at his cheeks before meeting the doctor's gaze. "She was
happy. No more lying about how she'd broken her arm
or where her black eye had come from. No more locking me in the bathroom to keep my father from making
me bleed. Life wasn't all sunshine and rainbows for me
and my mom, but we had each other. We loved each
other and looked out for each other. We were happy.
I'm not angry because my father abandoned me, doctor.
I'm angry because he had a choice. He had a choice not
to be a piece-of-shit husband and sorry excuse for a Human. He had a choice not to beat his wife and kid. He
had a choice not to put someone else's life at risk, same
as Fernando Ruiz. They chose wrong and were forced
to face the consequences of their actions." Calvin sat
back, exhausted. At least he'd calmed down. "They
both made their choice and left their families to pick up
the pieces, so yeah, I guess you're right. There's always
a choice. It's up to us which one we make."

ETHAN CLEANED up his and Calvin's desks, getting rid of the empty plates and food containers. When
they'd been filled, the office had looked like some kind
of lunch buffet. He'd called Dex and asked if he could
bring him a burger and fries from the canteen since
he'd be staying in his office. He couldn't handle going
into the canteen without Calvin. At that time of day, the
place would have been packed, and the thought of all
those people made him feel queasy. Dex said he'd take
care of it, and next thing Ethan knew, the whole team
was in his office with enough food to open a burger

business. How Dex knew he needed the distraction was beyond him, but it had been fun. Now it was time to go home. He'd finished his top-priority reports and checked up on his order for the new Packbot and X-Ray kits.

Once the office was clean, he showered and changed in the locker room before heading down to the employee garage. Calvin would take a taxi home sometime in the middle of the night. Ethan had no idea where Calvin went on nights like this. Tonight Ethan would be up listening for the sounds of Calvin's arrival. His evenings would be rather lonely for the next few days, but whatever Calvin needed, Ethan would provide. Things would be a little quiet on the team, but Dex would keep everyone's spirits up. Calvin didn't want anyone acting any different around him, and the rest of them needed to be distracted.

Once he got home, Ethan made himself a sandwich. He made another for Calvin and left it in the fridge like he always did. Calvin never ate it, but if his partner did wander out, Ethan wanted to make sure there was something already prepared for him to eat. After eating and washing up, Ethan watched a little TV, though his mind kept wandering off. It was far earlier than usual, but he decided to get into bed. He brushed his teeth and changed into his loose pajama bottoms and T-shirt before turning off the lights and climbing into bed. He faced the wall. Calvin's bedroom was on the other side. Today must have been rougher on him than he thought, because he'd about fallen asleep when he heard his bedroom door creak open, then close. He didn't get up or move, afraid of spooking Calvin. His partner had never come to him before. He had a bad habit of suffering in silence, holing himself up in the darkness to lick his wounds, hissing and lashing out like a feral Therian. His little wildcat, untamable yet sweet and unpredictable.

Calvin climbed into bed beside Ethan and rolled him over onto his back. His eyes were red and filled with need, a need only Ethan could fill. Ethan sat up, and Calvin brought their lips together in an ardent kiss, his hands going to Ethan's T-shirt. He scrambled to get Ethan undressed without having to pull back, and Ethan helped him, their lips parting only long enough for them to get naked. Calvin straddled Ethan's lap, his fingernails scraping down Ethan's biceps as he sucked Ethan's bottom lip before giving it a nip.

"Ethan...."

Calvin's broken plea squeezed at Ethan's heart. Ethan reached into the nightstand, his mouth still on Calvin's, kissing him, answering his desperation as he rummaged in the drawer and grabbed the bottle of lube. He handed it to Calvin, who poured some on his hand and lubed Ethan up, his strokes making Ethan moan and writhe beneath him. It felt so damn good, but this wasn't about him. It was about Calvin, about what his partner needed to soothe his bleeding heart. Calvin reached behind him and spent as little time as possible stretching himself. Ethan didn't have time to voice his concern before Calvin was pushing Ethan's cock inside him, the pain evident on his face, and the cry he let out when he impaled himself the rest of the way echoed Ethan's own.

Calvin faltered for a moment, his eyes glassy, but he quickly recovered. He smiled at Ethan and kissed him, bringing Ethan's arms around him. Ethan held on tight as Calvin started to move. He threw his head back, his eyes closed and his fingers digging into Ethan's shoulders. Their unsteady breaths mingled as Calvin picked up his pace, driving Ethan deep inside him faster and harder. Knowing what his partner needed, Ethan took hold of Calvin's hips and met his movements with his own thrusts, pushing himself up as he forced Calvin down. Calvin let out a surprised gasp. He took hold of his erection and pumped his fist as he bounced on Ethan, his skin flushed.

"Ethan, please...."

"I've got you," Ethan promised. "Always."

Calvin threw his arms around Ethan's neck and hugged him close, his fingers slipping into Ethan's hair. "Don't let me go. Never let me go."

"Never." Ethan shut his eyes tight as he fucked Calvin, his thrusts growing erratic as his orgasm loomed. He would have liked to take his time, but that wasn't what Calvin wanted. He slipped a hand between them and took hold of Calvin's cock, stroking him as best he could. Ethan's muscles tightened, and he buried his face in Calvin's hair as he came, his boyfriend coming shortly after. Ethan slowed his thrusts along with his hand, stopping when Calvin hissed at the touch. They remained in each other's arms until Ethan's legs began to ache. With Calvin held to him, he turned and lay down, their limbs intertwined. He brushed his lips over Calvin's kiss-swollen mouth before delivering a soft kiss to Calvin's wet cheeks, first the right, then the left.

"Thank you," Ethan said quietly, "for coming to me." He was well aware it wasn't just today's events that had Calvin feeling so vulnerable. The last few months had been emotionally and physically trying for the both of them, and Calvin was finally letting it all go, but there was something else too. Despite his heartache, he seemed... lighter. "Why do you do that?"

Ethan asked gently. "Why do you hold it all in until you're ready to burst? Suffering in silence? Growing up, you always wiped my tears, yet you never let me do the same for you. Not until tonight."

"I didn't have any tears to cry, Ethan." Calvin lowered his gaze, his thick blond lashes almost resting on his cheeks. "I couldn't let myself."

The words formed a lump in Ethan's throat. "Because of me?"

"And Mom." Calvin shrugged. He met Ethan's eyes. "I had to protect you both. You were all that mattered to me. Everything was so shitty back then, except you and Mom. You're the reason I never stopped fighting to get out of that place."

Ethan swallowed hard and nodded. He kissed Calvin tenderly, loving the feel of him, his softness. So much courage in such a small package. They lay down together, and Calvin cuddled up close. Within seconds, Calvin was asleep. Ethan stayed up watching him, enjoying having him there in his arms. Of course, that didn't last too long because Calvin moved around a lot. Ethan smiled at Calvin's sprawled position as he slept. How could a Human of Calvin's size take up so much space? For the first time in a long time, Ethan was still awake while his boyfriend slept.

Usually Calvin would be the last to fall asleep, an old habit from when they were kids. With Calvin's mom working late most nights, Calvin would sleep over at Ethan's. It had worked out for both their families. Calvin's mom was less frantic about leaving him on his own in the evening, and Ethan's mom was happy that Ethan had a friend like Calvin to look after him. Ethan stroked Calvin's hair, running his fingers this way and that. It was getting a little long. When they were kids,

Calvin always had it cropped short with a little spike on top, but in his teens he suddenly decided to grow it longer. There had been a time when he refused to be seen without a baseball cap, saying his hair looked gross. It had always looked cute to Ethan. Now it was still trim, but not as short as it once was.

Ethan frowned at the small, subtle bump he felt on the back of Calvin's head toward the top where his hair was longest. That was odd. It was raised skin. Like a scar. Ethan moved his finger, only to discover a similar one beside it and then another. Calvin had never told him about any scars. Ethan carefully parted Calvin's hair, stunned to find the jagged-edged white scars formed shapes.

Oh my God.

Ethan's blood ran cold. They weren't just scars. They were scars shaped into distinctive letters. FPT.

Ethan's tiger Therian classification.

Ethan jumped out of bed and paced the floor. *That can't be right.* Why did Calvin have scars in the form of his classification on the back of his head? How had they gotten there? Ethan felt sick to his stomach. How could Calvin keep something like this from him? The scars weren't placed there on purpose. They were too jagged.

"Ethan?" Calvin's sleepy murmur stopped him in his tracks, and he backed away from the bed as Calvin sat up. "What's wrong?"

Ethan ran a hand through his hair, his throat closing, choking him. He opened his mouth, but only a strangled cry came out. *Oh God, please don't let it be what I think it is.*

"Ethan, please talk to me." Calvin sat up, but he didn't approach Ethan. As much as Ethan wanted to shout and scream and demand to know what happened, he couldn't. His body refused to cooperate. He tapped the back of his head repeatedly before pointing to Calvin. His boyfriend's wide eyes told him he knew exactly what Ethan was referring to. "I'm sorry I didn't tell you. I didn't want to upset you."

Ethan shook his head. He didn't want to believe it. *Please, tell me it's not my fault. Please. Please tell me someone didn't do that to you.*

Calvin drew his knees up and wrapped his arms around them. "It was after the Halloween dance. Remember when I was supposed to bring you back candy, but I called and said I slipped on some eggs in the courtyard and was going to the nurse's office?"

Ethan nodded. He remembered it like it was yesterday. He'd been so worried about Calvin that night when he hadn't heard from him. Ethan was the only kid on their block who never went trick-or-treating. It was the worst holiday in the world for Ethan, terrifying on so many levels. He hadn't wanted to stop Calvin from having fun, but Calvin refused to go without him, saying he'd rather stay in with Ethan. So they reached an agreement. Calvin would spend a few hours trick-or-treating and bring back candy for both of them while Ethan put together a little party in his room with snacks and their favorite movies. Then they'd eat candy until they felt sick and fell asleep way past their bedtime.

"I was on my way home, and some of the seniors followed me. I thought they were going to talk shit and push me around, maybe take my candy. They said some fucked-up shit about you, and I got pissed. Punched their leader in the mouth. They ganged up on me, pushed me to the floor, and held me down. One of them had a switchblade. He said if I loved Therians so much, I should be marked like them. He carved the tiger Therian classification into the back of my head, said now I could be like my boyfriend. I knew you were waiting for me, and I didn't want to scare you. Mom was working, so I walked to the police station and asked for help. I made Mom promise me she wouldn't tell you."

Oh God. Ethan felt his chest tightening. His breath was coming out ragged. He was having trouble breathing. *Someone did that? How…? Ethan shook his head. He needed to leave. A wave of dizziness hit him, but he pushed through it. He left the room and ran down the hall to the front door, where he put on his sneakers and jacket. He turned to Calvin, who stood in one of Ethan's T-shirts, clearly the first thing he'd grabbed. Ethan's heart splintered.*

"I understand," Calvin said with a shaky smile. "Just be safe. I'll be here when you get back."

Ethan nodded. He ran out the door and outside, not bothering with his car. Where he was going wasn't far. He took off running, the cold air against his face helping him remain composed as he ran three blocks, then rounded the corner before running another two blocks until he reached Seb's house. He ran up the stairs and pounded on the door. His keys to Seb's place were on his key ring somewhere, but his hands were too shaky to hold anything.

Seb opened the door, and Ethan threw his arms around his big brother, holding on tight. He didn't know what else to do. How could this be happening? Seb held him close, running a soothing hand over his back like he did when they were kids. When Ethan could breathe again he pulled back, stepping inside so Seb could close the door.

"Talk to me. What's happened? Did you get into a fight with Cal? I thought things were good between you."

Ethan walked into the living room and dropped down onto the couch, unsure of where to start.

"It's okay, little brother, breathe." Seb took a seat beside him, breathing deeply in and out so Ethan would follow along. "That's it. Breathe. Good. I'm right here with you. Take your time."

Ethan opened his mouth, but he got choked up. He let out a frustrated grunt, and Seb put his hand on Ethan's shoulder.

"It's okay. There's no rush. It's you and me here."

Ethan nodded. He took a deep breath and let it out slowly. "Cal, he got hurt because of me."

"When? Is he okay?"

Ethan shook his head. "It was a long time ago. One Halloween. Remember the one where he didn't come over because he slipped on the eggs?"

"I remember. We watched movies all night. You were really worried about him. But that wasn't your fault."

"He never slipped on any eggs," Ethan replied, his anger rising. He jumped to his feet, his whole body practically vibrating with anger. "He got jumped. Some asshole seniors jumped him. They held him down." Ethan shook his head and shut his eyes. He didn't want to picture it. Didn't want to hear Calvin's screams in his head as they mutilated him. Ethan smacked his hands against his ears to make it stop. He was having trouble breathing again.

"Ethan, breathe. In and out."

Ethan dropped to his knees and closed his eyes tight. Why wouldn't the screaming stop? "So much blood."

"Explain it to me, Ethan." Seb took hold of Ethan's face, his words gentle but firm. "Open your eyes, Ethan. Look at me. It's Seb. Look at me."

Ethan opened his eyes, his brother's kind and loving gaze reminding Ethan of all the times his big brother had held him and promised to slay all the monsters for him. Seb nodded, breathing with him. He laid his hand on Ethan's head, and Ethan could breathe again. The touch was comforting, always had been. The letters…. Ethan dug his fingernails into his neck, wishing he could scrape the letters off. He'd do anything to get them off. He hated them.

"No. We talked about that, remember? Don't do that. Don't hurt yourself. It hurts me, okay? It hurts me when you try to hurt yourself."

"I'm sorry." He hadn't done that in years. It was like he was a kid again, so much pain, so much fear. "They took a knife and carved the letters into his head. He never told me. Why wouldn't he tell me? They hurt him because of me. He's scarred. They scarred him. They fucking scarred him!"

Seb stared at him before quickly shaking himself out of it. "What did Cal say?"

"That he didn't want to scare me."

"He's always protected you. He loves you."

"And what's that love cost him?" Ethan snapped. All his life, Calvin had been kicked around and beaten. It should have stopped when his dad left. Instead the pain inflicted on him by his father had been replaced by the pain inflicted on him for being with Ethan.

"It didn't cost him anything he wasn't willing to give. I'd have done the same, and you would have done the same for him. That's what love is. You're his whole world, Ethan. Do you think he would have stuck around if he didn't love you so fiercely?"

Ethan swallowed hard. He couldn't deny that. He would walk through the fires of hell for Calvin. He understood why Calvin hadn't told him, but he couldn't stop thinking of what he had endured for Ethan. "I bring him nothing but pain."

"If that was true, he wouldn't have fallen in love with you, Ethan. Call him. Tell him to come here."

"No. I can't. I can't see him."

"Ethan, you can't run away from this." Seb took hold of Ethan's face, his green eyes the same as Ethan's. His brother understood the kind of love Calvin had for him. His heart was burning for it, had been since Hudson. "Those scars are a part of him. You can't let the guilt eat away at you and ruin what you have with him, believe me. I know a thing or two about that. Do you love him?"

Ethan closed his eyes. "Yes."

"Then tell him. He *needs* you, Ethan."

Ethan nodded. Seb was right. Calvin had never run away. He stood up and faced whatever came his way, no matter how scared he might have been. Seb handed Ethan his smartphone, and Ethan called Calvin.

"Seb? What's wrong? Is Ethan okay?"

"It's me," Ethan said quietly. "I left my phone at home. Can you come to Seb's?"

"I'm on my way."

Ethan hung up and gave Seb back his phone. He got up and sat down on the couch to wait. He felt stupid for running away, but his heart hurt so badly. He hoped Calvin wasn't disappointed in him. It seemed like all he ever did was bring Calvin trouble.

There was pounding on the door, and Seb quickly answered. He said something to Calvin that Ethan couldn't hear. Even if he could, he was too busy worrying about what Calvin was thinking.

"Ethan?"

Calvin rushed into the living room, looking as if he were out of breath. His cheeks were red from the cold, and he looked more vulnerable than Ethan had ever seen him. There was so much he wanted to say, he didn't even know where to start. So he stood and opened his arms. Calvin didn't hesitate. He rushed into Ethan's embrace, and he did his best not to crush Calvin against him. When he could finally speak again, he pulled back.

"I'm sorry. I'm sorry for running."

Calvin cupped his face. "I understand, Ethan. I'm sorry I didn't tell you, I just… I knew how much it would hurt you, and with everything else going on at school, at home, I didn't want you to worry."

"No more secrets between us, okay?"

"Okay." Calvin moved his gaze to Ethan's neck, and he swallowed hard. "Please don't hurt yourself again. It breaks my heart when you do."

"I'm sorry." Ethan covered the sore spot with his hand, and Calvin gently moved it away. He stood on his toes and kissed Ethan's tattoo.

"You're beautiful. All of you. Just the way you are."

"I'd hate to become a burden for you."

Calvin took Ethan's hand and led him to the couch. He pulled him down with him as he sat. "Ethan, is your dad a burden for your mom?"

"No, of course not!" Even when she'd been told there was no hope, or that her life would become hell, his mom had stood her ground. She was the most courageous person he knew, next to Calvin. Despite everything his mom and dad had been through, their bond grew stronger. "She loves him more and more every day."

"It's been hell for them at times, but they persevered. They've stuck together. When your dad hurts, so does your mom, but she never once thought of him as a burden." Calvin put his thumb to Ethan's tattoo and stroked his skin. "When you hurt, I hurt, and I'll do everything to keep you from hurting, because every day I love you more and more."

Ethan pulled Calvin close and kissed his lips. "Thank you, for being my best friend and my partner. I love you, Cal. I'm sorry it took me so long to say the words, but I do. I love you."

Calvin's smile lit up his face, and Ethan had never seen anything more beautiful.

"I love you too."

Ethan brought Calvin up against him and put a hand to his cheek. How different would his life have been without this amazing man? He'd never take Calvin for granted again. With a smile, he placed his lips to Calvin's for a kiss, taking his time, enjoying the softness of Calvin's lips, the taste of him, the way he lit Ethan up from the inside. He made Ethan feel safe and loved. As long as he was in Calvin's arms, the world couldn't touch him. He pulled back and nuzzled Calvin's temple, his words quiet.

"Let's go home and go to bed."

Calvin kissed him in response before standing, their fingers laced together. He led Ethan to the door and paused to look behind them. Seb stood in the archway leaning against the wall, his warm smile on them.

"Thanks, Seb," Calvin said, giving him a wave.

"Anytime." He gave them a wink. "Stay out of trouble, you two. And lock up behind you." With that, he turned and left. Ethan's heart ached for his big brother.

They locked up behind them and headed down to the sidewalk, where Ethan couldn't help but look up at his big brother's house. He let out a sigh.

"I wish there was something I could do. I hate seeing him so alone."

"Yeah," Calvin replied somberly. "And you know it's going to get worse when he sees Hudson at Nina and Cael's birthday party."

Ethan stopped and turned to Calvin. "What birthday party?"

Calvin chuckled and pulled him along. "Dude, you really need to check your phone calendar more often. They sent out the invites to everyone a week ago. Nina and Cael's birthdays are a few days apart, right? So they're celebrating together by booking Dekatria for the night. All three floors. Seb was invited, and obviously Hudson's going to be there."

They crossed the street, and Ethan frowned. "That means Rafe's going to be there too."

Calvin cringed. "Yeah, I wonder how that's going to go down. I mean, how long do Rafe and Nina think they can hide their relationship from Hudson and Seb?"

The night was cold, and Ethan looked forward to getting indoors and under the warm covers with Calvin. He couldn't stop worrying about the party. "I guess there'll be enough people there so Seb won't have to be where Hudson is. It still sucks, though."

"Do you want to go?" Calvin asked. "You don't need to decide now. See how you're feeling that night."

Ethan playfully bumped Calvin with his hip. Calvin was always attuned to his needs. "I'll be okay. You'll be there. So will Seb and Dex and the rest of the team. You know I'll find the least crowded place. I can do it."

Calvin beamed up at him. "Whatever you want."

Ethan gave Calvin a wicked smile. He knew exactly what he wanted. "I think right now, what I want is you naked and sweaty."

"That can be arranged," Calvin said, his tone low and husky. He turned and let go of Ethan's hand. "Race you there."

Calvin bolted, and Ethan let him have a few seconds head start. He was so going to love pouncing on his sexy boyfriend. As soon as Calvin was at the end of the block, Ethan broke into a run. No way was he letting Calvin go. Not on their way to their apartment or any time after that.

Chapter Eight

"YOU DO realize this is training and not a pool party," Calvin said, shaking his head in amusement as Dex cannonballed into the deep end of Sparta's Therian-sized swimming pool. His crazy friend came up spurting water, a big dopey smile on his face. "Sparks is going to kick your ass."

"Hey, I'm training. Let's say I'm being chased by some huge feral Therian and there's a big body of water nearby. I'm going to jump, right? I'm not going to tiptoe in."

"That would be your second mistake," Letty offered as she leisurely floated by. "Your first mistake would be jumping in the water in the first place. Unless you got a motorboat in that water, your ass is grass, or in this scenario"—she motioned to all their Felid Therian teammates swimming toward Dex—"Felid chow."

Dex eyed Cael, Sloane, and Ethan as they swam circles around him, their tails in the air. They looked

like three huge kitty sharks. Calvin sat on the edge of
the pool, his bare feet in the water. Ash sat beside Rosa
on the edge of the pool looking unimpressed, but then
that was Ash's usual state of being, other than angry.
He clearly didn't fancy getting his regal mane all wet.
They watched Dex to see what his next move would be.
The moment he took hold of Sloane's tail, they cringed.

"North, Miss Tessmacher! North!"

Sloane hissed and dove under the water, taking
Dex with him, but not before he let out the manliest
of yelps. Had Dex considered letting go? Letty and
Rosa laughed their asses off. Ash closed his eyes and
chuffed with gratification, while Cael and Ethan swam
after Dex and Sloane. Somewhere in the middle of the
pool, the two popped up. Dex sputtered and moved his
hair from his eyes. He arched an eyebrow at his partner, who was doggie-paddling in little circles around
the pool, meowing happily, his head raised high.

"Proud of yourself, huh? Thanks for saving me
from being mauled by trying to drown me. That was
very helpful." Dex turned to Calvin with a frown.
"How come Hobbs lets you hold on to his tail?"

Calvin shrugged. "I don't know. It started when we
were kids. I think he likes knowing I'm there."

Ethan chuffed and rubbed his big furry head
against Dex's face.

"Yeah, I love you too, buddy, but you're all hairy
and... wet... with wet fur." Dex scrunched up his nose
when Sloane started rubbing up against him as well.
"Oh God, why? Someone want to help me? Anyone?
You're ferocious agents! Ferocious agents don't rub up
against their targets and purr!"

Cael swam toward his brother with a chirp. Dex's
hopeful smile turned into a frown when Cael bumped

his head under Dex's chin with a series of cheerful chirps. Dex was boxed in, a Felid to his left, right, and front. Next to Calvin, Ash chuffed, his tail swinging back and forth until it fell over the edge and landed in the water. He quickly plucked it up, caught it with his paw, and groomed it.

"Aw, you're such a precious princess," Calvin teased. Ash enjoyed the water as much as his friends, but only when he was in the mood. He was particularly fussy about his mane. That gave Calvin an idea.

Calvin cleared his throat and discreetly looked away. As expected, Ethan doggie-paddled over and mewed at him. "Hey, handsome." Calvin leaned in to scratch Ethan's ears before whispering at him. Ethan paddled around the pool, Dex flailing in the background as he tried to get away from Sloane and Cael. Had he not learned by now that Felids were exceptional swimmers? And unlike a good number of house cats, their larger counterparts loved water.

Ash's eyes were closed. It looked like he was taking a little lion nap. He really should have been paying more attention to their "training." Ethan bobbed up and snatched ahold of Ash's tail with his paws, tugging, and pulled the roaring lion Therian into the water. Ash hit the pool's surface so hard water splashed all over Calvin, but he was too busy laughing to care.

Ash resurfaced and scrambled to get out of the pool. His majestic mane was plastered down over his face and body. Calvin got up and quickly moved away to the other side of the pool as Ash shook himself from nose to tail. Everyone burst into laughter as Ash's mane puffed up. With the room having indoor heating, the warmth frizzed Ash's mane. Calvin doubled over laughing. Ash was so going to kick their asses, but it was worth it.

Seeing as he was already soaked, Ash jumped in and headed for his Felid teammates with a growl. Calvin hadn't seen Dex move that fast since the canteen announced they were handing out leftover cake from someone's birthday party. With Dex out of the pool, Ash turned his vengeance on Sloane and Ethan. They swam around, dove, and bobbed like giant apples. Felids were adorable when they swam. Well, unless they were feral Therians trying to kill you; then not so much.

Dex grabbed a towel from the rack and strolled toward Calvin all innocent-like. *Uh-oh. Rosa really should have been paying more attention. With a sweet smile, Dex crouched down behind her, nodded as if he was listening to her conversation with Letty, and pushed her in. Calvin winced. That was definitely going to hurt Dex later.*

Rosa emerged cursing at Dex in two languages.

Calvin shook his head in disbelief. "You got balls, man."

Dex shrugged. "Someone was bound to kick my ass for something today. Might as well get some fun out of it." He motioned toward the locker room. "Listen, got a minute? I want to talk to you about something while the guys are busy."

"Sure." Calvin headed for the male locker room. They might as well change and get dressed. The guys were going to need them to perform PSTC, and he'd rather not be half-naked while doing it. Having Ethan naked would be enough, especially since they'd have to wait until their shift ended to do anything more than a little kissing.

*Dex entered the shower next to him and spoke up.
"Listen, I have an idea for a tattoo, but I'm not so great
at drawing. Actually, I'm kinda shit. I was thinking
maybe you'd design it for me?" Dex asked hopefully.
"I'll pay you, obviously. Dollars, favors, snacks. You
name it."*

*Calvin peered at him as he removed his shower gel
from his toiletry bag. "I'm not sure if I should ask what
kind of favors you mean."*

*Dex eyed him in return. "What kind of favors do
you not want it to mean?"*

"Sexual." Too many weird coincidences lately.

Dex looked unimpressed.

*"You and Sloane, man. I am not looking for a
foursome."*

Dex hummed.

"Well, the evidence is kind of stacked against you."

*"No sexual favors. I can't believe I have to clarify
that,"* Dex said with a sad shake of his head. He turned
on the shower and tested the water's temperature. *"Favors like, I don't know, pick up your laundry or something. We'll figure it out later. So do you think you can
do that for me?"*

"You really want me to design your tattoo?" Calvin couldn't help how stupidly happy that made him.
He'd designed tattoos for plenty of people but never
for a friend.

"Yeah. Hobbs keeps going on about how awesome
you are, and we both know he's not one to bullshit.
Anyway, if you're interested, I'd love to run some ideas
by you. It would mean a lot to me." Dex stopped to put
his hand on his arm, the one carrying Sloane's mark. It
was pretty much all healed up, the scars from Sloane's
claw marks prominently displayed for all to see. "It's

for me, but really, it's more for him. Something to remind him I'll always be here when he needs me."

Aw, Dex was such a sappy romantic. Calvin couldn't help his smile. "Wow, that serious, huh?"

"Yeah," Dex replied, his wide grin almost shy. "It's kind of scary how much I love him, and this mark… it's weird. It's like when he's not around, I can still feel him, and I miss him like crazy. Like everything I felt before has been amplified. Does that make sense?"

"Makes sense. I don't know much about Therian marks, especially on Humans, but I know it's pretty powerful stuff on Therians. That's why you don't see a lot of it happening. No offense, but I'm surprised Sloane went through with it. That's pretty much as committed as you can get. It's more binding than a marriage, which isn't even very binding these days."

Dex cocked his head thoughtfully as he rinsed off. "I'm still kind of surprised too. My dad was all up in arms about it because of what happened with Hudson and Seb."

Calvin sighed. "Yeah, that's messed up." Marking was for life. These days there wasn't a whole lot that was permanent. Tattoos could be removed, cosmetic surgery could repair and replace, but Therian marks? That shit went deep. Even if surgery fixed the scar, the mark was still there, under the skin. It was so uncommon, it was still being studied and researched. A Human marked by a Therian was very rare.

"I can see why your dad would freak. I mean, if a Therian mate is no longer with their partner, it'll be tough to find another mate, especially Therian. But they could still potentially be in a relationship with a Human. For Human mates, that list of potential partners drops even more. There's a lot of stigma surrounding Humans who are marked. Not everyone is so open-minded. Mainly they tend to think it's some kind of kink."

"That's because there's still a lot of stupid out there."

"Preaching to the choir," Calvin grumbled. He'd been dealing with anti-Therianism most of his life.

Dex rubbed at his eyes and blinked. He stepped out from under the water and dried his face before rubbing his eyes again.

"You okay? Getting a little emotional?" Calvin teased.

"Fuck off," Dex said with a laugh. "Dick. No. My eyes are itchy. I think I must have gotten something in them at some point. They keep itching."

"You might want to get them checked out just in case. You know we're always walking through gross shit out there." Calvin cringed at the thought. Sometimes he didn't want to know what they were stepping in or walking through when they were called out to Greenpoint. Their equipment could only protect them from so much. Suddenly he felt the need to use a little extra shower gel.

"Yeah. It started a few weeks ago, but it's been getting worse. It's not unbearable or anything, just annoying. Sloane looked, but he couldn't see anything. It's fine."

"Okay, then. So tell me about this tattoo."

Dex's cheeks flushed, and he let out a shy laugh. "This is probably going to sound cheesy, but when he's feeling uncertain, or the world's coming down on him, I want him to look at my arm, see the artwork, know what's underneath, and know without a doubt that I'm there to guide him back home."

"That's not cheesy," Calvin assured him. It was incredibly sweet. "How about we hang out sometime soon, you pick a day, and we can get together to discuss ideas and styles. Then I can come up with some sketches, see what you think. Are we talking black and white or color?"

"Color. I'm thinking something kind of old-school. From my wrist to my elbow."

"You do realize that tattoos can get addictive. Once you'd have one, especially that size, you might want another."

Dex held his arms out and wriggled his eyebrows. "I got plenty of room."

"Okay, that's way more than I needed to see," Calvin said with a laugh. "I'd love to design your tattoo." The more he thought about it, the more excited he got. "This is going to be awesome."

"Thanks. And let's keep this between us. I want it to be a surprise."

Dex turned off the shower, and Calvin finished up. He joined Dex in the locker room just as Sloane and Ethan came trotting through the doorway. Ash and Cael most likely were already in the Therian changing rooms being helped with PSTC. Calvin got dressed, swatting at Ethan when his boyfriend swiped a paw at his butt.

"Hey, watch it, mister."

Ethan chuffed and sat down, his tail swaying and thumping cheerfully on the floor. Sloane had to get his scent all over Dex, rubbing his face against his partner's legs and circling him. Dex didn't even bat an eye anymore. It had freaked him out a while back. Now he went about his business while his lethal jaguar Therian partner rubbed up against him, purring like a big house cat. As soon as Calvin was back in his uniform, he opened Ethan's locker and removed his uniform, along with his duffel bag containing his boots, socks, and underwear. He threw it over his shoulder and turned to give Ethan's ear a playful tug.

"Come on, you." He waved as he walked out of the locker room, calling out behind him. "See you guys in a bit."

As he neared the Therian changing room, Ash and Cael were walking out. Ash narrowed his eyes at Calvin and thrust a finger in his face.

"I know you put him up to that."

"Me?" Calvin blinked innocently. "I would never." It's not like he didn't know Ethan could get away with it. Next to Cael, Ethan was the only one who wouldn't get his ass kicked by Ash.

Ash moved a menacing finger to Ethan. "That's sad, man. You are so whipped."

Ethan licked Ash's finger, and Calvin had to bite down on his bottom lip to keep himself from laughing. The scandalized expression on Ash's face was too much.

"You're a dick."

Ethan chuffed, and Ash grunted as he walked off, Cael chuckling beside him. Calvin turned to Ethan and held his hand out.

"Low five."

With a mew, Ethan smacked Calvin's hand with his huge paw. Calvin was in a good mood, despite knowing they'd be attending yet another one of Sparks's training sessions later today. He was looking forward to working on Dex's tattoo. The fun part, aside from the actual designing, was finding the right style. For Dex, something old-school would look great. Something vintage, maybe.

Calvin stood to one side of the empty changing station and waited for Ethan to go in before he followed and pulled the curtain closed. There was a little kitchenette-type station on one side with a small fridge and supplies the THIRDS kept stocked. The THIRDS might not be perfect, but they made sure to provide their agents with all the essentials, and that included keeping changing stations stocked with Post Shift Trauma Care kits and supplies.

As Ethan began to shift back, Calvin collected the supplies he'd need. A bottle of Gatorade from the fridge, some protein bars from the cabinet, along with hefty beef sticks. He flinched instinctively at Ethan's pained screams as he changed. He'd never get used to that. By the time Ethan was done, Calvin had set out everything they needed, and he'd hung up Ethan's uniform.

Ethan sat on the bench, his elbows on his knees and his head in his hands as he waited for the wave of dizziness to pass. Calvin sat next to him and placed a kiss on his boyfriend's shoulder. Ethan raised his head and smiled.

"Hi."

Ethan's smile was beautiful, and it reached his bright green eyes. He leaned in to Calvin and placed a kiss on his lips.

"Hungry?" Calvin asked him.

Ethan nodded. With a quick kiss, Calvin stood and grabbed the Gatorade and some of the beef sticks. He handed the beef to Ethan and tilted his head back, holding the bottle for him as he drank. When it was all gone, Ethan ate his snacks while Calvin fetched the protein bars. They'd head off to the canteen to get Ethan some real food as soon as his partner was able.

Of course, as soon as his partner was able, he had a different hunger in mind. Calvin was clearing up the small counter when Ethan slipped his hands around his waist, something hard poking into his back. Well, now. What's this? Okay, so he had a pretty good idea of what it was, but he really hadn't been expecting it. Ethan nuzzled Calvin's temple, his soft words in Calvin's ear.

"I might need a little more care."

Calvin turned in his arms, groaning when Ethan thrust his hips forward. "Is that so, Agent Hobbs?"

Ethan nodded. "And you're the only one that can give it to me." He took hold of Calvin's hand and moved it onto his hard dick. A shiver went through Calvin, and he all but melted against Ethan. Man, he was so in trouble. With a brush of his lips, Ethan walked to the bench and sat down. He leaned back on his hands and spread his legs, his pupils dilated as he watched Calvin. Damn, he was gorgeous. Powerful, muscular, yet so incredibly sweet and gentle, it took Calvin's breath away.

Calvin stopped in front of Ethan and stood between his knees. He bent down to kiss him, his tongue slipping between Ethan's lips as he explored and tasted every inch of his mouth. With a wicked smile, he got down on his knees and palmed Ethan's erection. It was a thing of beauty, much like the rest of Ethan.

"We can't be too long," Calvin told him, receiving a nod in response. He brought Ethan's cock into his mouth and swallowed it down to the root. A gasp escaped Ethan, but other than that, he was completely silent. Calvin did his best not to moan as Ethan huffed and writhed underneath him. Ethan clutched the edge of the bench until his knuckles were white, resulting in Calvin doubling his efforts. He loved driving Ethan crazy, loved watching the way his muscles tensed, the look of absolute ecstasy on his handsome face. Calvin drew back to the tip before plunging back down, his lips tight around Ethan. He sucked, licked, and laved when Ethan slipped his fingers into Calvin's hair with a quiet strangled noise. Calvin nodded, and Ethan came, folding over Calvin as he spilled himself inside Calvin's mouth.

Calvin swallowed, his fingers digging into Ethan's thighs. When Ethan was done, Calvin pulled off him, letting out a low moan as Ethan kissed him, tasting himself on Calvin's tongue. Calvin could have stayed here all day, but they'd already spent far too long here. Someone might come looking for them. A horrific thought struck him. He stood and grabbed Ethan's boxer briefs.

"You better get dressed before Dex shows up."

Ethan blinked at him before bursting into laughter.

"I'm glad you find that funny. He's already caught you once with your pants down."

Ethan stopped laughing and nodded somberly. He stood and pulled on his underwear before taking his pants from Calvin. As soon as he was dressed, they headed upstairs to the canteen so Ethan could have his favorite Therian-sized burger, cheese fries, and strawberry milkshake. As they took a seat, Sloane slid in next to Calvin.

"Hey, Cal."

"Hey. Are you looking for Dex, because I haven't seen him since the locker room," Calvin said, pilfering one of Ethan's fries. Ethan narrowed his eyes, but Calvin knew he didn't mind. Of course, he wouldn't recommend anyone else try it. Not unless they wanted to lose a hand.

"Yeah, I know. Sparks called him into her office to discuss his training schedule. I figured it was the perfect chance to come see you."

"Everything okay?"

"Are you designing his tattoo?"

"Um…." How did Sloane know that? Then again, Dex had seemed interested in their tattoo discussion that night at Dekatria when Bradley brought it up.

"Never mind," Sloane said waving a hand in dismissal. "I know you are. Dex isn't exactly subtle. Anyway, when the design is finalized, could you show it to me?"

"Well, he's got his heart set on surprising you." This meant a lot to Dex. Calvin didn't want to do anything to disappoint his friend, even if it was Sloane asking.

Sloane seemed to think about it. "Okay, how about this. When you finalize the design and you know exactly what he's going to get, can you let me know? Not what it is, just that he's set on something. I want to run something by you."

Calvin nodded. "Sure. I can do that."

"Thanks, man." Sloane clapped him on the back as he stood. "Don't tell him I spoke to you about it."

"Got it."

With a wink at Calvin and a wave at Ethan, Sloane was off. Calvin shook his head in amusement. Those two belonged together. They were each as crazy as the other. Calvin had an idea what Sloane wanted to run by him, and he was looking forward to it. It was sweet, how in tune they both were.

Ethan stuffed a couple of fries in his mouth before running a hand over his arm.

"Yeah, in the showers before you and Sloane showed up, Dex asked me if I'd design him a tattoo.

Something special for Sloane. You should have seen the way his eyes lit up when he talked about it."

Ethan smiled that dopey grin of his and made a heart shape with his fingers. Calvin chuckled. "Yeah, those two have got it bad."

Calvin chatted as Ethan finished his colossal meal. They were on their way back to their office when Dispatch put out a call for a Threat Level Orange. A shitload of teams were called in, including Destructive Delta. There was a demonstration that could possibly turn hostile. Calvin and Ethan hurried toward the armory to find the rest of his team already there, including Maddock. They suited up in full tactical gear while their sergeant filled them in.

"All right, team, the HPF and the THIRDS have been monitoring a small group of protestors, which has now tripled in size. The HPF will also be on scene, as there are some Human citizens protesting along with Therians. No feral Therians yet. We're going in for crowd control. You know the drill. Firearms stay in the truck, nonlethals only. Grab your batons. Letty and Ash will have the control rounds." Maddock turned to Ethan. "Hobbs, the second you see things are turning ugly, you get in the truck and shift. Hopefully it won't come to that, but if it does, maybe a couple of roars will get them to back off. Cael, you're running surveillance. Rosa, keep your medical kit on hand. Dex, I want you up front and monitoring the situation. Everyone be safe, and let's try and do this as low-key as possible."

Calvin secured his baton to his utility belt, when he caught Sloane's gaze. "Everything okay?"

Sloane looked uncertain. He turned to Maddock. "Sarge, maybe Calvin should sit this one out."

Shit. Calvin closed his locker. "This isn't a regular callout, is it?"

Maddock shook his head. "It's about the Ruiz case, and that's a negative on benching you. I already ran it by Sparks. She wants you out there. We can't hide every time we make a tough call, or people will believe we don't have the balls to stand behind our decisions. You've gotta be seen." Maddock's gaze was intense as he placed his hand on Calvin's shoulder. "Whatever happens, remember you're a damn fine agent, son. You keep this city and its citizens safe, even if at times they don't see it that way."

Calvin nodded. Lately, it felt like those times were happening more often than not.

Maddock gave him a hearty pat before turning toward the parking garage. "Let's move out."

By the time they arrived at Times Square, a huge mob had gathered. The majority were Therians, but there were Human protestors in the group as well. HPF was keeping its distance, but at least they were on scene. Beta Ambush and Theta Destructive were already there, with three more teams on the way. They stood close together between the US Armed Forces Recruitment Station and the HPF kiosk, visors down and shields in hand. Taylor and Seb approached Sloane. Seb's expression was grim as he spoke.

"This isn't looking good. The numbers have tripled in a little over an hour. There are roughly sixty-eight citizens, with a few instigators getting them riled up. The ones with the animal masks. A couple of the troublemakers are Human, and three are Therian, from what I can tell. I don't think they give a shit about what's going on. They're here to watch it all burn. Insults are the only things they've thrown at us so far."

Sloane nodded his understanding. "Okay. Let's secure the perimeter and keep this under control. Ash, Hobbs, keep an eye on anyone who looks like they might try to shift. Last thing we need is someone in their Therian form hurting anyone. Let's have Recon try and get the crowd moving along. If it goes sideways, we get in there."

They all verbally acknowledged Sloane's orders. Destructive Delta's Defense agents joined Seb's and Taylor's Defense agents in formation with their shields up while Taylor, Seb, and Sloane stood to one side to keep an eye on the situation. Each team's sergeant monitored from their respective BearCat, ready to call in backup should things take a turn for the worse. Their arrival wasn't welcome. Although no THIRDS agents carried firearms—a sure way to escalate things—their presence was enough to put people on edge. Some of the crowd chanted; some held up signs. Calvin took a deep breath and released it slowly through his mouth. Recon seemed to be doing a good job of getting the crowd to dissipate little by little.

The peaceful protest quickly went to hell when Ruiz's wife appeared. She marched straight through the crowd to the front lines where THIRDS agents were positioned. From the corner of his eye Calvin saw Sloane tense. Some of the protestors had started to leave, but Calvin knew things were about to take a turn. The hairs on the back of his neck stood on end, and his stomach felt like it was full of lead.

"Murderer!"

Mrs. Ruiz marched up to him, and Calvin felt his teammates inch closer. Sloane, Seb, and Taylor were busy keeping the crowd under control as the mob pitched forward under Mrs. Ruiz's exclamation.

"Asesino!" Mrs. Ruiz stopped before him, her nose almost touching Calvin's visor. He stared straight ahead, his gaze beyond the mass of citizens screaming for his blood. He couldn't focus on them. Couldn't look at the Therian woman with tears streaming down her cheeks telling him how worthless and evil he was. Calvin swallowed hard, his jaw clenched tight.

"You're a murderer! You deserve to be dead! I hope you die, pedazo de mierda. You are a Human piece of shit!" She spat at his helmet, but he barely flinched. He didn't move, simply stood there with his shield held firm in his grip as the saliva ran down his visor. She was in pain. He understood that. Her pain was focused on him. He'd killed her husband. She hadn't been told at the time he was the one who'd pulled the trigger. Protocol stated the officer visiting the victim's family was given only the necessary information until the report was written, confirming all the details of the incident. It would be shared with the necessary parties and used in court if he was summoned. Whether she recognized his name from the report her lawyer had presented her with or from his face plastered all over the news thanks to that damned piece-of-shit article, he was the source of all her pain.

"How can you stand there after what you did? Like nothing has happened? You should be locked up with the other killers. He was a good husband and a loving father. How could you?"

She cursed him out in Spanish. He understood most of it. The rest he was glad he didn't.

Would they really be satisfied at seeing his blood spilled? Was that what they wanted? An eye for an eye? Did it matter that someone else had died at Ruiz's hands? That another Therian was in the hospital fighting

for her life, that several more were badly injured? All
they saw was a monster who'd taken a life and not the
man who'd saved seven others. Calvin wasn't looking
for praise. Hell, he wasn't even looking to be acknowledged. He wished there wasn't a need for his position,
but the sad truth was that there was a need.

Someone would come and calm her. Or at least attempt it. He couldn't speak to her. That would only fuel
her anger. There was nothing he could say that she'd
want to hear. Another Therian woman appeared with a
little Therian girl and passed her off to Mrs. Ruiz, who
held her up to Calvin.

"Look at her! You took her father away! Murdered
him like an animal."

Mrs. Ruiz's grief had consumed her. Understand-
ably so. Calvin wished he could do or say something to
help, but he was well aware there was nothing. Her rage
and anguish wouldn't allow anything else in. He was a
heartless asshole hiding behind a badge.

The little girl's wailing was like knives in his ears.
She was clearly terrified and didn't understand what
was happening around her. Was she screaming because
her mother was yelling at the man who'd taken her daddy away? Did she understand why her father was never
coming home? Had it been explained to her? Had she
been told about the monster playing good guy?

Calvin cracked. "I'm sorry."

"You're *sorry*? *Pendejo*!"

She placed the little girl on her feet, holding on
to her while punching Calvin in the shoulder with her
free hand. His teammates made to move forward, but
he held a hand up. If they restrained her, she'd struggle,
and her little girl might get hurt. All it would do was
escalate the situation and possibly cause more harm.

"Hijo de puta! Sorry won't change what you did!"

He was doing his job, trying to keep the citizens of his city safe. This was his city as much as theirs. He'd been born here, grown up in a neighborhood where being out at sundown meant risking his life. Where refusing to be swept into the gang life had left him in the hospital more times than he could count. Where being friends with a Therian had left him with permanent scars. He'd bled for this goddamn city, and yet he loved it. They wouldn't take that away from him.

Ethan suddenly appeared beside them, and Calvin swallowed hard. His expression was stern yet pensive. *Ethan?* Ethan put a hand up in front of Mrs. Ruiz, who remarkably stopped short. She glared up at him and opened her mouth, when Ethan pulled down the throat guard of his tactical vest. He pointed to his classification.

"So what? You're a traitor to your kind, standing up for this Therian hater!"

Ethan grabbed Calvin's arm, and before he knew what was going on, Ethan unclipped Calvin's helmet and pulled it off.

"Ethan, what are you doing?" Calvin gasped. He was turned around and froze when he felt Ethan's fingers on the back of his head. There was another gasp, and he was stunned to discover it had come from Mrs. Ruiz. Calvin turned and took his helmet from Ethan to swiftly secure it on his head.

"What is that?" Mrs. Ruiz asked Ethan.

"He can't talk," Calvin replied so only Mrs. Ruiz could hear him. "He has selective mutism. Ethan and I grew up together. That was the result of real Therian haters. In high school, I was jumped by a bunch of senior kids. They carved the tiger Therian classification into the back of my head because I wouldn't stop being friends with Ethan." A lump formed in Calvin's throat, but he pushed through. "We've been fighting for our friendship since we were kids, and now we're fighting for more. I love him. And I would give my life for him. So you have to believe me when I say I didn't do what I did because I hate Therians. I did it to protect the citizens of this city. Whether they deserve it or not, I couldn't let anyone else die. When I say I'm sorry for your loss, I'm not quoting some procedural manual. I say it because I understand your pain, and I *am* sorry for what you've lost."

Mrs. Ruiz swallowed hard, tears in her eyes. She nodded. A tall, broad-shouldered young Therian pushed through the crowd, cursing at Calvin in Spanish. The venom rolled off his tongue as he called Calvin every filthy name in the book.

"*Lla callate*, Hector," Mrs. Ruiz ordered. "*Basta.*"

"*Pero, tía—*"

"*Vamos. Ahora.*"

Hector glared daggers at Calvin before thrusting a finger in his direction. "This isn't over." He marched off after his aunt, and it wasn't until they'd disappeared in the crowd that Calvin let out a huge sigh of relief. With Mrs. Ruiz's departure, soon the rest of the mob began to move along. Whether she'd said something to the protestors or not, Calvin was grateful everyone was leaving without incident. Not one arrest had been made. Once the crowd was gone, with only a few stragglers left, the teams broke up and gathered near their respective trucks. Calvin waited for Sloane to give the order before following the rest of his team into their BearCat. Everyone was silent, and Calvin subtly squeezed Ethan's hand. Ethan was about to step into the cabin when Maddock called out to him.

"Hobbs, take a seat on the bench. Ash, drive us back to HQ."

This couldn't be good.

Ash silently and quickly made his way into the front cabin while everyone buckled up on the bench. Maddock sat across from them. He was pissed.

"What the hell did you two think you were doing?"

Ethan held a hand up, and Maddock pinned him with a stare.

"No, this is on both of you, but what the hell got into you to make you think it was okay to remove your partner's helmet? We're in the middle of a possibly explosive situation, and you paint a target on your partner's head? For all we know, someone out there could have had a loaded weapon. You know better than that, Hobbs. Hell, rookies know better than that."

"He got through to her," Calvin said, hoping to take some of the heat off Ethan.

"And a bullet could have got through *you*," Maddock snapped, fuming. "You were strictly ordered not to engage. And with the widow, no less? How did you expect that to go? Tell me. I really want to know what the hell was going through your heads."

"I know, but that crowd was on the verge of rioting. They were waiting on a signal from Mrs. Ruiz. She'd already made physical contact."

"And you two decided to take it upon yourselves to break protocol on the chances she would listen?"

"The media's making out like I killed her husband because I hated Therians. The fact I was Human and had possibly killed him out of hate made me a monster. Monsters are easy to target. Ethan showed her she was wrong." He looked up at Ethan, who gave him a somber nod. There was only one way he could make his sergeant understand. "Okay, you might as well all know. Chances are it'll end up in the fucking news." He was pretty sure he'd seen a couple of cell phones out, probably recording him in the hopes of making him look even more of a dick. Everything always seemed to end up on the internet one way or another.

Calvin told his teammates about his scars and how he got them, sparing them the grisly details. They didn't need to know about the blood or stitches, or the nightmares he had for months after it happened. "That night, I thought I was going to die. The cops would have written me off as another victim of gang violence. It wasn't uncommon in our neighborhood, and considering my record for ending up in the principal's office for fighting, they might have even alleged I was part of a gang."

"Jesus, Cal."

Dex shook his head, and Calvin looked away from his team's horrified expressions. Even Maddock looked like he might be sick to his stomach. Calvin wasn't ashamed of his childhood, but he wanted to keep the ugly parts of his past where they belonged. He'd done what he had to for his mom and Ethan, for himself, including things he wasn't proud of, but his only thoughts during those times were on making it through another day because it meant he was another day closer to getting out of that shithole.

"Mrs. Ruiz needed to know her husband hadn't been killed out of hate," Calvin said. "That he mattered. By what she'd said to me earlier, it's clear her family had faced hate and prejudice before. My being Human hasn't spared me from the same pain she's experienced, but this was about her and her pain. Ethan saw an opportunity to bring this to an end, and he took it. That's our job, isn't it? Find a way to get through to people, connect, show them we're here for all our futures, not just one species?"

The truck was silent, with everyone lost in their own thoughts. Calvin had never meant for anyone outside of his mom to know what happened, but if it helped ease some of the pain Mrs. Ruiz was feeling, then it was worth it. He held his breath as Maddock looked from Calvin to Ethan and back.

"Next time, stick to protocol, or I swear I will suspend you both so fast you won't know what hit you. Got it? That goes for the rest of you."

Calvin replied his understanding, and Ethan nodded. He patted Ethan's knee and settled back against the truck's padded wall. The truck was quiet on the way back to HQ. They'd averted a potentially explosive situation, but Maddock was right. They knew better than anyone how difficult it could be to get through to people when they were hurt and angry. It was their job to listen and do what they could, but in the end when the talking stopped and the violence started, they had to do their duties and protect the innocent. Sometimes it seemed like the world was making progress, heading toward a future where Humans and Therians were treated as equals, but then his team would get called out, and Calvin would see how far they still had to go, and at times it even felt they were going backward.

It occurred to him then that things were about to change for him and Ethan outside of work. At the THIRDS their relationship wasn't a big deal. No one cared that Calvin was Human and that his boyfriend was a Therian. They'd have to be prepared for what they'd face out there. Dex was already experiencing it, and Calvin could see how it affected his friend. It was one of the few things that truly angered Dex, and usually Sloane was the one having to calm his partner. Sloane was used to it. He'd experienced hate and prejudice for being a Therian his whole life, and although it still stung, Sloane had learned how to deal with it.

For Dex it was harder. He'd dealt with it on a different level, sticking up for his little brother, but this was something else altogether. Dex had never had anyone verbally assault him for kissing his boyfriend out in public or for holding his hand. He'd never had someone threaten him for showing his boyfriend how much he loved him. Calvin did his best to help Dex work through his anger when Dex didn't want to worry Sloane. When he needed to let off some steam with someone who understood what it felt like. Calvin understood, and he was ready to face anything. He'd been doing it for years. This time it was a little different, but Calvin wasn't about to back down. He would always be at Ethan's side. Always.

Chapter Nine

"WOW. THIS is amazing."

Ethan nodded his agreement. Calvin was right. The place looked incredible. He was glad the team had been asked to come in early before the rest of the guests showed up. Once the lights dimmed and Dekatria filled up, Ethan was less likely to get a good look at the place. He'd be too busy trying to find somewhere he could feel comfortable for at least a little while. He hated that he couldn't enjoy parties like everyone else, because he really did want to, but he tried his best. The only time he even made the attempt to attend a big party was if he knew a good number of the people who'd be there. It meant stepping out of his comfort zone, but if he was having a good day and Calvin was with him, he could manage it.

When Cael told them his and Nina's birthday party was themed, stating they should all dress up in 1920s glamour, Ethan had no idea what to expect. He figured some party favors, a few banners, balloons, the usual party decorations. This was something else altogether. It was like they'd walked into some Hollywood club from yesteryear, from the white and gold gossamer curtains draped between white pillars—brought in for tonight—to the elegant table settings with extravagant centerpieces. Everything from the bar to the stage had been transformed in a bold art-deco style with a black, gold, and white color scheme. The speakers played modern tunes with vintage twists.

"What do you think?" Cael asked as he approached, dressed in a very Gatsby-inspired outfit, from his white shoes and white slacks to his red-striped jacket and boater hat angled on his head.

"Looking smooth, birthday boy," Calvin said. "The place looks amazing."

"Doesn't it," Cael said excitedly. "We hired Lou to do it. The guy's a party guru. Just don't get in his way while he's working. He will shank you with a toothpick. I'm serious. Ash nabbed a grape from one of the platters before I could warn him." He shook his head sadly. "Lou's still telling him off." Just as he said the words, there was a loud crash from out back. Ash came bursting through the kitchen doors to the sound of Lou's Spanish curses. He spun and thrust a finger at the swinging doors.

"You're fucking insane, you know that, Lou? It was *one* grape!" With a tug to his pinstriped vest, Ash headed in their direction. Ethan couldn't help his chuckle. Ash looked right at home in his pinstriped suit, complete with red carnation in his lapel, two-tone shoes, and a white felt hat angled on his head. He threw his arm around Cael and looked them over with a grin. "You two are adorable."

Calvin looked down at himself with a frown. "Hey, Baby Face Nelson was shorter than me. You wouldn't call him adorable."

"Probably because he was a cold-blooded murder-er. You, on the other hand...."

Ash leaned over to pinch Calvin's cheek, and he swatted Ash's hand away with a laugh.

"Fuck off."

Ethan had to agree with Ash. Calvin was the most adorable mobster he'd ever seen. Of course, he wouldn't tell Calvin that. The royal blue three-piece suit brought out his eyes, and the newsboy cap looked too cute on him. Ethan had chosen the same style hat, but he'd gone with a more casual look, opting for a green shawl collar sweater with deep auburn buttons that matched his bow tie and shoes, and a pair of gray slacks. He looked more like some twenties collegiate than a dangerous mobster.

This was so much fun! He couldn't wait to see what the rest of his friends were wearing. Just as the thought crossed his mind, Dex emerged from the back entrance of Dekatria, which Bradley had left unlocked for them. The drums of some swinging tune kicked up as Dex sauntered over. Ethan had to give the guy a slow clap.

"Aw shit. Well, look at what we've got here," Calvin said with a laugh. "It's Public Enemy Number One."

"More like Public Pain in the Ass Number One," Ash grumbled.

"Thanks, Cal."

Dex bowed gracefully, and Ethan put his thumbs up. His friend looked good in his navy blue three-piece suit and long black overcoat. He wore a black felt hat on his head with white spats over his shiny black shoes.

Dex grinned widely and opened the sides of his coat
to reveal the imitation Tommy gun hanging from his
shoulder holster. He motioned over his shoulder.

"My sugar daddy should be here any minute. He's
parking the Rolls Royce."

"So the delinquent falls for a class act. Not much
playacting involved there," Ash drawled.

"Bite me, Capone."

The back door opened, and Ethan let out a whistle.
Holy cow. Everyone broke into whoops and catcalls.

"Yeah, yeah. It's called a shave," Sloane said with
a smirk as he turned to show off his tuxedo with tails,
white vest, and bow tie.

His hair was slicked back and parted neatly to
one side, and he held a top hat in one white-gloved
hand. Ethan couldn't remember the last time he'd seen
Sloane without at least some stubble. Had his friend
ever been clean-shaven? Come to think of it, he'd never
seen Sloane in anything that resembled a suit either.

Dex walked over to Sloane and kissed his cheek.
"You clean up so pretty. Now how about wetting my
whistle, handsome?"

Sloane held his arm out, and Dex looped his
through it.

"Come on, kitten. Let's get us some hooch."

"Just stay away from the grapes," Ash warned.

Dex cringed. "Ooh, you ate from the platter before
he put it out? You're lucky to be alive, man. Lou is scary
when he's working. Seriously. Like, we're talking Temple of Doom, rip your heart out of your chest scary."

Ash threw his hands up. "It was one freakin'
grape."

Ethan chuckled and followed them to one of the
larger tables. Letty arrived draped in a faux fur coat, her

hair pinned up in curls, and a dazzling silver headpiece sparkling as she walked to the coatrack. She took her coat off, and everyone whistled.

"Holy shit, Guerrera's wearing a dress," Ash teased. "Never thought I'd see the day."

Letty flipped Ash off as she hung up her coat and walked over, the fringes of her glittering gold flapper dress swishing as she moved. "Fucking heels. I already want to throw them at someone."

"Looking smoking hot," Dex said, wriggling his eyebrows.

"Shut up." She tried to gather as much of her skirt fringe as possible in an attempt to sit, got frustrated, and plopped onto the empty chair beside Sloane.

"No really, you look good."

Letty peered at him. "You saying I don't always look good?"

"Um…." Dex leaned into Sloane, whispering hoarsely, "Help me out here."

Sloane took Letty's gloved hand and placed it to his lips for a kiss. "Letty, you always look beautiful."

"See?" Letty smiled sweetly. "That's why he's a gentleman, and you're a hood."

Dex slapped his hand over his chest. "Ouch! Mi corazone."

"*Corazón*," Letty corrected. "You're lucky you're cute, Daley."

"Now you sound like Sloane," Dex muttered, placing his hat on the table. He ran his hands over his slicked-back hair, but a small section fell over his brow, adding to his notorious-mobster look.

Ash looked around. "Where's Dimples?"

One of these days, they needed to find out what the guy's name was.

Letty rolled her eyes at the nickname. "He'll be here in a couple of hours. Sleeping off his last rotation."

"Sorry we're late."

Rosa walked in with Milena at her side. Both of them removed their long coats before hanging them up by the door. They looked stunning, and the team whistled and clapped, making Rosa and Milena smile. It was good to see Milena again, and Rosa was always so happy when her girlfriend was around. Milena greeted them each with a kiss, giving Ethan an extra-special hug. He beamed brightly at her.

"How are you, cutie?"

Ethan shrugged and nodded. *I'm good.* He gave her a gentle poke in the arm. *How are you?*

"Excited to be here. It's been too long since I've seen you guys." She took a seat next to Rosa.

"I had no idea the antique business was so demanding," Dex said.

"My employers are pretty ruthless. Their clients are pushy, demanding, and when time is of the essence, it's drop everything and acquire the item. These transactions move incredibly quick."

"Yeah, they don't care what time it is. If something needs doing, they're calling at all hours. Makes it hard to coordinate our schedules, but we do our best." Rosa's expression softened, and she leaned in to give Milena's cheek a kiss. With a shy smile, Milena turned her face and kissed Rosa's lips.

Aw. Those two were so sweet together. It was a shame their careers ate up so much of their time. It was clear Milena loved Rosa very much. Ethan could tell in the way she smiled at her and how it reached her sparkling gray eyes. Milena reminded him a little of Sparks, with her retro pinup curves and style, but unlike Sparks, Milena was a sweetheart. Granted, they only knew Sparks in a professional capacity. She was their superior and not a friend like Milena. Ethan had no idea what Sparks was like off the clock. Was she always so stern and focused? He recalled the email she'd forwarded him on shibari experts. *Why would you think about that now?*

Ethan quickly shook those thoughts from his head and turned his attention back to his friends.

"So where's the birthday girl?" Milena asked.

Cael shrugged. "She had to go pick someone up. A friend or something."

Bradley showed up, and everyone at the table ribbed him and whistled. He gave them all a little bow and chuckled. "Thanks, guys. You all look great."

"Rocking the suspenders," Dex said with a smile. "I like it."

Bradley had rolled his white shirtsleeves up his arms, his tattoos on display, but then Bradley always looked kind of preppy with a bit of a rockabilly vibe.

"So, how about some drinks?"

"Oh God, yes," Letty said with a cheer. "Bring on the booze!"

Ash held a hand up. "Can we get some snacks, since Señor Grape-warden tried to skewer me last time I got near the food?"

Bradley cringed. "Yeah, he doesn't like it when you touch the food before it's been put out."

"You get threatened too?" Dex asked with a chuckle.

"Of course not. I'm too cute to be yelled at," Bradley replied with a wink. "I ask. But I've seen terrible fates befall others." He shook his head sadly.

"Bradley?" Lou came out from the kitchen looking very refined in his tuxedo, a tablet in his hand. He smiled brightly at everyone. "Wow, look at you all. You look fantastic." He turned to Bradley. "Could you help me with something in the kitchen?"

"Sure. You think we could get the team something to nibble on?"

Bradley kissed Lou's cheek, making him blush.

"It's a little cruel to make them sit while the aroma from all that amazing food of yours floats out of the kitchen."

Lou put a hand to his chest. "You're right!" He turned to them and smiled apologetically. "I'm so sorry. I'll have the boys bring out some platters."

Ash sat up, and Ethan kicked him under the table. *I'm not losing out on tasty food because of you, so zip it.* Ash glared at him but remained silent.

Lou swiftly spun on his heels and hurried off to the kitchen. As soon as he was gone, Dex held his hand up to Bradley for a high five.

"And that's how it's done."

Bradley chuckled and high-fived Dex. They put in their drink orders, and soon their table was filled with cocktails, beers, champagne, spirits, and enough tasty food to make Ethan cry tears of joy. A good deal of it he had no idea what it was, but it tasted amazing. Ethan followed Dex's lead. He was familiar with Lou's catering and the different puff pastries. As they ate, the lights dimmed, and Ethan checked his watch. Guests would probably start arriving soon. The music switched to a romantic ballad, and Sloane stood. He turned and bowed to Dex, his hand held out.

"Would you care to dance, Mr. Daley?"

Dex took his hand with a bright smile. "I would love to, Mr. Brodie." He stood and walked his fingers up Sloane's chest. "I am so going to sex you up later."

Ash groaned. "I did not need to hear that."

Ethan chuckled. He turned his attention to Sloane and Dex on the dance floor, the way they stood so close together, the smiles on their faces as they murmured to each other, Sloane's head lowered so he was closer to Dex. Ethan remembered what Calvin had said in Sloane's apartment, how wistful he'd sounded. Ethan stood and took a deep breath. He turned and held his hand out to Calvin, who blinked up at him. With a smile, Ethan nodded to the dance floor. Calvin's smile stole his breath away, and he stood to take Ethan's hand.

"Sure, make the rest of us look bad," Ash grumbled before sweetly asking Cael to dance.

Ethan ignored his grumpy friend and led Calvin to the dance floor, the rest of his teammates following his lead. He pulled Calvin close and wrapped his arm around his waist, his free hand holding Calvin's. The song was a ballad from an era long gone, and Ethan enjoyed its sweeping melody and heartfelt lyrics. He closed his eyes and let his cheek rest against Calvin's head. Calvin squeezed his waist gently, and Ethan smiled, glad he'd done something to make him happy. He deserved it. Soon the place would get too crowded, and Ethan wouldn't be able to step foot near the dance floor, much less on it, which was why he cherished these moments. He was grateful to Bradley for sharing Dekatria with them. To Ethan, it was more than a bar or place to hang out. It was quickly becoming somewhere he felt comfortable, where he could be himself and not feel so anxious.

"Thank you."

Ethan opened his eyes at Calvin's soft words. He looked down, and Calvin stopped dancing to stand on his toes and kiss Ethan. Their friends cheered, and Ethan returned Calvin's kiss, pulling him up against him. Calvin laughed against his lips and threw his arms around him. He'd never been happier. They pulled apart and danced in each other's arms until someone knocked on the front door. It looked like the guests were finally arriving. Bradley emerged from behind the bar and went to open the door, greeting the group as they came in. A few Ethan recognized from work; some he'd never seen before. They came dressed up in suits and flapper dresses, feathers in their hair and gifts in their hands. As if sensing his unease, Calvin took hold of Ethan's hand.

"Come on. Let's get something to drink," Calvin said, leading him toward the bar. The end of the bar was always more comfortable for Ethan. It meant he was less likely to get boxed in. They ordered drinks from one of the waiters, and Calvin started chatting to him about ideas for Dex's tattoo. Ethan loved when Calvin talked about his art. He was always so passionate and excited when he talked about it. Like when they were kids and his mom would buy him a new sketchbook. One year, Calvin's mom had managed to save up enough money to get him some fancy colored pencils that professionals used. Calvin still had them. He'd been so careful with them, cherishing them, using them only for extra-special projects. Even though he could now afford to buy himself whatever colored pencils he wanted, he kept those safe.

Less than a few hours later, Ethan couldn't believe how packed the place was. The whole thing made him feel a little nervous, but he was okay. The music was good, with some fun eighties tunes thrown in the mix, courtesy of a certain loveable gummy-bear-eating nut-job who was bouncing around on the dance floor while his partner attempted to keep up. Dex was obviously already tipsy, but then again it didn't take much. Nina had finally shown up before the majority of the guests arrived. She looked dazzling in her white flapper dress and glittering silver headpiece with feathers. Ethan hadn't seen her come in, and she was alone. He had a sneaking suspicion Rafe was keeping a low profile. He had to admit, he was worried. Would Rafe be here as Nina's boyfriend or "work colleague"? Things were getting far too complicated for Ethan's liking. He didn't want to see anyone hurt, not even his brother. Rafe would never admit it to Ethan or Seb, but his brother cared about Nina.

Now that he thought about it, he hadn't seen Seb either. Hudson had arrived, looking snazzy in a blue three-piece suit and striped tie, and he'd disappeared sometime after. Occasionally he'd appear at the bar or chatting at one of the tables with coworkers and friends. Cael and Nina were dancing in the center of the crowded floor, blowing on their party favor horns. Everyone was having a great time. After a few more snacks and another beer, the music started getting a little loud for Ethan, and the bar was getting crowded. Calvin put his hand to the small of Ethan's back and nodded toward the stairs.

"Hey, how about we go up to the roof garden? It's a little quieter and less busy. I could use some fresh air."

Ethan's heart swelled at Calvin's thoughtfulness. Calvin didn't need a break; he knew Ethan did. Ethan took Calvin's hand and laced their fingers together. A blush crept into Calvin's cheeks, and Ethan leaned in to kiss him. It was the first time they were out in public as a couple. He led Calvin to the stairs and headed up. The second floor was packed, though not as much as the ground floor. They took the second set of stairs up to the roof. Ethan liked it up here. There was outdoor heating and a canopy that helped keep the cold out. It was pretty amazing, decorated with strings of lights and colorful lanterns. There were tables and a small bar, along with plenty of seating where folks could get cozy. Calvin had excused himself to say hi to someone when Seb and Taylor showed up. Seb grinned broadly when he saw Ethan.

"Hey, little brother. Rocking that cardigan."

He threw an arm around Ethan's shoulders and gave the side of his head a kiss. Ethan chuckled and playfully shoved him away. He made a drinking motion, and Seb poked Ethan's side with a chuckle.

"No, I'm not drunk, wise guy."

He ordered a drink for himself and one for Taylor, who was trying to chat up one of Nina's cousins. *Here we go.* Ethan motioned to Seb's brown three-piece suit before putting his thumbs up.

"Thanks. You know me. Not exactly the suit type, but it feels nice."

While Taylor was busy, Ethan leaned into Seb to whisper in his ear. "How come you're up here? Party's downstairs."

There were a number of people up there, but nowhere near the crowds downstairs. Everyone seemed to be having a great time, except his big brother.

Seb shrugged. "Just needed a break from the noise."

He smiled, but it didn't reach his eyes. Ethan's heart squeezed in his chest, and he whispered again.

"Hudson?"

"Can't hide anything from you, can I?" Seb replied with a sad smile. "Yeah. At work it's not so bad. I don't really see him around, and when I need something, I call Nina instead." Seb rubbed a hand over his face in frustration. "I thought it would get easier. It's *supposed* to get easier." He shook his head somberly. "But every time I see him, it kills me."

"Why do you do that to yourself?" Sure, there was something Seb could do. He knew it was especially hard with Seb having marked Hudson, but he couldn't go on like this. It was steadily getting worse. His brother was always so cheerful and playful, it broke Ethan's heart.

"I don't know how not to love him, Ethan."

Ethan swallowed hard. The anguish on his brother's face was hard to see. Before Ethan could reply, Taylor appeared, throwing his arm around Seb's shoulders.

"Listen, bro. I heard about what happened. Sorry things didn't work out with Cael. You two looked good together. Man, I can't believe he chose Keeler. Him and Daley have a hard-on for fucked-up guys. You took him home a couple of times before that. Tell me you at least got to bang him."

Unbelievable. Ethan glared at Taylor, when he happened to glance over Taylor's shoulder. His eyes widened, and a lump formed in his throat. Ethan tugged at Seb's sleeve. His brother turned around, and Ethan could almost feel his brother's pain when he saw Hudson standing there looking devastated. When Hudson spoke, his voice was barely a whisper.

"You and Cael?"

"It's not what you think," Seb said quietly, taking a hesitant step toward Hudson. "It was a few drinks. We didn't—"

Hudson held a hand up. "You don't owe me an explanation, Sebastian. You don't owe me anything."

"*Lobito*, please."

"Don't," Hudson warned sharply before seeming to get ahold of his emotions. He straightened and smoothed out his vest. "Please don't call me that. Excuse me." He started to turn, when Seb caught his arm.

"It was drinks and talking. Nothing happened."

Hudson tried to pull his arm out of Seb's grip to no avail. "Sebastian, please…."

"He's in love with Ash, and I'm—"

"Stop," Hudson pleaded.

His grief was as heartbreaking as Seb's, and Ethan wished he could do something to help. The despair filled the air like a thick fog. It made Ethan anxious. He hated seeing his brother hurting, and Hudson had always been a good friend to him. There was a time when Ethan believed Hudson would become part of their family. The two had been so in love, as if they'd always been together. From the first day they met, they'd been drawn to each other. Ethan cared about Hudson very much, but he couldn't understand why Hudson was determined to be apart from Seb when he clearly still loved him deeply. Why was he torturing himself? Especially since his pain would be greater than Seb's, considering he was the one bearing his ex-lover's mark.

"I love you." Seb put his hand over his heart, his grip still on Hudson's arm. "I told myself that I could move on, that my heart would heal, but after all this time, the wound's only gotten deeper. I need you in my life, *Lobito*."

Hudson swallowed hard. A tear rolled down his cheek, and Seb brushed it aside with his thumb. "Our bond is as strong now as it ever was. I can't stand to be away from you. Please, come back to me. I know you still love me."

Something flashed in Hudson's blue eyes, and his gaze turned hard. "You're wrong."

"And you're lying," Seb replied, moving his hand to Hudson's neck, his thumb stroking Hudson's skin. A visible shudder went through Hudson before he pulled away.

"I've moved on."

Seb flinched.

Ethan didn't know how much longer he could take this. The anger, hurt, and pain was overwhelming. Whoever had been on the roof garden when Hudson showed up, they were gone now. It wasn't some scandalous fight their coworkers would gossip about the next day. This was something that cut deep. Everyone in Unit Alpha felt for Seb and Hudson. *Please, Hudson. You love him.* Calvin placed his hand to the small of Ethan's back, and he felt himself calm.

Hudson straightened to his full height and lifted his chin. He pushed his glasses up his nose, his voice laced with a harsh tone unbecoming of him, one Ethan didn't like.

"It's time for you to move on, Sebastian. We can never get back what we had. It's over."

"Sweetheart…."

"We let a child die!" Hudson snapped. "We were so wrapped up in our perfect little world, we failed to protect those who counted on us. We swore an oath, and we bloody botched that up in spectacular fashion, didn't we?"

Seb shook his head. "That's on me."

"Listen to yourself! The guilt is still eating away at you." Hudson turned away from Seb, his voice quiet.

"Well, it eats away at me too. Can't you see that? What we had died that day with that poor boy. There's no bringing either back. Please, for both our sakes, let me go."

"I can't."

"Then I'll have to take the initiative." Hudson met Seb's gaze, his expression firm. "Unless there is no other option, considering we both work in the same unit, I'd like you to stay away from me. Good-bye, Sebastian."

Hudson walked off, and Ethan's heart sank. He'd thought that was it, but by the look on his brother's face, it was clearly not over. Seb followed Hudson.

"I know what you're doing, and you have to stop right now. You can't hide your emotions away in a little box and lock them up without losing a piece of you, without locking everything else up too. I know you. You shut your heart away until you don't feel anything at all. I won't let you do that to yourself."

"You really have no say in what I do or don't do to myself," Hudson replied sternly as he headed for the stairs with Seb on his heels.

Ethan quickly followed his brother, Calvin sticking close to him. He didn't like where this was heading. Hudson was determined to push Seb away, and his brother was having none of it. After years of Seb backing off every time Hudson asked him to, it would seem his brother was trying a different approach. Ethan wanted to do something, but he had no idea what. They followed Hudson as he pushed his way through the crowd on the ground floor toward the front of the bar, when the brewing shitstorm erupted into a tempest.

Nina and Rafe sat in a booth by the door, kissing.

Ethan could see the exact moment in which Hudson's heart finished shattering, but Ethan had bigger concerns than Hudson at that moment, and it was in the form of his seven-foot, three-hundred-pound brother launching himself at his even bigger brother, Rafe.

"You son of a bitch!"

Ethan took a step back, shaking his head as Seb landed a punch across Rafe's face.

"For years you blamed what happened on my being in a relationship with Hudson, giving me shit for it, and you're with Nina?"

"Get the fuck off me!" Rafe growled, pushing Seb away.

Hudson stood frozen, his wide eyes on Nina. "You and *him*?"

Nina quickly exited the booth and held her hands up. "Hon, please let me explain."

"Explain?" Hudson's pale skin flushed a deep crimson, his eyes reddened and glassy. "How could you keep this from me? I confided in you. You knew *everything*. You knew that bloody arsehole tried to get me sacked, and you're sleeping with him!"

Seb stared at Rafe in disbelief. "You tried to get Hudson fired?"

"He ruined your career," Rafe spat out heatedly. "He put you and our family through hell. We got death threats!"

"What?" Hudson looked aghast.

"That's right," Rafe replied through his teeth. "Seb never told you, but we got threats. Someone jumped him and tried to stab him, and that was after someone tried to run him down. Bet he didn't tell you that either. You ruined his fucking life!"

"He didn't do shit except put up with your disgraceful behavior time and time again. You're such a fucking hypocrite," Seb growled, shoving Rafe.

Having had enough of getting pushed around by Seb, Rafe pushed back. A fight broke out between them, both ignoring Hudson and Nina's pleas to stop. Ethan felt his anxiety bubbling up. He'd never liked it when his brothers fought. When he was little he'd cry at the top of his lungs, screaming until he was blue in the face and made himself sick. Soon the crying had become enough for them to stop, but when Ethan turned seven, he stopped crying, yet the horrible sick feeling it gave him remained.

During the really bad fights, he'd run to his room and shut himself in his closet with his headphones and his music so he wouldn't hear them. Seb would always come find him afterward and apologize. He'd make Ethan hot chocolate and explain why they'd fought. It didn't mean Ethan could stop feeling the way he did. For all of Rafe's faults, he was still Ethan's big brother, and he loved him.

Ethan wanted to shout at them to stop, but his throat closed up. He wished Sloane and Ash were here. Hudson wasn't big enough to pull two tiger Therians apart, and Ethan didn't want Calvin getting hurt. A crowd gathered, and Ethan felt his agitation growing. There were so many people, and the noise was hurting his ears. It was getting hard to breathe.

Seb punched Rafe, and Rafe tackled him to the floor. They thrashed around, cursing and shouting at each other, blaming each other, hitting.

Please, stop. Stop. Stop. Stop.

Rafe grabbed Seb and hauled him to his feet. Ethan shook his head. He started to tremble and wheeze. He knew he shouldn't fight it, that he could tolerate the discomfort. That it couldn't hurt him and would dissipate soon enough, but he couldn't stop himself. There was nothing he could do. His brothers needed him, and there was nothing he could do. He was a horrible, useless brother. Everyone probably thought so. They were probably watching him and wondering why he was so useless. Ethan's heart raced, and his fingers got tingly. Sweat dripped down his face, and he made a strangled sound.

Calvin and Hudson were at Ethan's side trying to calm him, but Ethan couldn't breathe. There were so many people. It felt like everyone was watching him, judging him. He was frozen to the spot, his chest tight.

"Seb, it's Ethan!"

Seb and Rafe pushed away from each other, and Seb hurried over just as Ethan heard a familiar "pop." On instinct he turned and grabbed Calvin, bringing him down to the floor as Rafe lunged for Nina and shouted to the crowd.

"Get down!"

Everyone hit the floor as a spray of bullets shattered Dekatria's glass windows and splintered the wooden beams, tearing through everything and anything. Screams and shouts echoed through the room as everyone scrambled and dropped to the floor. Ethan covered Calvin with his body, shielding him from the falling glass and debris. Tires shrieked as a car sped off. Ethan's adrenaline kicked in, and as soon as the noise stopped, he looked up and out the front. It was clear. He swiftly got to his feet and pulled Calvin up with him. They needed to check on everyone, see if anyone was—

"Oh God, please, no. No."

Ethan turned, a gasp caught in his throat. *No.*

"Lobito, what did you do?" Seb cradled Hudson in his arms, his lips pressed together in an attempt to keep

himself together as Hudson coughed and sputtered blood. "Why?"

Hudson smiled, tears in his eyes as he placed a bloodstained hand to Seb's jaw. "We both know why." His bottom lip trembled, and his face crumpled as the tears fell. "I'm so sorry. For everything."

Rafe pulled out his phone and called emergency services while Nina knelt beside Hudson, shouting for Bradley, who came running with the Therian First Aid Response kit. He handed it to Nina, the rest of Destructive Delta joining them. Rosa and Sloane rushed to Hudson's side.

"Shit." Sloane looked Hudson over, swiftly inspecting him. "I found an exit wound." He pushed his hand down against Hudson's side. "Where else is he hit?"

Rosa put her hand on Seb's shoulder. "Seb, you need to lay him on his stomach. One of the bullets is still in there, and he's losing a lot of blood."

Seb ran his hand over Hudson's head. "Please, don't leave me. Not like this."

"Seb!" Sloane ordered in his most authoritative voice, knowing it was the only way to get through to him.

Seb gently laid Hudson on the floor on his stomach. He removed his tux and folded it up, placing it under Hudson's head before taking hold of Hudson's hand while Rosa and Nina went to work trying to stop the bleeding. In the distance sirens wailed. Ethan joined Seb on the floor, kneeling beside him. He put his arm around his brother, letting him know he was there. Behind him Dex, Ash, Letty, and Cael were checking up on the rest of the guests to see who else might be injured and how badly.

"You're going to be okay," Seb told Hudson, brushing Hudson's hair away from his brow as Nina

and Rosa worked furiously to stop the flow of blood until the EMTs arrived.

Hudson appeared to be having trouble breathing, and he looked as if he were on the verge of passing out. His face had gone pale, his brow beaded with sweat. He looked over at Seb and smiled.

"I know it's... selfish, but... please stay with me?"

Hudson looked scared, but Seb held on to his hand, his expression determined.

"You know I will. It'll be okay."

The EMTs arrived on scene and rushed through the doors. Ethan stood to one side to give them room, but his brother remained at Hudson's side, though he was forced to step back while the team swiftly got to work preparing him for transport. The moment Hudson was on the gurney, Seb was beside him again, holding his hand. He followed them to the ambulance and climbed in after him. Before the doors closed Nina called out to him, telling him they were right behind. She ran off with Rafe close behind. Ethan wanted nothing more than to go after them. His brother needed him, but so did the people inside Dekatria. He had a job to do, and tonight's party had become a crime scene. Luckily, the majority of the guests were agents. They knew the drill. Ethan still couldn't believe this was happening. Had someone found out about the bar full of cops and decided to make a statement? Had it been personal?

Dex rushed over, wiping his bloodied hands on a cloth napkin. "How's Hudson? How bad is it?"

"I don't know," Sloane said, shaking his head. "One of the bullets went straight through, but the other is still in there. He had his back to the front of the bar."

"He was protecting Seb," Calvin said quietly. "When Rafe called out, Hudson threw himself at Seb.

He knew he wasn't strong enough to bring Seb down, but he did it anyway, protecting him. Even after telling Seb he wanted him to stay away."

Everyone went quiet for a moment. Hudson had tried to push Seb away, yet none of what he'd told Seb had been true. Hudson loved Seb as much now as he did then. Ethan hoped Hudson pulled through this okay and realized how much he needed Seb. For all he knew, this incident wouldn't change anything between them, but Ethan was hopeful. Sloane was the first to break the silence.

"Seb and Hudson will get whatever support they need from us, but right now we need to contain this situation and track down whoever's responsible for this. What have we got?" he asked Rosa.

"We've got several wounded, but luckily no fatalities or critically injured other than Hudson. The ones who heard the 'pop' first hit the ground, the rest the moment Rafe sounded the alarm. We're lucky we've got mostly agents and law enforcement here. EMTs are taking care of it."

Sloane nodded. "Did anyone see what happened?"

Ethan shook his head. He tapped his ear.

"Ethan heard the first shot. Then we heard the tires," Calvin replied.

"So this was a targeted attack."

Ethan frowned and put his hand on Calvin's shoulder. Are you thinking what I'm thinking?

Calvin sighed. "This is about me. I'm sure of it."

Sloane shook his head. "This is about all of us. We're a team, Cal. If someone decided to take matters into their own hands and express their opinion on what happened with Ruiz, then it's on all of us. Whoever did this has to answer for it."

Ethan put his hand to Sloane's shoulder and motioned out the door. He put his hand to his heart. *I need to check on Seb.*

"Yeah, of course. We'll meet you guys at the hospital. I'm going to call the sarge."

Ethan nodded his thanks and hurried out the door with Calvin at his side. If things had been tough for Seb before, they were about to get a whole lot tougher. Ethan had no idea how his big brother was going to handle this. He'd been struggling with it for months now. Not that he'd had it easy back when Hudson had ended things, but like Seb stated, things had been getting worse for him.

Calvin climbed in behind the wheel of his Jeep, and Ethan joined him in the passenger side. He buckled up and tried to wrap his head around everything as Calvin drove them to the hospital.

"Hector Ruiz."

Ethan glanced over at Calvin. "You think he did this?"

"Do you remember what he said to me the day of the protest? He said this wasn't over."

Ethan nodded. Calvin was right. Hector had motive. Just because his aunt had accepted Calvin's word didn't mean Hector felt the same. He'd been pissed. Ethan pulled out his smartphone and sent off a text to Sloane, letting him know about Hector Ruiz and his threat to Calvin that day. If Hector was responsible for this, the THIRDS needed to pick him up before he disappeared, if he hadn't gone into hiding already. The guy had opened fire on a room full of law enforcement. It also meant Hector hadn't been alone. Ethan put away his phone, noticing how Calvin's knuckles were tight over the steering wheel.

"This isn't your fault," Ethan said firmly. It was written all over Calvin's face. "You were doing your job. If it was Hector who did this, then he'll have to face the consequences of his actions, along with anyone else who was with him."

"What if Hudson—"

"Stop," Ethan ordered gently. "Hudson's going to be okay." He held his hand out, relieved when Calvin took it and gave it a gentle squeeze. They'd get through this, the same way they did everything else. Together.

Chapter Ten

HERE THEY were again.

Ethan and Calvin joined Seb, Nina, and Rafe in the emergency room at NYC Presbyterian Hospital. At least when they walked into a waiting room, Rafe and Seb weren't fighting. Rafe was holding Nina's hand and comforting her while Seb stood at the far end of the room by the doors, staring off into the distance like he was lost. His eyes were red, and Ethan could all but feel his brother's heart breaking. Ethan walked over and gently put a hand on Seb's shoulder, making him flinch. He hadn't even realized Ethan was there. His brother let out a heart-wrenching sigh.

"Hey, little brother. He's still in surgery."

Seb shook his head, and Ethan could see his brother fighting to keep his emotions at bay. Ethan brought Seb into his embrace and held him.

"What if I lose him for good this time? Having him away from me was hard, but it was better than this. Anything is better than this." Seb pulled back and wiped at his eyes. "I can't believe he did that."

Ethan put his hand to Seb's chest over his heart. *He loves you.*

"Yeah." Seb gave him a small smile when the rest of the team showed up. Sloane and Dex came over, their expressions filled with concern.

"How is he?" Dex asked worriedly. "Any news?"

"He's in surgery," Seb replied. "It's too soon to tell, but the outlook is promising."

Sloane nodded. He looked around the waiting room. "We've been seeing the inside of this place a little too often lately."

"Tell me about it," Dex huffed. He patted Seb's shoulder. "How about we bring you some coffee?"

"Thanks. That would be great."

Dex and Sloane headed off toward the café. Cael and Ash were huddled together talking quietly, while Rosa and Letty joined Nina. Ethan's mom wasn't able to come, but she called Seb every few minutes to check up on him and Hudson. Darla was putting an overnight bag together for Seb and would be there soon. Hudson was still considered family to them, even if he'd distanced himself some time ago. Ethan's mom refused to abandon Hudson the way his own family had. Seb had tried to get through to Hudson's parents in England, but they ignored his calls. When he tried calling from a hospital line, they hung up on him. Ethan had no idea why Hudson had been cast out of his wolf Therian family, but it was heartbreaking knowing his family didn't care that their son was fighting for his life.

Years ago Ethan's mom declared her family and Darla to be Hudson's new pack and refused to have it any other way. Ethan knew his mom missed Hudson.

He'd been like one of her boys, a quieter, calmer son. Whenever he could, he'd have tea with her, bring her celebrity gossip magazines so they could chat about the latest Hollywood scandal. They'd watch soap operas together, and he'd been there to help with Ethan's dad when Seb and Rafe were on call.

The waiting room was quiet at this time of night but still plenty busy. Ethan agreed with Sloane. Wasn't it time someone cut them a break? The job was dangerous, no doubt about that, but the last year had been unlike any other. Ethan was getting tired of ending up in the hospital, no matter which side of the doors he was on.

Seb refused to sit, so Ethan took a seat in the chair closest to his brother, Calvin at his side. He held Ethan's hand, and Ethan placed it to his lips for a kiss with a small smile. Having Calvin at his side helped put him at ease. He caught Rafe's surprised expression. His brother's eyes dropped to Ethan's hand in Calvin's before he shook his head and stood. He started to pace, something obviously weighing on his mind. Ethan had an idea what that something might be. Rafe was headed in their direction when the doors opened, and a wolf Therian doctor emerged.

"Agent Hobbs?"

All three brothers approached.

"Oh." The doctor checked his tablet. "Sebastian Hobbs."

"That's me," Seb said, holding a hand up.

"Agent Hobbs, you're listed as Dr. Colbourn's next of kin."

Seb nodded. "Yes, that's right."

Hudson still had Seb down as his next of kin? Why hadn't he changed it? Not that Ethan was opposed to

Hudson's decision, but if Hudson had truly wanted to sever ties with Seb, he'd have changed his records. If anything, having Seb listed as his THIRDS next of kin kept Seb in his life and in a decision-making capacity. From the looks of it, his brother knew it hadn't been changed.

"Dr. Colbourn is out of surgery and being transferred from ICU to a private recovery room. We were able to retrieve the bullet from his back with minimal tissue damage. Thankfully it remained intact, so there were no fragments. He'll be closely observed for the next forty-eight hours. Once he wakes up, we'll assess the situation and determine how long we'll be keeping him in recovery. We can decide on a timescale for his recuperation by then."

"Thank you," Seb said, shaking the doctor's hand. "When can I see him?"

"You can go in now, but he won't be awake for a few hours, and then he'll need plenty of rest."

Seb was still talking to the doctor and signing some forms when Dex and Sloane returned with coffee for everyone, and presumably a hot chocolate for Cael. Calvin updated them on Hudson's condition while they drank down a much-needed hit of caffeine. Everyone was relieved to know Hudson would be all right. While Seb finished up with the doctor, Sloane brought them all in close.

"I checked in with Maddock. Recon's picked up Hector's crew, but Hector's on the run. Unit Alpha has three teams out looking for him. In the meantime, Recon's trying to get his cohorts to talk. Sarge will let me know when he hears anything."

As soon as the doctor gave them the all clear, they followed Seb and one of the Therian nurses. They made sure to use plenty of sanitizer before going in. Ethan stopped by the door, a lump forming in his throat at the sight of Hudson hooked up to the various pieces of monitoring equipment. It hadn't been so long ago that Ethan had been in a similar position. Seeing how hard this was for his brother made Ethan realize what it must have been like for Calvin to see him lying there hurt, trying not to think about how much worse it could have been. They stood quietly as Seb pulled up a chair beside Hudson's bed and took hold of his hand. He spoke quietly to Hudson, his thumb stroking Hudson's hand.

Ethan turned to Calvin and pulled him into his arms. He let his head rest against the side of Calvin's, whispering in his ear.

"I'm so sorry for what I've put you through."

Calvin squeezed him tight. He pulled back and put a hand to Ethan's cheek when Rafe appeared beside them, a deep frown on his face.

"So when were you two going to tell me?"

"It's not like we announced it," Calvin replied quietly. "It's complicated."

"Yeah, I'll bet." Rafe turned to Sloane, his eyes narrowed. "What kind of team are you leading here, Brodie? Is there anyone on Destructive Delta who isn't sleeping with a teammate?"

"You're one to talk," Ash scoffed.

"Nina and I aren't on the same team. It's not against the rules," Rafe growled.

Sloane's jaw clenched. "Now's not the time for this, Rafe."

"Oh? When's the right time?" Rafe thrust a hand toward Hudson. "When someone ends up dead? Is there anyone on your team who hasn't ended up in this hospital? Is there anyone you know how to keep safe?"

"That's enough," Sloane warned.

Rafe shook his head in pity before moving his gaze to Dex. "I feel sorry for you, man. With his track record, you'll be lucky if he doesn't get you killed."

"You son of a bitch."

Sloane charged Rafe, and it took Ethan, Cael, and Ash to hold him back. Seb stood and rounded on Rafe.

"What the fuck is the matter with you? Haven't you caused enough pain? Now you have to attack my friends too?"

"If he's such a fucking good friend, why do people keep getting hurt on his watch, huh?"

"Are you fucking kidding me? Because no one's ever gotten hurt on your watch, right?" Seb spat out. "Oh, I forgot, you're fucking perfect."

Rafe turned his attention back to Sloane. "I don't know why Sparks has let this team—has let *you*—get away with the shit it has. When Gabe died, your ass should have been benched. You haven't been fit for duty since."

Ethan, Ash, and Cael grabbed Sloane when they should have been keeping an eye on Dex. None of them saw it coming, least of all Rafe, who reeled back after Dex managed to punch him square across the jaw with a jump and punch move Ethan had never seen him do before. Where the hell had he learned that?

"Jesus, Daley." Ash stared at Dex. "Where the fuck did that come from?"

"Training," Dex replied, his eyes narrowed at Rafe. He positioned himself between Sloane and Rafe. "I've had enough of your attitude. You wanna go at it? Let's step outside."

"You little shit." Rafe took a step toward Dex, when he let out sharp cry and fell to his knees.

"Rafe!"

Nina ran to his side, and Ethan joined her. He tried to help his brother, but Rafe pushed him away.

"Don't touch me. I'm fine," Rafe growled.

Jesus, really? Ethan threw his arms up in frustration and put some distance between him and his brother before he ended up following Dex's lead. Like they weren't already going through enough. He was surprised they hadn't gotten themselves kicked out.

"Are you okay? What's wrong? Should we call someone?" Letty asked.

"I said I'm fine."

Rafe was on his knees, his brow beaded with sweat. Whatever he was, he wasn't fine. Why wouldn't he let them help?

"Tell them." Nina cupped Rafe's face, her deep brown eyes pleading.

"Nina," Rafe warned.

Nina shook her head. "No. I'm sick and tired of everyone treating you like shit."

"Here's an idea," Dex said. "Stop acting like an asshole all the time and maybe people wouldn't think you were such a dick."

"Fuck you, Daley. I don't give a shit what anyone thinks."

Rafe winced, and Ethan knew something was wrong. He wanted to go to his brother, but Rafe would push him away.

"That much I gathered," Dex muttered.

"Rafe, it's not right."

Nina ran a hand over his head, her expression filled with concern, but Rafe shook his head. He pushed himself to his feet, the pain caused by the movement evident on his face. He limped toward the door, head held high.

"I'm going for some coffee. You do what you want."

He walked out the door, and Seb went back to his chair beside Hudson. He closed his eyes and sighed.

Dex turned his attention to Nina. "How can you go out with that guy?"

"How can *you* be so judgmental?"

"Judgmental? He goes out of his way to be a certifiable prick to everyone, even his own brothers!"

"Because he's hurt and angry and scared. His life is crashing down around him, and no one gives a fuck. They're too busy talking shit about him behind his back about what an asshole he is."

Dex looked affronted. "Hey, I've never said squat about him behind his back. Anything I've got to say to him, I say to his face. I'm sorry he's going through whatever he's going through, but maybe if he actually talked to someone about it rather than pissing on any and every effort someone makes to get along with him, then he wouldn't be going through it alone."

"He's not going through it alone," Nina replied angrily. "He has *me*. I'm the one who wakes up in the middle of the night to him screaming in pain. I'm the one who holds him when it gets so bad he passes out. When he wakes up and he's shaking so bad he can't hold his own glass of water, I'm the one who helps him. All you see is the asshole. You don't see the guy who dropped out of high school and took night classes while working two jobs so his family could put food on the table, so his dad and little brother had the medicine they needed."

Ethan stood stunned. He wasn't sure which part of Nina's outburst left him the most hurt and confused.

Just what the hell was going on with his brother, and why hadn't Rafe said anything?

Nina turned to Ethan, tears in her eyes. "You and Seb have always been so angry with him for never being there, but did you stop to think about why? Everything he did, he did for his family, without complaint and without even bringing it up, because he didn't want anyone feeling guilty. When Seb applied to the THIRDS, who do you think put in a referral for him to get hired? When you applied, who fought tooth and nail so you'd get hired? The THIRDS is inclusive, but they were unsure if you could perform out in the field as a specialist with your mutism. They wanted to give you a desk job, Ethan. Rafe fought for you to receive equal treatment. He told them they'd be losing out if they didn't put you out there." She turned to Seb, her expression softening. "After the shootout, when everyone was out for your blood, demanding you be let go, who do you think went to the very top to fight for you? Rafe gave everything he had, put his own reputation on the line so they would give you a second chance." Her resolve strengthened, and she wiped a tear away from her cheek.

"Rafe's health has been deteriorating for some time, and he's been trying everything to prevent...." She took a deep breath and released it slowly. "He has two years left out in the field. Three at most. The doctors have already confirmed it. Rafe's going to end up in a wheelchair. Permanently. Like your father. He inherited your dad's Therian Acheron Syndrome."

Ethan's heart dropped. He shook his head. *No. That can't be right.*

"That's why he's so angry all the time. He's been hiding it for years. The symptoms started appearing back in college, but they weren't so bad, so he tried to ignore it. Then three years ago... the pain got too bad to ignore. It hit him hard."

Ethan couldn't believe what he was hearing. His heart squeezed in his chest. Seb stood, but Ethan shook his head. He turned and left, grateful when Calvin stayed behind. He needed to see Rafe alone, needed to know if it was true. Ethan tried not to think about Rafe going through what his dad went through. The doctors said it was what had set off Ethan's mutism. The trauma of seeing and hearing his father in so much pain, watching how it contorted his body. Worst of all was the flash of resignation in his father's green eyes. That slip of a moment where it had been evident that he wanted nothing more than to end his own suffering. It didn't last long before his father's determination set in, but it was enough to haunt Ethan for the rest of his life.

Ethan rounded the corner and found his brother leaning against the corridor wall that led to the café. Rafe cut him off and held a hand up.

"I don't need your pity parade. I can take care of my own shit. Always have."

Rafe tried to limp off, and Ethan grabbed his arm. *Please don't go.*

"Fuck off, Ethan. Don't pretend like you give a shit. You and Seb made it pretty clear ages ago that I'm not part of your little club. Just because I'm going to end up a spaz like you and Dad doesn't change anything."

Ethan flinched at Rafe's callous words. They hurt, but he knew his brother was hurting worse. Stepping up to Rafe, Ethan wrapped his arms around him and hugged him close, refusing to let go when Rafe tried to push him away. His brother wasn't really trying.

He could have pushed harder. Ethan leaned his head against Rafe's and whispered in his ear.

"I'm sorry."

Rafe stiffened. It was the first time Ethan had spoken to him. Ever. Rafe wrapped his arms around Ethan, giving him a squeeze before burying his head against Ethan's shoulder. Seeing Rafe so vulnerable was difficult. Rafe had never been anything but fearless and stoic. He made it a point never to show any weakness, or rather what he deemed weakness, in front of anyone. It was difficult for Ethan to hear Rafe's quiet sobs.

When Rafe was ready, he pulled back and wiped at his eyes. The tears were gone, and his somber expression returned, but his eyes gave away the despair he was feeling. He cleared his throat and smoothed out his shirt.

"I always resented the fact you spoke to Seb and not me. I know I'm not fun like Seb, and that I've never been there for you, but you have to know it's not because I didn't want to be. I didn't know what to do to help you, and that frustrated me. I'm not so good with feeling helpless. Seb always knew what to do when you got upset or scared. I made things worse."

"That didn't mean I didn't need you," Ethan said softly.

Rafe gave him a nod. "Thanks. That means a lot to me."

"Is it true? You have what Dad has?"

Rafe inhaled deeply and nodded. He motioned over to the large fountain and the tiled seating around it. They walked over, and Ethan took a seat beside his brother.

"I was diagnosed years ago, but I was in denial. Seeing Dad struggling with his meds, confined to his wheelchair, how hard it was for Mom, for everyone, and knowing there was nothing I could do to prevent it… I couldn't handle it. It made me furious, and I know it was wrong to take that out on you and Seb, but I was so angry. I was the oldest. It was my job to look after everyone, to provide for our family. This wasn't supposed to happen."

"Do Mom and Dad know?"

Rafe shook his head, his lips pressed together. "I don't know how to tell Mom. It'll be like Dad all over again, and that almost killed her. And now with this…." He motioned toward the corridor they'd come from and ICU.

"He saved Seb's life."

"I know. And I know it wasn't his fault. It would make me so angry seeing Seb hurting like that." Rafe let out a humorless laugh. "Anger seems to be the only thing I can feel these days. It was easy to hate Hudson for what he did. For breaking Seb's heart, for leaving him when he was at his lowest, after Seb had risked his life and his career for him. I couldn't understand it. Why the hell would Seb do something so stupid? Now I understand."

"Nina."

A smile came onto Rafe's face, and it warmed Ethan all over. His brother didn't smile nearly enough, if ever. It made him look like a different person. Someone not so angry at the world.

"It took me a while to realize she wasn't going to go anywhere. I figured once she found out, she'd leave me. The first time I woke up screaming, I told myself she was out the door. Instead, she was focused and helped me through it. She wouldn't put up with any of my shit. I tried to break it off, and she refused."

Rafe chuckled at the memory. "She actually refused. Just said 'Nope, not happening,' and then she made me soup." He narrowed his eyes. "There was a fish head in it, but it was surprisingly good."

Ethan laughed. He knew how much his brother hated eating things with eyes still attached. Rafe took a deep breath, and Ethan could have sworn his cheeks were flushed.

"You love her," Ethan said as it dawned on him.

Rafe gave Ethan a sideways glance before his lips curled into a smile. "Yeah, I think I do."

Ethan threw an arm around his big brother and hugged him. "I'm happy for you. Really."

"Wow, you making up for not talking to me all your life?"

"I'm sorry." And he meant it. "It wasn't that I didn't want to. I couldn't."

"I know." Rafe stared off at nothing in particular. "I read up on it, you know. On your selective mutism and social anxiety. I wanted to understand. And I did. I couldn't get past the fact that you could talk to Seb and not me."

"I don't get to choose," Ethan murmured quietly. "I either can or can't. I wish I could talk to Mom. I know how much it would mean to her. To Dad. I've tried so many times. But I can't. I open my mouth and my throat closes up. I start to panic. Then I think about how disappointed she must feel, and it makes things worse. I passed out once." He'd tried so hard. His mom had so many worries, so much going on with their dad. Even at a young age he knew how happy it would make her if he talked to her, but no matter how much he pushed himself, he couldn't. He'd tried so hard one day he'd blacked out.

"I remember," Rafe said gently. "I was the one who found you."

Ethan stared at him. "But I was in Seb's room when I woke up."

"I put you there. Figured you'd feel better if Seb was there when you woke up."

Ethan couldn't help feeling guilty. How many times had his brother placed Ethan's needs before his own and simply kept it to himself? "Seb told me I didn't have to talk. If one day I did it would be great, but not to force myself. Things got a little better after that."

"See, I would have fucked it all up." Rafe frowned down at his fingers. "Speaking of fucking up, I'm sorry about Thanksgiving. I had a bad episode that morning and said 'fuck you' to the world. I didn't mean for you to get hurt or Cal. Not that I'm excusing what I did, but I had no idea what was going on with your meds. I hope that motherfucker rots in hell for what he did. Anyway, yeah, I was a shitty brother, and there's no excuse for what I said to you that day. I'm really sorry."

"I forgive you."

Rafe's brows drew together, and his eyes grew glassy. He pressed his lips together and nodded, his hands clasped tightly between his knees.

"What are you going to do now?" Ethan asked softly.

Rafe shrugged. "There's nothing I can do. There's no cure for it. Maybe one day. All I can do is prepare myself for the day my legs stop working."

"When that day comes, I'll be there to help you in every way I can," Ethan promised.

"Me too."

They looked up to find Seb standing to one side looking uncertain. Rafe stood, and they faced each other, neither one seeming to know what to do. Seb shoved his hands into his pockets.

"I'm not here out of pity. I wanted to say I'm sorry. I accused you of being an asshole, and I was no better, always expecting you to be the one to make all the effort."

Rafe stepped up to Seb, and Ethan braced himself. He hoped they wouldn't get into a fight here of all places. To Ethan's surprise and relief, Rafe pulled Seb into a hug. The two wrapped their arms around each other, and Ethan smiled. He couldn't remember the last time his brothers had hugged. They stood like that for a long time, and Ethan met Seb's gaze. He gave him a nod and smiled.

"We'll get through this together," Seb promised. "No more pushing us away, okay? We're your brothers, and we love you. Let us help you."

Rafe nodded. "Okay." He cleared his throat and motioned to the corridor they'd come from. "When Hudson wakes up and he's better, I'll apologize. I doubt he'll forgive me, but I need to at least try. I know how much he means to you."

"Thank you."

The three of them made their way back to Hudson's room, and everyone got up when they entered. Calvin looked relieved when he saw them. Most likely because they'd returned without bruises.

"I don't want anyone treating me different," Rafe grumbled as he walked in.

Nina ran over to him and hugged him.

Sloane shook his head. "We don't treat Hobbs any different. Why would we treat you differently?"

"Sorry I punched you," Dex added. "But you did deserve it."

"Fair enough. I'll try not to be so much of an ass-hole." Rafe stopped in front of Sloane and met his gaze. "I'm sorry for always giving you such a hard time. I guess I felt a lot of resentment towards you. I've always respected you, and when I found out about my condition, I needed to vent, and I guess you were an easy target." Rafe shifted uncomfortably, but he carried on, determined to say what he needed to say. "You were the kind of team leader I always wanted to be, and it got hard, seeing you doing so well, knowing where I was going to end up. I looked for any reason to drag you down, and I'm sorry."

Sloane looked surprised. He quickly snapped himself out of it and held his hand out to Rafe, who took it without hesitation. "I appreciate your honesty. If you need anything, just ask."

"Why would you help me?" Rafe's expression was wary. "After all the shit I've said to you? After everything I've done?"

"Because Destructive Delta is family, and that includes anyone connected to Destructive Delta." Sloane took a deep breath and shoved his hands into his pockets, looking somewhat embarrassed. "The truth is we can be stubborn asses. We're so used to doing things our way that when things change, we have trouble keeping up. It's easy to think that putting our trust in others makes us weak, when really it makes us stronger."

Rafe pulled Nina close and smiled down at her. "I'm starting to see that." He kissed her, his public show of affection unexpected. Ethan was happy to see his brother smiling. It was obvious how much he cared about Nina, and that was something Ethan never thought he'd see. Ethan worried about Hudson and Nina's relationship. Hudson had been deeply hurt. He and Nina were close friends. If only Nina had confided in Hudson, things might have gone a little differently.

Nina stepped up beside Seb. "Not a day goes by when he doesn't think about you."

"He told me he didn't love me," Seb replied softly, bringing Hudson's hand to his lips for a kiss.

"We all know that's bullshit. There's no one but you, Seb. There hasn't been since he left you, and there won't be. I tried to get him to move on, to at least go out on a date, and he tried."

"He dated?"

"I said he tried. He sabotaged them."

"What do you mean?" Seb asked, his eyes on Hudson.

"Whenever someone asked him out, he told them he was marked. They'd bail. There were a couple of Humans who didn't, but they never made it past the first date. Nothing worked because none of them were you, Seb."

"Then why won't he come back to me?"

"Because you can't just pick up where you left off." Nina knelt beside Seb, her hand on his arm. "Until you both forgive yourselves for what happened and find a way to leave it behind you, you can't be together. He knows that. As painful as it's been for him, there's always this little flicker of hope. If you come together and it doesn't work, that's it."

"He's scared," Seb said, nodding his understanding.

It made sense to Ethan. He'd never thought of it that way. All these years, Hudson stayed away from Seb, afraid a reconciliation would lead to confirmation their relationship was never meant to be. So instead he suffered in silence, living with the hope that someday things might change.

"We should give them some time," Rafe told Ethan, motioning for everyone else to follow. Ethan agreed. Seb needed some time alone with Hudson. He'd gone pensive, and Ethan had no doubt he was considering Nina's words. Ethan took Calvin's hand, and they left the room with everyone following close behind.

Outside in the waiting room, Sloane was getting ready to check in with the sarge when they heard it. Shots fired.

"Shit." Sloane put his phone away and ran over to reception. "I'm Agent Brodie with the THIRDS. Where's your security office?"

The anxious nurse put in a phone call, and seconds later a security officer came running.

"Agent Brodie?"

"What's going on?" Sloane asked.

"I'm Riviera, head of security. We have a hostile situation in the lobby. The shooter says he's looking for an Agent Summers."

Sloane turned to Calvin. "Hector Ruiz."

Chapter Eleven

SHIT. RUIZ had come looking for him.

If there had been any doubt about who was responsible for the shooting at Dekatria, this pretty much confirmed it. Ruiz was out for Calvin's blood. If Ethan hadn't knocked Calvin to the ground when he did, Ruiz might have had it. Instead Hudson was lying in a hospital bed with two bullet wounds.

Calvin joined Sloane, along with the rest of their team, including Nina and Rafe, as they followed Riviera to the security office. They had to take a number of long corridors, since the office was located near the entrance of the emergency department, outside the lobby. When they reached the office, several other officers were there. Riviera brought up the camera feed in the lobby, where Hector Ruiz held a security officer hostage, a gun aimed at the leopard Therian's head.

"The THIRDS are on their way," Riviera said.

Sloane studied the screen. "Okay, we've got a major containment problem. We need to find out if Ruiz showed up with anyone else. Can you show me his arrival?"

Riviera nodded and got to work bringing up the footage of Ruiz's appearance. Ash stepped up beside Sloane. "If Ruiz makes it out of that lobby and into the hospital, we're talking hundreds of rooms, multiple exits. If he's not alone, we have an even bigger problem. We're going to need as many agents on this as possible."

"Here." Riviera brought up several camera feeds of Ruiz entering through Emergency before he grabbed the nearest security officer and removed his firearm, shouting at the citizens in the lobby and firing a warning shot.

"What about exterior footage?" Sloane asked.

Riviera brought up footage from the parking garage and outside the hospital. A taxi dropped Ruiz off.

"Looks like he's alone." Sloane turned to the team. "Dex, get ahold of the sarge and tell him where we are. Meet him at the side entrance. I want as many agents as possible securing the entrances and exits. Put an agent on every floor. Cael, Nina, keep an eye on the security feeds. I want to know about anything or anyone that looks out of place. Rosa, stand by for possible medical assistance. Letty, Ash, Rafe, you're backup. I'm going to go talk to him. Cal, you know what to do."

It was what he feared. Calvin faced Sloane. "Let me talk to him."

"I don't think that's a good idea, Cal. This guy's trying to kill you. If we—"

Ruiz's voice came in through the security office speakers. "I know you're listening, Summers! If you don't get out here, I'm going to start shooting!"

"It's me he wants, Sloane. I don't want anyone getting hurt because of me. Let me try to talk him down," Calvin pleaded. The last thing he wanted was to put a bullet in another Ruiz family member. He needed to give Hector a chance to do the right thing. "He's angry, and he's hurting."

"And he put Hudson in the hospital," Ash argued heatedly. "He could have fucking killed someone! He could have killed you. He tried to kill you."

"I know that, but does that mean we take the easy route and take him out? If I have to, I will, but I want to make damn sure I've given him every opportunity to turn himself in."

"Or an opportunity to shoot you," Ash scoffed.

"That won't happen." Calvin turned to Riviera. "Do you have any equipment?"

Riviera nodded and motioned to the far wall and the large weapons locker secured shut. "Vests and firearms."

"Okay, good." Calvin turned to Sloane. "Please, you have to let me do this."

Sloane seemed to think about it for a moment before giving him a nod. "All right. Suit up and head out. Letty, Ash, and Rafe will be on the sidelines and out of sight in case this goes south."

"Got it." Calvin turned to Ethan as Riviera went to the weapons locker to get him the equipment he needed. "I have to do this," he told Ethan.

Ethan pulled him close and gave his lips a quick, gentle kiss. He nodded his understanding. Calvin strapped himself into the tactical vest Riviera handed him before taking one of the Glocks and checking the magazine. With a full clip and one in the chamber, he headed for the lobby with Letty, Ash, and Rafe. They made sure to stay tucked away as Calvin approached the swinging doors leading to the lobby. He nudged one side open.

"Hector, I'm coming out. Don't shoot. I want to talk."

"Well, let's go, then," Hector called out. "Let's talk."

Calvin held the Glock in his hand and raised his arms at his sides as he slipped out. Hector tensed at the sight of the gun, but he remained where he was, jerking the security officer in front of him and using him as a shield. Letty, Ash, and Rafe were concealed to Calvin's sides, waiting in the shadows.

"You wanna talk, but you bring a gun?" Hector growled. "Typical THIRDS pig."

"It's for my protection, Hector. You tried to shoot me tonight, remember?" Calvin slowly lowered his arms, his gaze never moving from Hector. The guy was sweating and fidgeting. He looked to be in his early twenties. Something told Calvin Hector wasn't as self-assured as he made himself out to be.

"I ain't saying nothing."

"You put one of my friends in the hospital," Calvin said, his voice calm. "A really good guy who does a lot for this city. I know you saw an opportunity. A room full of THIRDS agents, me being one of them. But they're more than that, Hector. They have families like you. You had a room full of Humans and Therians who fight to keep this city safe."

"Like you kept my uncle safe?"

"He left me no choice, Hector. He killed someone and injured two others. Yes, he had every right to be upset for what they did to him, but that didn't give him the right to take someone's life. We tried to get through to him. We did. But he was too distraught to listen. He was going to shoot someone. I couldn't let that happen. I don't want to shoot you, Hector. Please, you have to believe that."

Hector let out a scoff. "What makes you think I won't shoot him or you first?"

"Because this is what I do. It's what I'm trained for. You'll never see it coming. You'll be dead before you get a shot off. Is that what you want, Hector? Do you really want to put your aunt through that after all she's suffered?" Hector was unsure. Whatever had happened at Dekatria, Calvin was certain Hector had help, someone to push him into the decision, perhaps from his friends. It was easier to set something into motion when you had your friends backing you up. The THIRDS would get to the bottom of it. Right now Calvin would do his best to give Hector a second chance.

"Shut up! Don't bring my aunt into this."

"She's still mourning your uncle's death. Do you want to add yours to her grief?"

Hector swallowed hard, and Calvin continued, hoping he could get through to the angry young Therian. If Hector had really wanted to shoot Calvin, he would have done it by now.

"Think about your family. They're suffering, in pain. Think about your little cousin. She needs you, Hector. She needs all of you right now."

"Stop!" Hector shook his head, tears in his eyes. "You're trying to manipulate me so I don't shoot."

"I'm trying to save your family from another loss," Calvin replied sincerely. "They don't deserve that."

"My uncle didn't deserve to die!"

"You're right. He didn't. But he made a choice. He hurt his family. Is that the choice you want to make here today, Hector? Because you have a choice. The same one he did."

"You think I'm gonna punk out?"

Calvin shook his head. "No one who makes a sacrifice for their family is punking out. Think about it. Really think. Is the chance that you might get a shot off worth the pain you'll cause your family? Worth your life?"

Hector pressed his lips together. His face and eyes were red. He looked tired, like he hadn't slept in days. The seconds ticked past as Hector thought about his next move. His eyes darted around the place, at the hostages on the floor, some crying softly, others rightfully terrified. Hector turned his attention back to Calvin. "How do I know you won't shoot me?"

Calvin kept his eyes on Hector as he lowered his gun to the floor. He stood slowly, hands out in front of him, and kicked his gun to one side. "Now it's your turn."

Hector hesitated, and for a split second Calvin thought he might back out. Instead he slowly lowered his gun to the floor. He stood and kicked it over. Letty, Ash, and Rafe rushed out, guns in hand.

"Get on the floor now!" Ash shouted as they rushed him. Hector dropped onto his stomach and put his hands behind his head. Ash and Rafe restrained him while Letty secured his wrists with Therian-strength zip ties. Calvin approached as they dragged Hector to his feet. He stopped in front of him.

"I know it might not seem like it, but you made the right choice. Tell your family you made a mistake and you're sorry. You all need each other."

Hector let his head hang before giving Calvin a nod. Teams of agents rushed in as Ash and Rafe escorted Hector out of the hospital to one of the awaiting BearCats. It was over. For now at least.

Sloane stood beside Calvin and smiled at him. "Good job, Cal. You did real good."

"Thanks. I'm glad no one was hurt."

"It's been one hell of a long night. Why don't you and Hobbs head home. We'll finish up here. You can write your report in the morning."

"Thanks, man." Calvin wasn't about to turn down Sloane's offer. He was exhausted. The place was crawling with agents, and the EMTs were checking on the hostages. As tired as Calvin was, all he wanted to do was get Ethan home. Ethan had been on the verge of a bad panic attack before the shootout. He needed to make sure Ethan was all right.

Calvin dropped off the vest and gun with Riviera, thanking him before letting the rest of his team know he'd see them bright and early Monday morning. Tomorrow was Sunday, so he could just fill out his report from the comfort of his living room while in his pajamas. He smiled at Ethan and motioned toward the door.

"Let's go home."

Ethan smiled widely and followed him out. They headed for the parking garage and Calvin's Jeep on the second floor. Ethan was quiet, and Calvin knew it was exhaustion finally setting in. Ethan had been through a lot today. The party itself had been draining enough, but with his brothers, what happened to Hudson, and his panic attack, Ethan would be feeling it soon.

When they got home, Ethan disappeared into his room. Calvin let him go. In the meantime, he got a nice hot bath ready in their Therian-sized bathtub. He added scented bath salts and lit a few candles before turning on the small bathroom radio to some soft tunes. In his bedroom he undressed, hanging up his clothes behind the door. He wrapped a towel around his waist, then walked to Ethan's bedroom. His boyfriend was most likely going over everything that had happened tonight, wondering if he could have done something different. His anxiety would be trying to get the better of him, and he'd be worried about what everyone else might be thinking of him.

Calvin knocked, smiling warmly after Ethan hesitantly opened the door. He held his hand out to Ethan.

"I could use a nice warm bath to unwind in. Join me?"

"Okay."

Ethan quickly finished undressing and took Calvin's hand. They walked into the bathroom, where the bath was nice and full. Ethan was going to get in first when Calvin stopped him. He tossed his towel and turned to Ethan.

"Let me take care of you."

Ethan's expression softened, and he put his hand to Calvin's cheek. "You always take care of me."

"That's not going to change, Ethan." He stood on his toes and kissed Ethan, loving the feel of Ethan slipping his arms around him, pulling him close against his hard naked body. Before things could get heavy, Calvin stepped back. He smiled at Ethan before climbing into the tub and sitting back. "Come on. Before the water gets cold."

Ethan climbed in and carefully sat. Even though their tub was Therian-sized, with both of them Ethan had to bend his knees, and they stuck out of the water as he slid down so he and Calvin were chest to back. Calvin took the shampoo and washed Ethan's hair, telling him to close his eyes and relax. Ethan had done the same for him over Valentine's Day, and now it was Calvin's turn. The soft sigh Ethan let out squeezed at Calvin's heart. It scared him a little how much he loved Ethan, especially since that love would only grow with time.

Calvin rinsed Ethan's hair, using the tips of his fingers to massage his scalp. Then he poured shower gel into Ethan's pouf and soaped him up, using his hands to caress Ethan's body as he washed him. He slowed down, taking his time as his fingers explored Ethan's skin, his sculpted muscles and firm abdomen. He moved his hand lower until he had Ethan's half-hard cock in his grip. Leisurely he stroked Ethan, smiling when Ethan let his head rest back against Calvin's shoulder.

"I love you," Ethan said softly.

Calvin turned his head and kissed Ethan's lips, savoring the taste of him. There was no telling what the future might hold for them, so Calvin would make it a point to cherish what he had while he had it. He'd never been much of a dreamer, always focused on goals and what he could do to achieve them. Life had taught him not to take anything for granted, and he had no intention of starting now, especially with Ethan in his arms.

"I love you too," Calvin replied, pulling away to smile down at Ethan before kissing him again. Never in a million years would he have imagined having what he had with Ethan. Deepening his kiss, he stroked Ethan's cock, quickening his pace just enough to make Ethan moan. They kissed for what seemed like ages but wasn't really. The water was still warm. Calvin picked up his pace. This was about Ethan and making him feel good.

Ethan arched his back, a shuddered sigh escaping him as Calvin tweaked one of Ethan's nipples. His skin was flushed, his breath coming out quicker. His fingers dug into Calvin's thighs as he thrust his hips against Calvin's hands.

"Cal…."

"It's okay," Calvin murmured, kissing the side of Ethan's head.

Ethan groaned, his muscles tensing as he came. A shiver went through him, and Calvin rained kisses up the side of Ethan's head.

"I got you."

Ethan stood and turned. He climbed out of the tub and held his hand out to help Calvin. He followed Ethan without question, his heart skipping a beat as Ethan dried them off before leading Calvin to his bedroom. He closed the door and pulled Calvin against him, kissing him with a passion Calvin hadn't known Ethan possessed. It curled Calvin's toes and sent the most amazing shiver up his spine. He stood there, floating on a cloud as Ethan stepped away to turn down the bed, then the lights. He took Calvin's hand, and like every other time in their lives, Calvin followed Ethan blindly and willingly. They climbed into bed and huddled close together, their limbs intertwined. Calvin paid close attention to Ethan's signals. Whatever his boyfriend needed. Ethan rolled Calvin onto his back, mindful of his weight. He was always so attentive, so careful with Calvin.

Ethan's expression turned troubled, and Calvin ran a thumb across Ethan's bottom lip.

"Talk to me."

"I could have lost you tonight."

"But you didn't," Calvin said gently. "I know this is going to be hard for us. All these close calls, the job, but we can't let our fears come between us. I want to see where this takes us, Ethan." He felt his cheeks grow warm, and he was having trouble looking directly at Ethan. "I can see us, I don't know, growing old together. Complaining how music isn't what it used to be."

Ethan took hold of his chin and turned his face so he could look him in the eye. He smiled warmly. "I'd love nothing more than that." He plucked at a lock of Calvin's hair. "I think I see some gray already."

"Fuck off," Calvin said with a laugh, smacking his hand away. "You're going to get gray hair before me because that shit's hereditary. Look at Rafe and Seb."

Ethan narrowed his eyes. "Yeah, all right Mr. Smarty-Pants."

Calvin chuckled. He planted a kiss on Ethan's chin, then his jawline. "I think it'll just make you look even sexier."

"Yeah?"

"Mm-hm. My sexy silver fox. Or silver tiger, rather."

Ethan pressed his lips to Calvin's, and Calvin opened his mouth, inviting Ethan to slip his tongue inside. He'd never grow tired of this. He loved the feel of Ethan's heavier weight on him, of Ethan's warm breath against his skin, the way Calvin felt loved and needed. Ethan had always needed him, but now things were a little different. Being loved by Ethan, being in his arms was more than he could have hoped for.

CALVIN WAS startled awake in the middle of the night by Ethan's cell phone buzzing away. It took a moment for the sleepy haze to pass. He sat up and groaned. He was sore from their sex earlier. The thought brought a smile to his face. Ethan had been sweet and gentle, and then he'd rocked Calvin's socks off. The phone continued to buzz from the nightstand. Who would be calling at this time of night? *Shit. What if it was Thomas or Seb? He grabbed Ethan's smartphone, frowning when he saw Letty's picture and number on the screen. Ethan was fast asleep, so Calvin answered for him. It wasn't like they didn't often answer each other's phones.*

"Hey, Letty, it's Cal. Everything okay?"

"Cal, thank God. I tried calling your phone, but you didn't pick up."

Calvin hadn't expected Letty's unsteady voice. "Shit, sorry, I left it in my room. I'm, uh, not there right now. Is everything okay? What's wrong?"

"You and Hobbs need to get over to Dex's house right now."

Calvin jumped out of bed. "What happened?" *He gently nudged Ethan until he stirred awake.* "Are Dex and Sloane okay?"

"Just get over here."

"On our way." *Calvin hung up as Ethan sat up, his expression both sleepy and puzzled.* "We have to go to Dex's. Something's wrong. Letty sounded worried."

Ethan scrambled out of bed, and they both quickly dressed. Nothing ever rattled Letty. Whatever it was, it was serious. The fact she wouldn't tell him over the phone didn't bode well.

As soon as they were dressed, they put on their shoes, and Calvin grabbed his jacket and keys. They locked up and ran downstairs to the Jeep parked at the curb. Shit, it was almost four o'clock in the morning.

What the hell was going on? Luckily there was very little traffic at this time, and Calvin sped through the streets trying to get them to Dex's as quickly yet safely as possible. Ethan was quiet, undoubtedly worried for their friends. Calvin was too. Had Sloane lost control of his Therian form again? That seemed to have stopped after the whole mess with the medication had been cleared up.

In ten minutes they were at Dex's house. They climbed out of the car and ran up the front steps, where they knocked on the door. Letty answered and stood to one side as they went in. Calvin stopped so suddenly Ethan almost ran into him. The living room had been ransacked. Cushions were torn and scattered around, with the stuffing strewn all over. The shelves were bare, their content strewn all over the floor. Even the furniture had been turned upside down. The rest of the house looked to be in just as bad a state. Cael looked beside himself, and Sloane was pacing while Ash tried to calm him.

"How can I calm down? He's gone, Ash!"

"What's going on?" Calvin asked.

"Dex is gone," Sloane replied, his hands going to his head. "I can't believe this. Look at this place."

Wait, that couldn't be right. Calvin walked over to Cael. "What do you mean he's gone? Gone where?"

"We don't know," Cael replied worriedly. "Sloane woke up, and Dex was gone."

"Something's wrong." Sloane ran a hand through his hair. "I can feel it. In my gut, deep down, like… I just know he's in trouble. God, what if he's hurt or…." Sloane shook his head as Ash grabbed hold of his shoulders.

"Stop. We'll find him. Whatever's going on, we'll figure it out."

"Did you see the guys who did this?" Calvin asked. He didn't dare touch anything. This whole place had just become a crime scene.

Sloane took a deep breath and released it slowly. "That's what's most fucked-up about this. I didn't hear a thing." His eyes grew glassy, and he breathed in once again. "I didn't even feel it when they took him out of our bed. He was in my arms." Sloane blinked away his tears, anger swiftly taking over. "How is that possible?"

Rosa stepped up to Sloane, looking him over. "My guess is someone injected you with something. How else would they be able to do all this without you waking up?" She inspected his fingers, his arms, then neck, before she motioned for him to lean in. Gently turning his head, she checked behind his ear and cursed under her breath. "They injected you with something."

Calvin wasn't sure what scared the shit out of him more, someone managing to get close enough to Sloane to inject him with something without him knowing it, or the feral gleam in Sloane's amber eyes.

"They took him from my arms, and I didn't feel a goddamn thing. When I get my hands on whoever did this, they're going to regret ever stepping foot in this house."

"You're going to have to find them first."

Everyone spun around to find Sparks at the front door. She was dressed in a black leather catsuit with a host of weapons tucked in her thigh rig and utility belt. Was that a crossbow attached to her back?

"What did you do?" Sloane growled as he stormed over to Sparks. "You had something to do with this, didn't you?"

Sparks serenely walked past Sloane and into the living room, then took a seat on the coffee table. "I had hoped to be further along in his training before this happened, but unfortunately, the timeline seems to have been moved up."

"What are you talking about?" Sloane demanded. "Where's Dex?"

"I don't know."

Calvin tapped Ethan, letting him know to be ready in case they needed to subdue Sloane. Their team leader's amber eyes were blazing with fury. He knew his mate was in danger. There was no telling what Sloane might do.

Sloane marched over to Sparks and threw out a hand, his fingers closing around her neck. Calvin swallowed hard and waited. He prayed this didn't get ugly. As pissed off as Sloane was, they all knew Sparks wasn't to be messed with.

"Don't lie to me!"

"If I knew, I would tell you. Dex has been taken. I don't know where or by whom exactly."

"Exactly? What does that mean? I swear, if you don't start giving us some fucking answers, I don't give a shit who you are or who you work for, I'm going to start causing you some pain," Sloane demanded.

Sparks looked up at Sloane as if she were searching for something. Everyone waited with bated breath until Sparks finally spoke up.

"Dex was taken by those responsible for his parents' murder."

Calvin stood stunned. The rest of his team was no better off. How was that possible?

"Wait, what?" Calvin shook his head. "Dex's parents weren't murdered. They were caught in a shooting that broke out in the movie theater they were at during their date night. Right?" That's what Dex had told him. Would Dex have lied? No, Dex wouldn't have lied about something like that.

Sparks tapped Sloane's hand, and reluctantly Sloane released her.

"That's what everyone has been led to believe, but the truth is, Gina and John Daley were there to meet with someone. Before the meeting could take place, they were killed."

Cael sank down onto the floor across from Sparks. "I can't believe this. They were murdered?"

None of this made any sense to Calvin. "Why would they take Dex now? I mean, his parents were killed when he was just a little kid."

"That's a good question. We believe Gina Daley had something in her possession before she was killed. Something important. It was possible she was going to pass this information on to whoever she was meeting. However, there was nothing on her at the time of her death."

"That doesn't answer why now," Ash said. "Why, after all these years, are they making a move on Dex now?"

"We'll have to ask Shultzon."

Sloane threw his hands up. "What the hell does Shultzon have to do with any of this?"

Sparks stood, her steel blue eyes meeting Sloane's. "Shultzon is the one who ordered the hit on Dex's parents."

An icy chill went up Calvin's spine. He couldn't believe what he was hearing. And here he'd hoped they'd heard the last of that son of a bitch. Ethan grabbed Calvin's hand and squeezed. The entire room was silent.

"I hope your team is ready, Sloane," Sparks said as she headed for the door. "You're going to have to be if you want to get Dex back alive."

KEEP READING FOR AN EXCERPT FROM

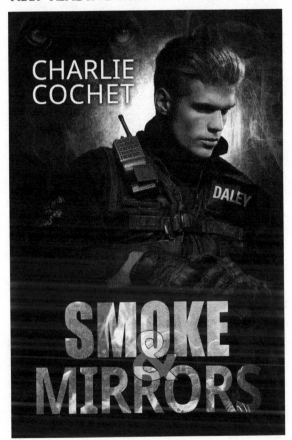

CHARLIE
COCHET

DALEY

SMOKE
&
MIRRORS

Sequel to *Catch a Tiger by the Tail*
THIRDS: Book Seven

Life for Dexter J. Daley has never been easy, but he's always found a way to pick himself back up with a smile on his face. Taken from his home and the arms of Sloane Brodie, his boyfriend and THIRDS partner, Dex finds himself in a situation as mysterious and lethal as the Therian interrogating him. Dex learns what he's secretly believed all along: his parents' death wasn't an accident.

Discovering the whole truth about John and Gina Daley's homicide sets off a series of events that will change Dex and Sloane's life forever. As buried secrets rise to the surface and new truths are revealed, Dex and Sloane's love for each other is put to the test, with more than their relationship on the line. If traversing the waters of murder and secret government agencies wasn't enough, something inexplicable has been happening to Dex—and nothing will ever be the same.

Chapter 1

SOUND EXPLODED in Dex's ears. His head throbbed and his face hurt. He tasted blood, and his body didn't feel like his own as he struggled through the lethargy. His limbs felt heavy, like he was swimming in molasses. With a groan, he forced his eyes open. It was dark save for the halo of light floating somewhere above his head. Where was he? The last thing he remembered was Sloane's strong arms around him, wrapping him up in warmth, holding him close. Sloane had nuzzled his face in Dex's hair, then kissed him good night, followed by a soft "I love you."

Sloane....

Dex bolted upright, a gasp caught in his throat as he surfaced through the haze. His eyes widened, and his heart beat furiously as he realized his wrists and ankles were zip-tied to a chair.

"What the hell is this?" He looked up and reeled from the stabbing white light. It seared his vision, and he shut his eyes tight for several seconds. A halo was all he could see before he was finally able to focus on the stretch of nothingness around him. Shadows surrounded him on all sides, the only light coming from the lamp hanging over his head. "Hello?" It struck him then.

They'd taken him from his home.

Oh God, where was Sloane? His blood ran cold, and he jerked against the restraints. "Somebody answer me!"

"You're awake. Good."

Dex froze. He peered into the shadows and could just about make out an outline, along with the glow of eyes. A Therian.

"Who are you? What is this?" Dex demanded, his voice hoarse from his dry throat. It was like his mouth was full of cotton. Most likely a result from whatever they'd given him to knock him out. He did his best to ignore the queasy feeling in the pit of his stomach. Someone had broken into his house and taken him from his boyfriend's arms. He had no idea where Sloane was or the condition he was in. Was he hurt... or worse? *Please let him be okay.*

"I'll be the one asking the questions here, Agent Daley."

"Where's Sloane?"

A tall wolf Therian in an expensive gray suit emerged from the shadows. "Looking for you, I imagine. I don't really care. My interest lies with you, not Sloane Brodie."

Dex had expected a thug or a raging psychopath. The Therian before him didn't appear to be either, but appearances could be deceiving. Refined, smooth, chiseled jaw, and handsome, with rich black hair neatly styled, he looked to be in his late thirties, maybe early forties. The Therian cocked his head to one side, his sharp gray eyes studying Dex. He seemed to come to some kind of conclusion and pulled a chair out from the darkness to place in front of Dex.

Dex studied his adversary, noting how nonchalantly he unbuttoned his tailored suit jacket and took a seat. He crossed one leg over the other and placed his laced fingers over one knee, as if he were about to have an informal business chat.

"Where is it?" he asked smoothly.

"Why do you spooks always start with such cryptic questions?" Dex frowned down at himself. "Why am I in a suit?" He was pretty sure he'd gone to bed in a T-shirt and pajama bottoms. The suit was tailored to fit. Everything from the black dress pants to the pristine white button-down shirt to the black jacket fit like a glove. Even his shoes hugged his feet comfortably. "How do you know my shoe size?"

"I know everything about you."

Dex glanced around the room. There were no cameras, windows, nothing but the bare concrete floor and walls. "Why?"

"Where is the file?"

"Why the tie?" This was bizarre. Someone had painstakingly fixed a tie around his neck while he'd been unconscious. Who kidnapped people and dressed them up in fancy clothes?

"Answer the question."

"How about we start small," Dex offered. "What do I call you?" He needed to figure a way out of this. There had to be a door somewhere behind the Therian. The guy hadn't just materialized out of thin air. Of course, first Dex would have to get himself out of the chair. It was steel and bolted to the floor.

"Don't act cute with me, Agent Daley." The wolf Therian smiled pleasantly. "And you can call me Mr. Wolf."

Mr. Wolf. Right. "Now who's being cute?"

Wolf chuckled. "I do appreciate a man with a good sense of humor. You're very charming." He looked Dex over and smiled warmly. "You're taller than I imagined, and your photo hardly does you justice. You're far more handsome in person." He motioned to his own eyes. "Beautiful color. Absolutely stunning."

Dex leaned forward, his lips curling up wickedly. "You trying to get information out of me or date me?"

Wolf chuckled. "I can see you're going to be a handful. All right, Agent Daley—May I call you Dex? Agent seems so formal."

"Sure."

"Dex, your little 'I'm just a ditzy blond' act isn't going to fly with me. I know perfectly well who you are and what you're capable of."

Dex sat back with a smile. "Do you now? FYI, I'm more of a *dirty* blond."

Wolf arched an eyebrow at him. The man wasn't quite sure what to make of Dex. Despite Wolf's calm and nonthreatening demeanor, something in his eyes warned Dex to tread lightly.

Wolf cleared his throat before continuing. "Dexter Justice Daley, born August 18, 1980. Only child to Gina and John Daley. Adopted by Anthony Maddock. Adopted brother, Cael Maddock. You were an HPF officer before becoming a detective like your father before you. Then you testified against your partner for shooting an unarmed Therian youth in the back. Your boyfriend at the time, Louis Huerta, walked out on you.

"You were hired by the THIRDS and appointed a Defense agent for Unit Alpha's Destructive Delta. Your team leader is Sloane Brodie, a First Gen jaguar Therian who spent the majority of his youth in the First Gen Research Facility being prodded and poked like a lab rat. You've been together for a year and roughly two and a half months—he had a few commitment issues to work out. This month he moved in with you. He thinks you need to eat healthier, and he's correct. You consume copious amounts of caffeine, sugar, and red meat, have a somewhat unusual obsession with the eighties, and enjoy karaoke. Have I left anything out?"

Who was this guy, and how did he know so much? Dex smiled widely. "Yeah, I love dancing, sadly can't hold my liquor, and give great head."

Wolf's eyebrows shot up before his expression returned to its previous impassive state. He shifted in his chair, and Dex held back a grin. He could use this. Dex held Wolf's gaze.

"Did you know I can make my boyfriend purr in Human form? And I don't mean figuratively. I mean, I can literally make him purr."

Wolf peered at him before brushing some nonexistent lint from his suit jacket. "Not possible."

"Oh, but it is," Dex replied, his voice low and husky. "I'm good with my mouth."

Wolf smoothed down his tie before meeting Dex's gaze. He carried on as if he hadn't heard Dex. "I know you would risk everything for your loved ones. Your career, your heart, your life. You have a fierce sense of justice. I know at this very moment you're considering your options and how you can get out of that chair. Those are Therian-strength zip ties, Dex. You won't be going anywhere, and unlike most, I won't underestimate you. You're quite good at discovering your opponent's vulnerabilities. Fortunately for me, I have none. I know you play the fool, act the class clown, hiding who you really are."

Dex cocked his head to one side and smiled. "And who's that?"

"A very dangerous man."

Here he was tied to a chair, and *he* was dangerous? "That's funny."

Wolf stood and shoved his hands into his pockets. "It is funny, because even you don't realize it." He leaned forward, his gaze holding Dex's. "Others may not see it, but I do. There's darkness lurking behind those pale blue eyes. You never did quite recover from your parents' murder."

Dex opened his mouth to reply when the words sank in. His gut twisted. *No. Absolutely not.* "My parents weren't murdered. They were killed in a shoot-out. Wrong place, wrong time."

Wolf moved his chair closer to Dex and sat. "You didn't believe it then, and you don't believe it now. It may be what you were told, what you *wanted* to believe, but deep down inside, you know the truth you buried long ago."

"What do you know about my parents?" Why was he asking? It wasn't as if he could trust Wolf. For all he knew the guy was making shit up to rattle him, to make him talk.

"Do forgive me. I seem to have deviated from my intended path." Wolf let out a pleasant laugh, as if he were conversing with a friend. "You're very easy to talk to. Let's try a different approach. Gina Daley was killed for interfering in business that was no concern of hers. Sadly, she dragged your father into it. I want the file she had in her possession the night she was killed."

Dex closed his eyes, suddenly nauseated. He needed the room to stop spinning and his stomach to stop turning over. Wolf was right. Deep down, he'd always known, but this... this was just too much. All these years he'd tried denying the fact there might be more to his parents' deaths than mere coincidence, but he'd never delved deeper. He'd been scared to. Afraid of what he'd find. To him, his parents had been two regular people who'd loved him very much and who'd been taken from him far too early in life. He'd wanted to preserve their memory. Dex opened his eyes and took a deep breath. There was no running from it now. He needed answers.

"It's been almost thirty years. Why are you looking for this file now?"

"That information is inconsequential. I would very much like that file."

"If there is a file, I don't know where it is," Dex replied truthfully. "This is the first I'm hearing about it. If you've been watching me, studying me, you'd know that."

Wolf stood and removed his suit jacket in no particular hurry. He took hold of his chair, placed it to one side, and draped his jacket across the backrest. Dex observed him, the way he moved, how he smiled warmly as he removed the cuff links from his sleeve cuffs. Once he'd slipped the cuff links into his jacket pocket, he rolled up his sleeves. Not in a half-assed way either. He wasn't in any kind of rush. The fabric was folded meticulously. First one sleeve, then the other. From his pants pocket he pulled out a pair of black gloves and slipped them on.

"I hear you have quite the pain threshold."

Dex sat up straight and rolled his shoulders. His heart raced, and his muscles tensed. He subtly closed his hands into fists to keep Wolf from seeing them shake. When he spoke, he made certain his tone gave away nothing of the fear shooting through him. "Moving on to the kinky stuff already. That's not really my scene, but whatever floats your boat."

With a chuckle, Wolf stepped in between Dex's knees. He took hold of Dex's chin, his smile turning apologetic. "Forgive me, but I'm going to have to bruise this pretty face of yours. I hoped to avoid it, but you've left me no choice. It's nothing personal."

Dex shrugged. He wouldn't give Wolf the satisfaction of knowing he was scared. No point in him losing his shit. Wolf wasn't like anyone he'd faced before. He was a professional given a job to do, a job he took pride in. The steel of his gray eyes told Dex all he needed to know. There would be no mercy coming from Wolf. Any and all pain inflicted on Dex was of his own making for not cooperating.

"Just part of the job description. I get it."

"Thank you for being so understanding." Wolf ran his thumb over Dex's bottom lip. "I like you, Dex. In fact, I like you so much I'm going to start small."

"That's really kind of you." He swallowed hard, his eyes never leaving Wolf's.

"I know," Wolf replied sincerely. "Now brace yourself."

Dex nodded. He clenched his jaw and inhaled deeply through his nose, his fists balled so tight his knuckles were white. *Think of home.*

The first blow had him seeing stars. For all of Mr. Wolf's sophisticated charms, he was a Therian, and one skilled in the art of causing pain. That much was evident right away. Wolf also managed to inflict damage without incapacitating. After all, if he wanted information out of his prisoner, a method of communication was key. The most intriguing part was how Wolf managed to beat the shit out of Dex while keeping himself looking impeccable. Even with Dex's blood splattered over his white shirt, he looked elegant. Dex would have commended him if he could talk.

The worst of it wasn't the blows to the face, the split lip and brow, the throbbing, or even the taste of his own blood inside his mouth as well as the blood trickling down from his nose. It was the fiery concoction that must have been brewed with the devil's piss, because it burned like a son of a bitch when Wolf applied it to one of Dex's open wounds. It scorched his flesh, and when Wolf applied it to Dex's brow, he cried out. Tears pooled in his eyes from the sting, but he quickly blinked them away and gritted his teeth, pushing through the pain. His heart was pounding, and he jerked in his seat, sucking in gulps of air. Jesus, it burned.

"I know," Wolf cooed. "I'm so sorry."

He pressed his lips to Dex's. It was brief but gentle, startling Dex. He tugged at his arm, instinct propelling him to punch Wolf in the face, but all that did was send more pain up his arm.

"Shhh, it's okay." Wolf wiped Dex's blood from his lips with his thumb before he ran a hand over Dex's head, soothing him. "Please. You can make this stop. Just tell me what I want to know." He crouched down between Dex's knees and slid his hands to Dex's thighs, then to his hips. Wolf's dark brows were drawn together, his lips pulled down in a frown. "I'm really not enjoying this. You're a good man, Dex. I don't like hurting good men."

"You could stop," Dex said with a shaky laugh that verged on a sob, but he pushed past it. His vision was growing blurry again, and he shut his eyes tight. For weeks his eyes had been bugging him, itching, blurring, and until recently it had been a minor inconvenience. He'd put it down to fatigue, but Sloane had been worried, so Dex promised he'd make an appointment with the eye doctor. He wished he'd done it sooner. Now was not the time for his vision to be giving him problems.

"I wish I could, but I have a job to do, and once I give my word, I follow through. Dex, please. Help me help you."

Dex gazed down at Wolf, his voice a low growl. "You know what? Fuck you. At this point, even if I had the goddamn thing, I wouldn't give it to you."

"Such language." Wolf tsked.

Dex let out a laugh. "Well, get used to it, Buttercup, because it just gets prettier from here on out."

"I was afraid it would come to this." Wolf stood and leaned in, pressing his cheek to Dex's as he slipped one hand around the back of his head. He murmured softly as he stroked Dex's hair. "I'm going to ask you one more time. Where is the file Gina Daley had in her possession the day she died?"

When Dex didn't reply, he received a punch to the kidney. *Fuck.* At this rate he'd be pissing blood for a week. If he survived.

"All right." Wolf straightened and released a sigh. "Just remember, you brought this on yourself." He slipped into the shadows and returned with a long, narrow wrap of dark leather. After moving his chair closer to Dex, he pulled the ties loose and unrolled the leather on the chair's seat. Dex's jaw muscles tightened at the neat row of long, fine needles. They looked like the kind acupuncturists used. Dex twisted his wrists, the sweat on his skin only allowing for minimal movement, not enough for him to free himself.

Gently, Wolf took hold of Dex's left hand and bent to give his fingers a kiss before taking hold of his middle finger. Dex's body betrayed him, trembling under Wolf's touch in anticipation of the pain. Nothing he'd experienced before could prepare him. All he could do was endure. Pray he could somehow find a way to get out of this. To survive. Wolf slipped one of the needles out, crouched down in front of Dex, and placed the tip under Dex's fingernail. Wolf's steel-gray eyes met Dex's. "This is going to hurt a great deal. It's all right to scream. Again, you've left me no choice."

Dex's eyes watered as Wolf began to push the needle in. His heartbeat skyrocketed, and he jerked against the restraints. *Oh God....* He'd endured a hell of a lot in his life, in his career at the HPF and then the THIRDS, but never anything like this. He focused on his breathing, on finding a safe place inside his head. *Sloane....*

The needle plunged deeper, and Dex jolted, a strangled cry torn from his lips. He pushed against the floor with his feet, jerked his arms, and twisted his body in an attempt to get away from the agonizing pain, but nothing he did would ease his suffering.

"This is just the beginning, Dex," Wolf assured him softly. "I *will* break you."

"Fuck you," Dex spat. Sweat beaded his brow, and his fingers shook. It was only going to get worse. With a sigh, Wolf moved on to the next finger, and Dex closed his eyes, his muscles straining and sweat dripping down the side of his face as the second needle was pushed in under his fingernail. Sometime between the third and fourth needle, everything went black.

"Stop! Stop, I can't take anymore!"

Tears ran down Dex's cheeks. His face hurt from laughing so hard.

"You give up?"

Sloane's smile brought little creases to the corners of his amber eyes, making Dex's heart skip a beat. He was so damned beautiful. New silver strands had appeared in his beard and at his temples, adding to his sex appeal. Sloane was one of those guys who grew even more gorgeous with age, and Dex's heart swelled at the thought of growing old with the man he loved.

Those amber eyes had been filled with so much pain not long ago, and now they lit up with affection and laughter. With every passing day, despite the darkness they sometimes encountered on the job, Dex witnessed Sloane embrace the growing lightheartedness within him. It was their day off, and they'd been too tired to go out, so they decided to lounge around the house reading, watching TV, eating, and cuddling. In the afternoon they'd made love, then took a nap. Dex had never been happier.

"I give up," Dex said with a husky laugh, drawing his knees up and pressing them to Sloane's hips. "I'm tickled out. I'll eat the rabbit food."

Sloane planted his elbows on either side of Dex's head, his eyes bright with laughter. "Am I going to have to tackle you every time I ask you to try a new vegetable dish?"

"If I'm going to start gnawing on bark, I should get something out of it."

Sloane laughed. "You are getting something out of it. Good health."

"But why does healthy food have to taste like boiled grass?"

"Hey, my veggie dishes do not taste like boiled grass." Sloane's expression softened, he stroked Dex's hair. "Do you know why I'm always trying to get you to eat healthy?"

"Because eventually I have to be a grown-up and realize gummy bears are not one of the four basic food groups? Even though they should be. I mean, some are green, right? Like vegetables."

"That's not why." Sloane lowered himself onto Dex, mindful of his weight. He held Dex close and planted a tender kiss on his brow. "Because I want you to live a long life. I want to have you with me as long as possible."

Dex blinked up at him, surprised by Sloane's heartfelt confession. "Really?"

"Yes, really."

Sloane kissed Dex's lips, a soft, lazy kiss that had Dex letting out a sigh. He was so madly in love with this man.

"Are you trying to guilt me into eating healthier?" Dex teased, nuzzling Sloane's neck.

Sloane's rumble of a chuckle sent a delicious shiver through Dex. "Maybe a little."

"You're evil."

"I know." Sloane nibbled on Dex's earlobe before whispering in his ear. "Time to wake up, babe."

"What?"

"Wake up, Dex."

Dex snapped his eyes open, and his body shrieked with pain. A jolt went through him, and he cried out. His cheeks were wet from tears, his fingertips bloodied and throbbing, his hands shaking. His body was like one giant nerve ending, exposed and in agony. He started to shiver horribly. He was cold, his skin crawled, and sweat dripped down his face. Inside his blood boiled, and he was having trouble breathing. Swallowing past the bile in his throat, he glanced down at the five needles sticking out from under his fingernails on his left hand. His right hand had another two. Oh God, why the hell had he looked?

"Were you dreaming of him?" Wolf asked serenely as he began to slowly remove the needles one by one.

Jesus, what now? Please don't let me throw up. Please. Wolf sat in the chair again, the wrap of needles now on the floor by his pristinely shined shoes.

"It sounded like a good dream. Your man's quite something, isn't he? Despite his time in the First Gen Research Facility, he's managed to lead a relatively normal life. Friends, love, a successful career? Not everyone who survived was so lucky. Granted, he wasn't able to leave the demons behind, but it would seem he's learned how to cope with the darkness inside of him. How are the nightmares, by the way? Better? I think they're better now that he has you at his side." Wolf's smile faded, his expression becoming troubled. "He's lived through so much pain. I hate to think what would become of him if you were torn from his life."

Dex didn't reply. He was pretty sure Wolf could see the loathing in his eyes.

"I know what you're thinking," Wolf said with a sigh. "What kind of person feels nothing when bringing another so much pain?" He dropped the last needle onto the floor by his chair.

What time was it? Better yet, what *day* was it? How long had they been at this? Dex had lost track of how many times he'd passed out. Wolf liked to change things up. He'd alternate between the needles to his fingernails and the ones to various pressure points around his body, to beating the shit out of him one vital organ at a time. His body was bruised inside and out, his skin was caked in blood, and his left eye was all but swollen shut. Dex groaned, feeling his empty stomach lurching. He reeked of sweat, blood, and bodily fluids he couldn't give a second thought to or he'd retch. Fuck, was Wolf still talking?

"I feel no remorse, take no pleasure in what I do. Breaking you is akin to picking up a gallon of milk at the grocery store or doing my laundry." Wolf shrugged. "It's a talent I suppose. Perhaps a rather unorthodox one, but a talent nonetheless."

"Well, that's nice," Dex muttered, feeling his eyelids growing heavy. It was easier to give in to the darkness. It didn't hurt there, and he could dream about being in Sloane's arms. He tugged at his wrists and his ankles. Nothing. Maybe if he took a short nap, tried to regain his strength....

"I'm sorry, Dex, but I'm going to need you to stay awake a little longer." Wolf stood and reached into his jacket pocket—Mary Poppins's pocket apparently— and pulled out a syringe with a clear liquid.

Fuck me, seriously?

Dex wavered on the edge of the abyss, slightly aware of his head being gently tilted to the side, his hair stroked absently before he felt the tiniest prick to his neck. One minute he was ready to surrender to the encroaching blackness, and the next he feared his heart would explode. He gasped for air and twisted in his seat, his muscles straining as he pulled. Tears welled in his swollen eyes as his senses sharpened. Every dull ache and throb flared into a shrilling agony. His eye-sight sharpened, and his breath came out in pants.

"Fuck!" Dex blinked a few times before shutting his eyes tight. Everything was so bright. Even the shadows seemed to fade. "What did you give me?"

"Just a little concoction of mine. Not at all dissimilar to Therian epinephrine. The dose was lower, of course. I don't want your Human heart to give out on me."

Dex squinted and tried to open his eyes again. It still hurt, but he was stunned that he could see all the way across the room to the closed door, as if someone had turned up a dimmer switch. There was a steel table next to the door Dex hadn't seen before because it had been too dark. On it was a pitcher of water and a stack of plastic cups. Whatever Wolf had given him seemed to clear his vision enough to see past the shadows.

"You continue to surprise me, Dex." Wolf shook his head. "Would you like some water before we move on?"

Dex nodded. At least Wolf was keeping him hydrated. He placed the plastic cup of cool water to Dex's lips and helped him drink. When he was done, Wolf smiled at him before returning the cup to the table across the room.

"As much as I'm enjoying your company, Dex, we're going to have to hurry this along." Wolf came to stand before him. "Your boyfriend or your brother?"

Dex stared at him. "What?"

Wolf walked over to his chair. "I was hoping you would be like the others, eventually look to save yourself and thereby give me what I want, but I see now you're every inch the man I believed you to be. You have no trouble sacrificing yourself for your cause." He removed his gloves before turning them inside out, then tossing them onto the chair. With a sigh, he rolled down his sleeves. "I can't get through to you like this. The only way to get to you is through someone you love."

Dex's heart almost stopped.

Wolf finished with his cuff links, then slipped into his jacket. "I'm going to bring back your boyfriend or your brother, I'll let you choose which, and then I will take him apart piece by piece until you give me the information I want."

"I'm telling you the truth! I don't know what file you're talking about. There was nothing like that left behind. No letter, note, nothing addressing a file. Please." Dex struggled against the restraints. The thought of Sloane or Cael in this room terrified him. "I'll do what you want. Just leave them out of this."

Wolf walked over and bent forward, his gaze holding Dex's. "Who's it going to be? The love of your life or your baby brother?" A thought seemed to strike him, and he snapped his fingers. "I have a better idea. How about I bring them both, and then you can look them in the eye when I make you choose who lives and who dies. Either way, I'll make them both bleed."

Rage erupted through Dex like a fiery geyser. He let out a fierce cry and wrenched at the zip ties with all the strength he could summon. They snapped. The ones around his wrists first, then his ankles.

Wolf's eyes went wide, and Dex thrust his head forward, head-butting Wolf and sending him stumbling back. He rubbed his forehead before staring at Dex.

"How did you do that?"

"Guess you don't know everything," Dex growled, lunging at Wolf.

The two of them hit the floor, thrashing and trying to do as much damage to the other as possible. Wolf was undoubtedly cursing his luck right now. If he hadn't pumped Dex with that Therian shit, Dex wouldn't have had the strength to stand, much less fight.

Wolf was a trained professional and a Therian, but Dex wasn't without skill. Thanks to Sparks, the months of special training, of getting his ass handed to him by TIN specialists, of pushing himself beyond his limits, were finally paying off. He was never more grateful to Sparks for kicking his ass like she had than he was at this moment.

They got to their feet and circled each other. How many people had Wolf tortured and killed? And who the hell did the guy work for? Whoever he was, Dex couldn't let him near his family.

"How did you get out of those restraints?" Wolf demanded.

Dex had no idea, but he wasn't about to let Wolf know that. "Who are you working for?"

Wolf charged him, using his elbows in the hopes of inflicting as much damage as possible, but Dex remembered Sparks's training. Wolf's blows were continually blocked, with Dex quickly picking up on the guy's technique. He matched Wolf's speed, anticipating where Wolf would hit rather than reacting. It was something Dex discovered he was good at. Sparks had noticed right away, so rather than simply teaching him new techniques, she had him mimic his opponent's and use what he'd learned against them. Dex threw his hands up, blocking the blow Wolf intended for Dex's ears. Recovering swiftly, Dex threw an uppercut, catching Wolf under his chin, followed by an onslaught of fierce punches before Wolf could get his bearings.

Dex's muscles pulled and burned, but his adrenaline had spiked. He was so close to freedom he could taste it, so he reached even deeper, putting all his strength behind every blow, making sure not to get too cocky. Wolf let out a fierce growl and lashed out, snatching a hold of Dex's jacket. Dex went with the momentum, spinning and pulling his arms out of the sleeves. With a frustrated grunt, Wolf chucked the jacket to one side and lunged at Dex, who spun out of the way. If Wolf got his hands on Dex, it'd be over. He couldn't allow that. Sloane…. He had to get back to Sloane.

"You won't make it out of here," Wolf warned, his breath unsteady.

Dex met Wolf's eyes and grinned. "Like how I wouldn't be getting out of that chair? How'd that work out for you?"

Wolf smoothed back his hair, and Dex readied himself. The guy was rethinking his strategy. Dex gingerly inched away from the door, his eyes locked on Wolf. He didn't have to wait long. Wolf's gray eyes turned hard, empty, and he charged Dex, fangs elongated as he attacked, just as Dex had hoped.

Dex had maneuvered Wolf exactly where he wanted him. Before Wolf could grab him, Dex snatched hold of Wolf's chair, swung it around, and slammed the steel piece of furniture into Wolf. The guy hit the floor hard, his head banging against the concrete. He didn't stir. Dex quickly rummaged through Wolf's pockets. There was nothing.

Leaving the guy on the floor, Dex ran farther into the shadows, and he immediately spotted the faint light coming in from under the door. He grabbed the handle and carefully cracked it open. There was no one on the other side. Slipping out, he closed the door behind him. More darkness and more concrete walls. Where the hell was he? Why was it so damned dark?

It was time to get the hell out of here. His body protested every movement, his head was killing him, but he got moving, sucking in a sharp breath and holding on to his side in a feeble attempt to keep some of the pain at bay. His ribs were bruised, and his lungs burned as his breath quickened. He wouldn't be able to stay on his feet much longer, but the thought he might blow his only chance at getting out of there, at getting back to Sloane, had him pushing forward.

The corridor seemed to stretch on forever, and he stilled when he caught a whiff of something familiar. It was faint, but he could smell it. Something mixed with licorice. Dex hated licorice. One too many shots of Sambuca in college. Ahead of him in the shadows, he spotted movement. *Shit.* Had he really thought he could just walk out of here? Several pairs of glowing eyes grew nearer, and Dex stopped, leaning against the wall for support as the figures stalked forward, their shapes soon becoming visible. Three Therians. Dex grinned. One of them had a tranq gun holstered to his belt.

Dex pushed away from the wall and put his hands up in front of him. "I don't want any trouble, fellas." He turned his gaze on the lion Therian with the tranq gun and motioned to his face.

"You know, I got a friend with that same scowl. Is that, like, a lion Therian thing, or are you both members of the same Scowler's Association? No? Okay."

The guy was short-tempered. Not surprising. The lion Therian lunged at him, and Dex dropped to his knees, twisting his body despite the cry from his muscles. He swiped the guy's tranq gun, then shot him in the back and sent him stumbling forward. Not skipping a beat, Dex jumped to his feet and fired at the two Therians charging him. One managed to grab him by the neck, lifting him off his feet. Dex grabbed the guy's wrist while shooting him a second and third time in the chest. Another gasp for air later, Dex was released. He dropped to the floor and coughed before staggering forward. A red light flared to life up on the ceiling, and Dex cursed under his breath. The jig was up.

"Time to get out of Dodge," Dex grunted, willing his feet to move faster. It was like running through a fog. His vision blurred, and he alternated between squinting and shutting his eyes tight in an attempt to clear them. He took a wrong turn and ended up in a dead end.

"Fuck." He doubled back quickly, the tranq gun held close. Rounding a corner, he was met with two more Therian goons. He fired, taking one down, and then he was out of darts. *Fucking fuck fuck!* Tossing the gun to one side, he charged the leopard Therian. He had no idea what the hell he thought would happen, but when he tackled the guy and sent him slamming into the wall behind him, Dex was just as surprised as his foe. Swiftly recovering, Dex pulled back a fist and punched the guy across the head. The guy crumpled to the floor, out cold.

"Holy shit." Had Wolf given him fucking steroids or something? Whatever it was, Dex was glad for it, though he feared what the repercussions would be. Pushing that aside for now, Dex hurried down the corridors. Up ahead he saw the Exit sign. He could have cried, he was so happy. Not waiting for any more goons to show up, he pushed through the door and ran down the dark corridor, not questioning how it was he could see through the darkness. He rushed up the stairs, ignoring his burning lungs.

Bursting out into the night air would have brought him to his knees if he hadn't kept pushing. He had to get away from this place. Phone. He needed a phone. Trees surrounded him on all sides, and he glanced back to find the door he'd come from was set in a brick wall hidden by grime, moss, shrubbery, and foliage. In the distance he heard the faint sounds of city traffic. Was he still in the city? He was certainly in *a* city. As he moved quickly through the trees, he spotted a small road with a narrow sidewalk at the bottom of an incline and beyond that, homes. He'd never make it to any of those houses. Voices carried through the air, and Dex hurried down the incline to the sidewalk, trying his best not to fall, because if he did, he wouldn't be getting back up.

Hunching himself over, he stumbled by the two Humans walking by, bumping into one of them.

"Watch it, asshole," one guy grumbled as he kept moving. Yep, definitely still in New York City.

"Sorry, man." Dex staggered toward the small hill he came from and climbed back up, his legs growing shaky. Normally the darkness would make him nervous, but now it was his sanctuary. There was plenty of light for him to see movement, in case someone tried to get the drop on him. The expanse of trees stretched on for miles, and he kept going as long as he could. When his knees gave out from under him, he dragged himself over to a tree and sat up against it. He pulled out the phone he'd swiped from the guy he'd bumped into. After one ring, Sloane picked up.

"Who is this?"

"It's me," Dex choked out, tears filling his eyes. It was so damned good to hear Sloane's voice.

"Oh thank God. Dex, where are you?"

"I… I have no idea. There's lots of trees. I don't see any signs. There was a road, but I don't know what it was. Can you get Cael to find my location using the phone's GPS?"

There was some faint murmuring before Sloane's voice returned.

"He's on it. Are you okay? Talk to me. What happened?"

"It's a really, really long story. I just… I need you." He let his head fall back, and a tremor went through him. His need for the man he loved was crushing, and he blinked back his tears.

"I'm on my way, sweetheart. Are you somewhere safe?"

"Home was safe."

There was a long pause. "We'll sort that out. Right now, let's get you to me, okay? I'm your home."

Dex smiled despite his split lip. That's right. Sloane was home. It didn't matter where they were. As long as Sloane was with him, he was home. "Thank you. I really needed to hear that right now."

"We have your location. I'll be there soon. Stay on the line with me."

"I'm tired."

"Stay awake, sweetheart. Please."

"I don't think I can. I'm kinda in bad shape here." His adrenaline was crashing and with that his strength, causing his whole body to shake violently. He'd be lucky if he didn't go into shock. It was so cold all of a sudden.

"Sing with me."

"What?"

"Come on. Listen."

Sloane turned up the radio, and Dex smiled at the familiar sounds of strumming guitar followed by clapping. It was the Romantics' "What I Like About You." Sloane sang and urged Dex to sing with him. Dex did his best to keep up with the lyrics. He loved this song. He'd danced to it around the kitchen last week while making dinner. Sloane had even joined in after Dex grabbed him and begged him to dance with him. It was the most fun Dex had ever had making baked potatoes.

"Keep singing, sweetheart," Sloane pleaded.

Dex tried. His voice was rough, his words barely audible, but he tried to keep from slipping into the darkness threatening to drag him under. He wanted to be awake for Sloane, wanted to see his beautiful smile and glowing amber eyes. The light around him seemed to dim, and he couldn't tell if it was the last of whatever Wolf had given him leaving his system or if he was beginning to lose consciousness. It was all so quiet, or at least it appeared that way, as if time had stilled. His sharpened senses dulled, and he tried to push himself up, but his body refused to cooperate. He had no idea how much time had passed or at what point the phone had slipped from his blood-caked fingers.

"Dex! Dex, where are you?"

"Sloane," Dex croaked.

Was Sloane really there, or had he simply heard what he was desperate to hear? One moment there was quiet, nothing but shadows, and the next dozens of lights burst through the trees. Sloane emerged alongside three figures in black suits, and when he spotted Dex, he sped over. He dropped to his knees and cradled Dex in his arms. Dex was aware of more people calling his name. Cael? Ash? Thank God they were safe.

"Dex, I'm here, sweetheart. I'm here." Sloane gently hugged him close, one hand around Dex's back, the other cradling Dex's head to him, enveloping Dex in warmth. Sloane was always so warm.

"I stayed awake," Dex murmured, nuzzling his face against Sloane's shirt, inhaling his scent. He smelled so good.

"You did good, babe. It's okay."

Dex nodded, or at least he thought he did. There was chaos around him, quiet chaos. He could hear the many whispers, the orders given to span out and search. All Dex cared about was that the man he loved had come for him and he was once again in Sloane's arms. Now safe, the darkness came for him.

CHARLIE COCHET is an author by day and artist by night. Always quick to succumb to the whispers of her wayward muse, no star is out of reach when following her passion. From adventurous agents and sexy shifters to society gentlemen and hardboiled detectives, there's bound to be plenty of mischief for her heroes to find themselves in—and plenty of romance, too!

Currently residing in Central Florida, Charlie is at the beck and call of a rascally Doxiepoo bent on world domination. When she isn't writing, she can usually be found reading, drawing, or watching movies. She runs on coffee, thrives on music, and loves to hear from readers.

Website: www.charliecochet.com
Blog: www.charliecochet.com/blog
Email: charlie@charliecochet.com
Facebook: www.facebook.com/charliecochet
Twitter: @charliecochet
Tumblr: www.charliecochet.tumblr.com
Pinterest: www.pinterest.com/charliecochet
Goodreads: www.goodreads.com/CharlieCochet
Instagram: www.instagram.com/charliecochet
THIRDS HQ: www.thirdshq.com

Would you like to receive news on Charlie Cochet's upcoming books, exclusive content, giveaways, first access to extras, and more? Sign up for Charlie's newsletter: bit.ly/CharlieCochetNews

Follow me on BookBub (www.bookbub.com/authors/charlie-cochet)!

HELL & HIGH WATER

CHARLIE COCHET

THIRDS: Book One

When homicide detective Dexter J. Daley's testimony helps send his partner away for murder, the consequences—and the media frenzy—aren't far behind. He soon finds himself sans boyfriend, sans friends, and, after an unpleasant encounter in a parking garage after the trial, he's lucky he doesn't find himself sans teeth. Dex fears he'll get transferred from the Human Police Force's Sixth Precinct, or worse, get dismissed. Instead, his adoptive father—a sergeant at the Therian-Human Intelligence Recon Defense Squadron otherwise known as the THIRDS—pulls a few strings, and Dex gets recruited as a Defense Agent.

Dex is determined to get his life back on track and eager to get started in his new job. But his first meeting with Team Leader Sloane Brodie, who also happens to be his new jaguar Therian partner, turns disastrous. When the team is called to investigate the murders of three HumaniTherian activists, it soon becomes clear to Dex that getting his partner and the rest of the tightknit team to accept him will be a lot harder than catching the killer—and every bit as dangerous.

www.dreamspinnerpress.com

Sequel to *Hell & High Water*
THIRDS: Book Two

When a series of bombs go off in a Therian youth center, injuring members of THIRDS Team Destructive Delta and causing a rift between agents Dexter J. Daley and Sloane Brodie, peace seems unattainable. Especially when a new and frightening group, the Order of Adrasteia, appears to always be a step ahead. With panic and intolerance spreading and streets becoming littered with the Order's propaganda, hostility between Humans and Therians grows daily. Dex and Sloane, along with the rest of the team, are determined to take down the Order and restore peace, not to mention settle a personal score. But the deeper the team investigates the bombings, the more they believe there's a more sinister motive than a desire to shed blood and spread chaos.

Discovering the frightful truth behind the Order's intent forces Sloane to confront secrets from a past he thought he'd left behind for good, a past that could not only destroy him and his career, but also the reputation of the organization that made him all he is today. Now more than ever, Dex and Sloane need each other, and, along with trust, the strength of their bond will mean the difference between justice and all-out war.

www.dreamspinnerpress.com

CHARLIE COCHET

BRODIE

THIRDS

RACK&RUIN

Sequel to *Blood & Thunder*
THIRDS: Book Three

New York City's streets are more dangerous than ever with the leaderless Order of Adrasteia and the Ikelos Coalition, a newly emerged Therian group, at war. Innocent civilians are caught in the crossfire, and although the THIRDS round up more and more members of the Order in the hopes of keeping the volatile group from reorganizing, the members of the Coalition continue to escape and wreak havoc in the name of vigilante justice.

Worse yet, someone inside the THIRDS has been feeding the Coalition information. It's up to Destructive Delta to draw out the mole and put an end to the war before anyone else gets hurt. But to get the job done, the team will have to work through the aftereffects of the Therian Youth Center bombing. A skirmish with Coalition members leads Agent Dexter J. Daley to a shocking discovery, and suddenly it becomes clear that the random violence isn't so random. There's more going on than Dex and Sloane originally believed, and their fiery partnership is put to the test. As the case takes an explosive turn, Dex and Sloane are in danger of losing more than their relationship.

www.dreamspinnerpress.com

CHARLIE COCHET

RISE&FALL

Sequel to *Rack & Ruin*
THIRDS: Book Four

After an attack by the Coalition leaves THIRDS
Team Leader Sloane Brodie critically injured, agent
Dexter J. Daley swears to make Beck Hogan pay for
what he's done. But Dex's plans for retribution are
short-lived. With Ash still on leave with his own injuries, Sloane in the hospital, and Destructive Delta
in the Coalition's crosshairs, Lieutenant Sparks isn't
taking any chances. Dex's team is pulled from the
case, with the investigation handed to Team Leader
Sebastian Hobbs. Dex refuses to stand by while another team goes after Hogan, and decides to put his
old HPF detective skills to work to find Hogan before
Theta Destructive, no matter the cost.

With a lengthy and painful recovery ahead of him,
the last thing Sloane needs is his partner out scouring
the city, especially when the lies—however well-in-
tentioned—begin to spiral out of control. Sloane is
all too familiar with the desire to retaliate, but some
things are more important, like the man who's pledged
to stand beside him. As Dex starts down a dark path,
it's up to Sloane to show him what's at stake, and finally put a name to what's in his heart.

www.dreamspinnerpress.com

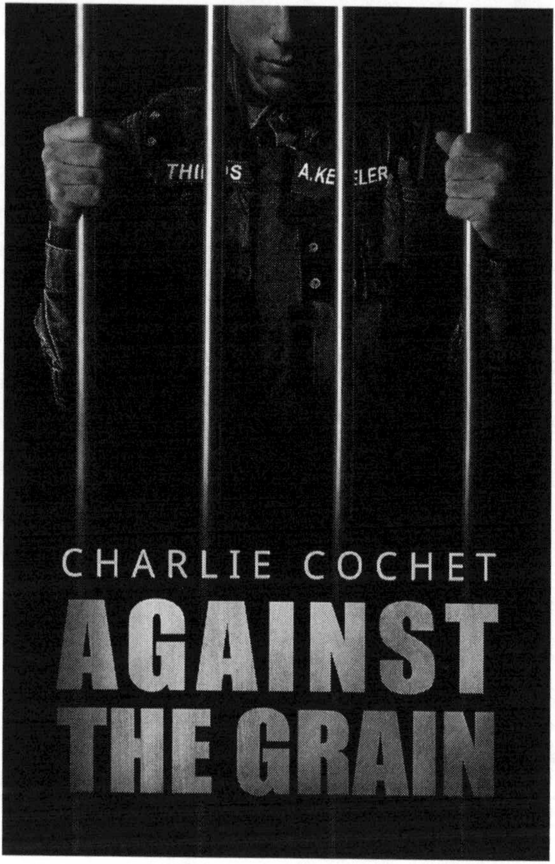
THII S A.KE LER
CHARLIE COCHET
AGAINST
THE GRAIN

Sequel to *Rise & Fall*
THIRDS: Book Five

As the fiercest Defense Agent at the THIRDS, Destructive Delta's Ash Keeler is foul-mouthed and foul-tempered. But his hard-lined approach always yields results, evident by his recent infiltration of the Coalition. Thanks to Ash's skills and the help of his team, they finally put an end to the murdering extremist group for good, though not before Ash takes a bullet to save teammate Cael Maddock. As a result, Ash's secrets start to surface, and he can no longer ignore what's in his heart.

Cael Maddock is no stranger to heartache. As a Recon Agent for Destructive Delta, he has successfully maneuvered through the urban jungle that is New York City, picking up his own scars along the way. Yet nothing he's ever faced has been more of a challenge than the heart of Ash Keeler, his supposedly straight teammate. Being in love isn't the only danger he and Ash face as wounds reopen and new secrets emerge, forcing them to question old loyalties.

www.dreamspinnerpress.com

FOR **MORE**
OF THE
BEST
GAY
ROMANCE